# Alan Robertson

# Lila

outskirtspress
DENVER, COLORADO

This is a work of fiction. The characters and events in this book are the product of the author's imagination. Any similarity to real persons, living or dead, is coincidental and not intended by the author. The opinions expressed in this manuscript are solely the opinions of the author and do not represent the opinions or thoughts of the publisher. The author has represented and warranted full ownership and/or legal right to publish all the materials in this book.

Lila
All Rights Reserved.
Copyright © 2014 Alan Robertson
v2.0

Cover Photo © 2014 Paulita Korby. All rights reserved - used with permission.

This book may not be reproduced, transmitted, or stored in whole or in part by any means, including graphic, electronic, or mechanical without the express written consent of the publisher except in the case of brief quotations embodied in critical articles and reviews.

Outskirts Press, Inc.
http://www.outskirtspress.com

ISBN: 978-1-4787-2509-1

Library of Congress Control Number: 2013920511

Outskirts Press and the "OP" logo are trademarks belonging to Outskirts Press, Inc.

PRINTED IN THE UNITED STATES OF AMERICA

For
Francey Rothschild

I think you'll like this one.

Al

# Lila

PERFECT SNOWFLAKES FELL from a perfect sky, and in the eyes of Lila Barzoon, all was right with the world. Her lover was waiting when she arrived. They laughed and danced and told stories with friends, and later, in his home on the shore of frozen Lake Independence, made passionate love on the Navaho-print couch as a warm fire crackled in the hearth. He was everything she'd ever wanted. She longed to spend the night, to sleep in his bed and to wake next to him, to smell his scent and touch his skin, but she knew she couldn't, not yet. So late, very late, she brushed the snow from the windshield of her blue Jeep, kissed her lover goodbye, and began the long drive home.

\* \* \*

Lila lay on her side, slightly curled, as though asleep in the freezing snow. Paralyzed with pain, she gasped for breath that would not come. She sensed the Jeep, rolling . . . *closer* . . . *closer* . . . . She knew that it would roll on top of her. She knew she was going to die. *Why? Why now, when everything is right?* She felt the pressure. Her last breath was crushed out. Then she didn't feel anything at all.

# Orville Dorian

Thirteen months later.

*SEARCH ENDS FOR Contractor Missing in Snowstorm*—eighty point Benicia font above the fold in the Peninsula Journal, tossed on the bar by a departing patron. When the drunk saw it, voltage passed through him and his hunched frame jerked straight. Too thin to be healthy, with gnarled workman's hands and a weathered face capped by a hurricane of graying hair, the man who'd only moments before been buried under a dozen bleary layers of thought was now alive with rejoicing. "Bartender, round for the house!" he bellowed. "The sonsabitch is dead. Burn in hell, Barzoon! *Burn...in...hell!*" His curses echoing off the amber walls of the suddenly quiet room.

The bartender, a large, rubbery-faced man with a graying Fu Manchu, frowned and angled toward him, offering a few quiet words, but whatever he said didn't work. "Shoulda killed him myself," slurred the drunk in loud response.

"Too late now," came a taunt from the far end of the rail. It was a beer-bellied Mutt of a Mutt and Jeff pair. The lanky, hatchet-faced Jeff couldn't resist. Voice like a rusty viola, "Orville, only thing you're good at killing is time."

"One pint at a time," chortled Mutt.

The drunk glared. "Shut your mouth, Lamont! Justice, that's all I ever wanted. *Justice!*"

Gliding around the end of the bar, the bartender shepherded the man to the door. "Come on, Orville. It's over now, all right? He's dead, isn't he? It's over. Go home and take a rest, get something to eat, you can come back later."

The drunk didn't resist but continued his rant out the door and beyond. "Got away with murder, he did. *The sonsabitch!* If he weren't such a damn big shot, he'd be in prison. But nooo, not him. Not mister moneybags. Not in this town. Killed my baby girl, he did. *Killed her!* And no one even cared! *Rot in hell, Barzoon!* You can *rot . . . in . . . hell!*"

"Sorry about that, folks," said the bartender striding back to his station. "Orville's a bit excitable."

Drama over, former FBI agent Mike Tate's attention was drawn back to his date, the lovely Gayla Jackson. With Nordic blue eyes, hair the color of sunshine and a face that would forever be cute—coupled with a personality barely contained in her five-foot four-inch body—Gayla was far too energetic for the dour Tate, but he'd found her relentlessly upbeat nature to be curiously habit-forming and this was their third date. "So much for a quiet drink."

"Orville Dorian," said Gayla, with the offhand ease of stating the obvious.

Tate's brows converged. "Is it true that you know everyone in town?" He'd lived in Marquette just short of a year, assigned to the touristy enclave on the southern shore of Lake Superior in Michigan's Upper Peninsula after burning out in Detroit. Seven months later, with his minimum twenty in, he'd retired. The city had 21,355 residents. The reserved Tate knew only a handful.

"Just the ones who eat," replied Gayla. She'd resided in Marquette her entire life and had been waitressing at the Omelet Eggspress going on four years and the Villa Italia before that, which is how they met. Tate loved to eat. With a walking-around weight of two-twenty (with the scale adjusted to minus ten), his five-eleven frame carried enough muscle to be called burly rather than fat. At least that's what he hoped. In his late forties, his face had the clean-cut, squared-off look of a longtime cop—straight brown hair, cut sharp and combed back, graying at the temples, hazel eyes, a nose that had only been broken once, and a smile that—when Gayla could pry one out of him—had a genuine warmth. She'd tagged him as the strong, silent type the first time he entered the O.E., and she was right. Attracted from the beginning, she knew he was attracted to her as well. But Tate was painfully slow to make a move, and that made it all the more exciting as they improvised their way through the courting ritual, a word, a look, a touch, until he finally asked her out.

"Sad case," she said.

"Oh?"

"The guy he was talking about, Harlan Barzoon, Orville's daughter was married to him." Before she could explain further, a waitress materialized next to their booth. Her thin, jet-black hair was streaked with florescent blue and intentionally cut much shorter on one side than the other. Tate thought unless repelling people was her objective, whatever she was trying to do wasn't working.

"What can I get you?"

He noted she had a lisp. She flicked her tongue and he caught sight of a faux pearl the size of an industrial ball bearing. Repressing a gag reflex, he nodded toward Gayla. "Vodka gimlet. Beam for me, neat." As the waitress strode away, Tate shook his head.

Gayla grinned. "Going to comment on her jewelry?"

"No."

Coyly. "Think *I* should get one?"

"No way! Why would a person do that?"

"It's supposed to be sexy. Do I need to explain?"

Tate rolled his eyes. "Guess the definition has changed since I learned."

"Maybe you could explain *your* definition to me sometime . . . in detail." She gave him a wink.

He grinned. "I will. That's a promise."

Flirting accomplished, Gayla returned to the subject. "About Orville's daughter. Hmm, if I remember correctly she died in a car accident in February of last year. Or was it March? Sometime around then. Anyway, it's no secret Orville blamed it on Harlan. Word was, Lila and Harlan weren't getting along. She was a wild one, and he was more of a duck hunting, Rotary Club kind of guy. Big age difference too. Lila was the sexy young trophy wife. Dumped number one in an ugly divorce."

"Wouldn't happen to have his prints on file, would you?"

She feigned offense. "So sue me for knowing what goes on."

At 9:15 the next morning Tate was in the kitchen of his modest beach home east of town on the shore of Lake Superior. He was polishing off his second cup of coffee and perusing the newspaper when he heard a car drive into his yard. Pulling a curtain aside, he saw the drunk from the previous evening climb out of a purple Dodge that had seen better days. His worn chore-coat hung open displaying white painter's bibs spattered in a rainbow of colors. After pausing to appraise the layout, he made his way to the front porch. Tate was opening the door as the man's work boots clomped up the snowy steps.

"You Mike Tate?"

"That's me."

Orville Dorian ran fingers through mussed hair in an effort at dignity. "Name's Dorian. Ran into your friend Gayla at the Omelet Eggspress. She said you're a private eye. Said you might take my case."

Tate's shoulders slumped. He wished she hadn't. His retirement income wasn't much and he'd been thinking about finding part-time work, but he hadn't made up his mind yet. Freezing air swirled around his legs, filling the porch and kitchen beyond. He opened the door wider. "Might as well come in, Mr. Dorian."

Dorian stomped the snow off his boots and stepped inside. Tate sealed the port against the artic chill and led Dorian into the kitchen. "What exactly are we talking about?"

Dorian didn't mince words. "Harlan Barzoon killed my daughter. I don't want him to get away with it. It's not fair. It's not right. He should pay."

Tate's face morphed into puzzlement. "Have I missed something? According to the newspaper, Barzoon's dead. Not much you can do to him now."

"That's right, the sonsabitch is dead." He said it as if expectorating. "But it's like he was some kinda hero.

Weren't nothing of the sort. Murdered my Lila, he did. I know it as sure as I'm a foot high. All's I want is for everyone else to know it too."

"It's over, Mr. Dorian. What good can it do now?"

"It's about justice, Tate. I want the truth to come out. I want people to know who he really was." His face twisted in anguish. "People said bad things about my girl, but now they're talkin' 'bout him like he was some kinda saint. Bullshit! Weren't nothin' of the sort. He was scum, and I want 'em all to know it."

"Is this about money from his estate?"

Dorian's bloodshot eyes flashed with anger. "I don't want nothin'. Wouldn't take it if offered. Anyway, it'll be goin' to the kids."

"There were children?"

"Yeah. He and Lila had a daughter. And there was a boy and girl from his first wife too. I suppose whatever money there is will be split up between the three of them. So no, Tate, this ain't about money. It's about my Lila, and it's about the truth."

"What about your granddaughter? Don't you think this could hurt her?"

He shook his head. "She's still young. She won't know."

Tate sighed. "Mr. Dorian, I'm truly sorry about your daughter, but she's dead."

Dorian balled a fist and pounded his chest like a drum. "She's not dead in here."

Tate knew that trying to prove a woman was murdered by a man who's dead is a fool's errand, but Dorian had driven all the way out to see him so the least he could do is listen to his story. "How about a cup of coffee, Mr. Dorian? We'll sit down and you can tell me what you think happened. That sound okay?"

Orville Dorian relaxed. "Yeah. That'd be fine."

Tate expected a fragmented, emotion-laden screed against Dorian's son-in-law, but to his surprise the story told was coherent and reasonably straightforward. Barzoon was a successful real estate wheeler-dealer in his fifties who'd met Dorian's daughter while still married to his first wife. The two began an affair that went on for a year or so before the wife found out and filed for divorce. It was messy, and once everything was split up, Barzoon wasn't rich anymore, if he ever was.

By that time Lila was very pregnant, so Harlan and Lila were married. They began building a plush house on Nash Lake, west of Marquette, and several months later Lila had the baby. For a while everything was sweetness and light, but there was alimony and child support to pay, and the new house was costing a fortune, and Harlan had expensive toys and habits. So, as it happened, about three years after their marriage Lila confided to Orville that they had money problems, and that Harlan would get drunk and argumentative and spend nights away from home. Not long afterward, when everything seemed hopeless, Harlan's business partner, Kevin Adams, died in an end-loader accident. As a result, not only did Barzoon receive a hefty payoff from an insurance policy, but as a bonus, ended up gaining his partner's share of the business.

Harlan and Lila were back in the money and everything was fine for a couple of years until the cycle started again. Barzoon would stay out late and Lila suspected he had a girlfriend. The construction business was slow. The insurance money had run out. Then in March of last year Lila was killed in a car accident and Barzoon collected on another policy, hers, and once again he was living high.

"You see, Tate? It ain't right. There's too much coincidence in it. Maybe his partner, Adams, *wasn't* careful. Maybe the loader tipping on him *was* an accident. Then again, maybe not. But lightening don't strike twice in the same place. Once I can believe, not twice. He did it. I know he did."

"Tell me about your daughter's accident."

"Sure. She was up in Big Bay at a bar. The Lumberjack. They say she had some drinks. She was driving home on 510. Know the road?"

"Sort of. Gravel most of the way from Big Bay to Negaunee Township."

Dorian nodded. "It was 'bout a year ago, late March, sometime after midnight. It was snowing but the road had been plowed that afternoon. Maybe four or five inches of fluff sittin' on it, but that weren't nothin'. She was drivin' her Jeep. It had four-wheel drive, and she woulda used it. Lila lived here all her life, driving in snow weren't no big deal."

"How'd it happen?"

"Cops said she was going too fast for conditions. Went around a corner, skidded, Jeep hit the snowbank, threw her out, rolled on top of her."

"Any problems with the vehicle? Brakes, steering, lights, tires? Anything like that?"

"Cops said it was driver error. Not sure they even looked for anything else."

"So, what do *you* think happened?"

"I think he did it."

Tate frowned. "I got that part. But *how* did he do it? Seems like a typical accident."

"That's the way it's *supposed* to seem, Tate. The guy wasn't stupid. He *had* to set it up to look like an accident or else he couldn't collect."

"Mr. Dorian—"

"Think, Tate! Two accidents. Both dead people was insured. Both paid off to Barzoon. Both had vehicles roll over on 'em. Yeah, I know, one was an end loader and the other a Jeep, but they're still almost the same. And both times was when Barzoon needed money. Think about it, that's all I'm askin'. Just think about it."

Tate sighed, flinched, twisted in his chair, his eyes wandered, he sucked in his cheeks and then grudgingly said, "Okay . . . I'll think about it. I'll do some digging and get back to you in two days with my decision."

"I'm not rich, Tate, but I'll pay. I'm not what you think. I got a job. I work. I own my place free and clear."

"We can talk about that later."

"You'll call me?"

"Yeah. Two days."

# Two Days

AFTER DORIAN LEFT, Tate was hungry. The obvious answer: Drive to the Omelet Eggspress. Donning his parka, he opened the door to leave but stopped short. Facing him was a young boy bundled in a royal-blue snowmobile suit with black rubber boots and a multi-colored chook. The chook had a red ball on top. It bobbed as he spoke. "My dad said you're in the FBI. Is that true?"

"I was, but not anymore."

"That's what I wanna do when I grow up. My name is Greg, what's yours?"

Tate smiled. "Mike Tate. Pleased to meet you." He extended his hand. Greg gave him a mitten shake. "How old are you, Greg?"

"I'm nine," he said pridefully. "Almost nine and a half."

Tate nodded. "You're lucky, son. Nine and a half is a good age to begin preparing for a career in the FBI."

"Really?" said Greg, beaming. "You mean I should start learning how to shoot and fight bad guys?"

"Oh, yeah. That too," said Tate. "But the most important thing is to study hard in school because, as you know, the FBI only takes the best of the best. They do it by testing you on things you learn in school. They already know you have courage, otherwise you wouldn't be applying. So what they really want to know is if you're smart. Real smart. Smart enough to outfox the bad guys and get them in jail without even having to use your gun or do any fighting." Seeing the crestfallen look on the lad's face, he quickly added, "But sometimes being smart isn't enough, then you have to fight and use guns."

The smile returned. "That's good." Having all the information he needed, Greg spun and bounded from the porch, charging down Tate's long tree-lined drive and across the lane to his home.

"Thanks a lot," said Tate.

"It isn't going to kill you," replied Gayla. She was standing next to him in her light-blue waitress uniform. It had wide white lapels and a cinched waist, showing off her figure. Her body was curvy and feminine and although she avoided exercise and ate whatever she pleased, because of her hummingbird metabolism, her weight never varied by more than a pound.

Tate was hibernating in his regular corner booth at the Omelet Eggspress with the house special, the Ore Boat, in front of him. The Ore Boat was by far his favorite breakfast because it consisted of a steaming heap of every artery-clogging item on the menu. His mouth was watering, his food was getting cold, and Gayla was treating him like a child. He scowled, thinking, I should never have gotten involved with her, the O.E.'s the best breakfast place in town, and if I don't humor her, I won't be able to eat here anymore.

"Please, Mike, just check into it for him. If you don't find anything, tell him. He'll understand."

"No, Gayla, he won't understand. He has his mind all made up that Lila was an angel sent from heaven and

Barzoon the devil incarnate. Nothing I say will change that."

Gayla made a 'you're not a nice man' face, turned on her heel, and marched away. Tate knew what that meant: He knew he'd have to do it. No sense worrying about that now, he reasoned, as he began uploading precious cargo into the hold.

Later, on his third cup of coffee, Gayla seated across from him, shoe off and her toes working their way up his leg, he said, "Two days, Gayla, that's what I told Dorian and that's what I'm telling you. I'll give it two days. If something feels off, I should know it by then. Anyway, Barzoon's dead. Even if he did what Dorian claims, what's the law going to do to him now?"

She beamed a smile. Little Miss Sunshine. It made Tate happy. The thought disturbed him. She said, "Thanks, Mike, two days is fine. Why don't you come by for dinner tomorrow night? I'll fix something special and you can tell me what you've found."

"Tomorrow? I thought we were on for tonight?"

"Let's make it tomorrow, hon. You're going be busy."

That's how it starts, thought Tate.

Leaving the restaurant, the new P.I. slid his bulk into the driver's seat of his Lincoln Town Car. He wasn't a car guy and didn't give a rip about image. He'd purchased the champagne behemoth seven years back because it was one of the few vehicles he'd ever found that was easy to get in and out of. Soon after buying it, though, the smooth ride and powerful V-8 made him a true believer. Since then, in an era of fuel efficiency, he'd stoically suffered countless jibes about his gas-guzzling land-yacht. Gayla had already dubbed it the Brontocarus.

Down Third Street and left on Ridge, on a bluff overlooking Lake Superior, the Peter White Library was the first stop on his quest. Entering the granite fortress, he went straight to the computers. After finding the web site for the Peninsula Journal, he typed *Lila Barzoon* in the search box and tapped the enter key. There was a pause while data was summoned from cyberspace then three hits appeared: Lila's wedding to Barzoon, her accident, her obituary.

The accident was roughly ten miles from her home at about the mid-way point on County Road 510 between Negaunee Township, west of Marquette, and the village of Big Bay, to the north. The police report cited alcohol and excessive speed as factors resulting in the failure to negotiate a curve. Lila was thrown from the vehicle and pinned underneath. The coroner cited asphyxiation as the cause of death, ruling it accidental. A lifelong resident of Marquette County, Lila had graduated from Marquette High School and was a homemaker. Thirty-one at the time of her death, she left behind a husband, Harlan Barzoon, and a daughter, Jenna. The obit had a picture: A black and white of an attractive woman with flowing dark hair whose eyes and smile had a 'come hither' quality that would take effort to resist.

Tate printed the articles and then did a search on Harlan Barzoon, coming up with over a dozen stories going back ten years. They painted a picture of an entrepreneur with his fingers in numerous pies in and around the city of Marquette. A sportsman in his leisure time, he was active in hunting and fishing. There were clubs and good works too, the kind that get your name in the paper.

Among the articles on him were two about the death of his business partner, Kevin Adams. It restated much of what Tate already knew: Adams had been working late, alone, moving a pile of gravel with an end loader. He ran the loader up the side of a pile and it tipped over. Adams fell out and was crushed beneath the machine. Cause of death, massive trauma.

Tate printed the articles and sat in the overheated cubicle mulling what he'd read. Coincidences occur all the time. Just because Barzoon's partner and wife were both killed in rollover accidents doesn't mean Barzoon engineered them. And a rollover would be extremely difficult to plan and execute. How could it be done? Nothing came to mind. Of course, there's the sticky subject of insurance. It'd be interesting to know when the policies were written and the payoff amounts. And there was Dorian's contention that both deaths occurred when Barzoon was in financial difficulty. A red flag, but not definitive. During his twenty years with the Bureau, Tate learned he had to peel away the layers of a person's life until he reached the core. Only then would he know someone's true character. He was still on the outer layer of Harlan Barzoon—businessman, husband, father—a few more layers would have to come off before he could say goodbye to Orville Dorian.

Pulling a leather-bound notepad from his pocket, he jotted a list: Kevin Adams widow, Lila's friends, the Lumberjack, insurance policies. Leafing through the articles until he came to the one about Adams' death, Tate noted his widow's name was Monica and her address 8299 Morgan Heights Road. Folding the documents, he shoved them in a pocket then went searching for a phone. He didn't have a cell, hated their intrusive nature, and couldn't use the library's phone for a personal call, so he hoofed it across the street to the stately Landmark Inn. There was a pay phone in the lobby. She answered on the second ring. Tate identified himself as an investigator looking into the death of Lila Barzoon. Would she mind if he stopped by and asked a few questions? After a pause, she said, "Sure. Come on over."

# Monica Adams

FIFTEEN MINUTES LATER Tate was maneuvering the Lincoln up a long plowed drive to a white clapboard ranch-style with a blue metal outbuilding set behind and to the right. The picture said I'm in construction and take pride in my home and property. But there was snow piled high in front of the shop's overhead door and the siding on the house needed paint, a clear indication that the person who'd cared was gone.

He rang the bell. After a short wait, a chemistry blond wearing charcoal slacks and a coral top answered and led him into a tan country-style living room with shag carpet that hadn't recently known congress with a vacuum cleaner. The furniture was low-budget Early American and the walls were embarrassed by racks of ceramic knickknacks. At the end of the room was a brick fireplace fitted with a wood-burning insert. The mantle above it held photographs. All adults, no children. Prominent among them, a wedding shot of Monica Adams and her late husband, Kevin. Beside it, another of them, but this time in a foursome standing on a dock with a lake in the background. Barzoon was in the picture. Tate recognized him from a photo in the Journal archives. The woman next to him was younger than the others by twenty years. With a full smile and a rough-and-ready posture, Lila appeared mischievous, almost taunting.

Tate sat on the couch, sharing it with a disinterested gray cat. Across the room a picture window glared at him, displaying a bleak panorama of an open snow-covered yard guarded by the spindly, leafless arms of sugar maples. He ached for summer.

Monica Adams seated herself primly on the edge of a patterned chair. He guessed she'd been quite attractive when she was younger, and except for some excess on the thighs and the normal accumulation of road miles on her early-fifties face, still was.

"What would you like to know, Mr. Tate?"

"I'll get right to the point. Lila Barzoon's father asked me to look into her death. Frankly, ma'am, he thinks it's more than curious that both she and your husband died in the same way, a vehicle accident, and that both had insurance policies paying off to Harlan Barzoon."

Any joy in residence on Monica Adams' face was summarily evicted. "Harlan was a wonderful man. I can't understand why Dorian would want to start digging around. Harlan didn't do anything wrong. Things just happen, that's all. He should let it go."

"I tend to agree, Mrs. Adams, and maybe this will help him do just that. If he gets some answers and finds there's nothing there, perhaps he'll have a measure of peace." Tate waited, but Monica Adams didn't respond, so he went on, "I understand your husband was working alone at the warehouse when the accident occurred."

"Yes. He was moving gravel around the yard and the loader went up the side of a pile and tipped over."

"And the insurance paid off to Harlan?"

"They had a standard business policy, the kind partners have so if one dies, the other will have a way to keep the business going. They depended on each other. With Kevin gone, it was going to be harder for Harlan. Anyway, the bank encouraged them to take out the policy when they took out their first joint loan. There's nothing sinister about it. Nothing at all."

"What's going to happen to the business now? Are you still involved?"

"After Kevin died, I sold my share to Harlan."

"So he was the sole owner?"

"He and the bank."

"At the time of your husband's death, was the business doing well?"

She shrugged. "Like all businesses, it had its ups and downs."

"How was it when your husband died, up or down?"

Her posture stiffened. "I don't like where this is going, Mr. Tate."

"Ma'am, I'm just asking how the business was doing. It doesn't mean his death was anything other than an accident. I'm just trying to get a handle on the facts."

With a tight face, "It was fine. The business was fine. There was nothing wrong. They were busy all the time."

"So it was in an up phase, not a down phase?"

"Yes, an up phase."

Glancing at the picture of the foursome, "Is that Harlan Barzoon with you and your husband?"

Monica Adams softened a degree. "Yes, better times, at our cottage on Shag Lake."

"I take it the other woman is Lila?"

Reluctantly. "Yes."

"Were the two of you friends?"

She pursed her lips, hesitating. "It's not polite to speak

ill of the dead. But, if you must know, Lila wasn't the kind of person I wanted to be friends with."

Tate wasn't surprised. "Why's that?"

"To be blunt, Mr. Tate, she had low moral character."

"Low moral character? As in?"

"Ask around, you'll find out soon enough."

"Was she cheating on her husband?"

"Like I said, ask around."

"So you weren't all broken up when she died."

"No, I wasn't. Harlan deserved better."

"Had you known him a long time?"

"Yes."

"I take it the two of you were friends."

"Yes."

"Do you happen to remember where Harlan was when your husband had his accident?"

"After he left work, he went to his camp at Echo Lake. It was a Friday. As I recall, he went there for the weekend."

"Was Lila with him, or was he alone?"

She hesitated again. Her eyes never leaving his. "I'm not sure."

"How about the night Lila died? Do you know if Harlan was alone or with others?"

"I really don't have the slightest idea," she said brusquely, then stood up. "Now, if you don't mind, I have an appointment."

"Sure," said Tate, rising. "Thanks for your time."

Without a further word, she showed him to the door.

Tate pulled out of the drive reviewing his conversation with Monica Adams. In the thousands of interviews he'd conducted for the FBI, he'd found a pattern. There was a 'right now' feel to an interview, and an 'overall impression' later on. The right now feel had been animosity—stop asking questions and get out. The overall impression was a mixed bag. He found it strange that Adams hadn't once mentioned her late husband, Kevin. There was no 'I miss him' or 'he was a wonderful man'. All of her compliments were lavished on Harlan Barzoon. And it would be an understatement to say she didn't have great affection for Lila. Maybe she was close to the first wife, Theresa, or simply jealous of the younger, more attractive woman. That gave him an idea. If you really want the dirt on someone, talk to the ex.

# Theresa

UNLIKE MONICA ADAMS, Theresa Barzoon was more than willing to talk. They were in the stylish kitchen of her late 1900s two-story sandstone on a bluff lot in the upscale section of East Marquette. Tate sat on a leather-covered barstool in front of an island of black Italian granite. She leaned against a matching counter six feet away, a glass of cabernet sauvignon held in one hand, curls of smoke rising from a cigarette in the other. It was one in the afternoon on a Monday.

About the same age as Adams but thinner and with a more sophisticated air, Theresa Barzoon was dressed expensively casual in navy slacks and a scoop-neck sweater the color of tumbleweeds. She had long brown hair, a sun-bed tan, and a face accentuated by intelligent eyes but flawed by lips too thin to be sensual. Her voice was slightly coarse, almost husky, from cigarettes and alcohol. Unlike Monica Adams, Theresa Barzoon was animated, witty, and caustic.

"What can I say? The little slut ruined my marriage. Always meant to thank her for that. Did me a huge favor. Harlan was a real shit. Two scoops in a cone. I can't imagine what I ever saw in him. Bad husband and terrible father. What more can I tell you?"

"Do you know how the construction company was doing when Kevin Adams died?"

"You mean, were they making money?" She shrugged. "Who knows? Harlan was always late with his alimony payments, so they may have been having problems. But really, Tate, he was so full of bullshit that it was impossible to tell. He was a tremendous salesman but could never back it with action."

"What about Kevin?"

"Oh, Kevin knew what he was doing all right. He was a hard worker. I'm sure he did all the real work. Harlan didn't know shit from Shinola about construction, but he was able to talk Kevin into letting him buy into the company, telling him he'd *grow* it."

Tate's eyebrows went up. "Oh? I was under the impression they'd started it together."

She shook her head. "Uh-uh. Kevin did. Harlan weaseled his way in later."

"Him being a talker, I suppose Harlan did most of the sales work and Kevin took care of the actual construction."

She emitted a derisive laugh. "Yeah, something like that."

"I spoke to Monica Adams. She seemed to think Harlan was a saint."

"No surprise there. Monica always had the hots for him. Didn't try very hard to hide it either. At first I was angry, told her to keep her pants on. Later, when I didn't care anymore, I was embarrassed for Kevin."

Tate thought he'd get to the heart of the matter. "Orville Dorian, Lila's father, thinks Harlan killed Adams for insurance money. And after he'd chewed his way through that, killed Lila for the same reason."

Theresa Barzoon's eyes moved off at an angle while she considered it. "Umm . . . seems like a stretch."

"Why's that?"

"Because of the way they died. I don't see how he could have done it."

"But you wouldn't put it past him?"

"Tate, the only person Harlan Barzoon ever cared about was himself."

Tate was back at the Omelet Eggspress. Gayla slid in the booth next to him and gave his thigh a squeeze. "What'd you find out?"

"Happy little town. Mayberry with snowdrifts."

Her mouth formed an o. "You found something!"

"Not really."

"Yes you did. What is it? Don't keep me in suspense."

"Am I that easy to read?"

"Uh-huh."

"Wonderful, and all these years I thought I was inscrutable."

"Forget it. You're an open book. Tell me."

"It's nothing incriminating. Harlan Barzoon was a jerk, that's all. A jerk with limited business ability and questionable morals. According to the ex-wife, he talked his way into Kevin Adams's construction company, I'm guessing maybe with the help of Monica Adams, who seems far more concerned about the death of Harlan than of her late husband, Kevin."

"He did it," said Gayla, excited. "I can feel it."

Tate's mouth fell open. "On exactly what basis have you formed that opinion?"

"I just know," she replied. "Orville will be so pleased."

"What! There's nothing to be pleased about. One woman loves him, another hates him. That makes him just about normal. Where's the crime?"

"Ohhh, that's right. You're the *P.I.* here. So what do you need, a signed confession?"

"Gayla, I'm thinking maybe a teensy-weensy bit of evidence might be a start. Say, for instance, documents showing a big payoff to Harlan from insurance policies on Kevin and Lila. And maybe a crumb of a theory explaining how a man who apparently wasn't even there could have engineered an end-loader accident *and* an automobile accident. The guy must have been a criminal genius! I can't imagine how he'd do it. Can you?"

"Well . . . no. But that doesn't mean he didn't."

"We need the terrible trio, hon: means, motive, and opportunity. Barzoon may have had insurance money as a motive, but whether he had the opportunity depends on if he had alibis for when Kevin and Lila were killed. Even so, in this case, the toughest element to prove would be means. We know how they died, but *how* did he do it? I sure as heck don't know how someone would stage an end-loader accident. What do you do? Do you say, 'Ah, Kevin, I'm going to tip this loader on an angle and I want you to lay right there on the ground to see if I can balance it?' And then a car accident after that? C'mon, Gayla."

"If he could figure out one, he could figure out the other."

"Huh?"

"Sure, Mike. Barzoon finds a way to kill his partner and make it look like it an accident. Then, since the means, as you call it, is so convincing, he does it again to his wife."

"Modus operandi," said Tate reluctantly. "Criminals tend to find something that works and stick with it. Much as I hate to say it, you're right about one thing. If he *did* kill Adams by staging his death as an end-loader accident, since there was never any suspicion cast his way, he'd be inclined to try the same stunt over. Not an end loader, of course, but something similar, like a car."

"Of course he would," replied Gayla, as though it were obvious. "And that's exactly what happened." She beamed a satisfied smile. "What's next?"

"Well, if it were a Bureau job, the next item on the agenda would be to talk to everyone who had anything to do with the suspect or victims. We'd interview the cops who responded to the accidents, read the reports, including the coroner's, and have forensics go over any evidence that still exists. If we came up with anything incriminating, we'd visit a friendly judge for a subpoena to check out the financial angle. Insurance payoffs, dates written and amounts, construction company finances, personal finances, that sort of stuff. But it's not a Bureau job, and no sane judge is going to give me a subpoena, and without one, no one is going to let me go poking around in their records. Definitely not at the bank or insurance company."

"Maybe you should forget about the Bureau, Mike, and start thinking like a TV detective. They don't have subpoenas or writs or things like that. They pry things out of people by being friendly or clever or pushy. They use phony business cards and tell people they're the gas man or from the IRS. And they sweet talk the secretaries and bully the tough guys. That's how it's done."

Tate's shoulders sagged. "All those years wasted showing my badge and asking questions under the color of law."

"Don't be a wise guy. That was then and this is now."

He let out a slow breath. "The only other people are Barzoon's kids. The girl he had with Lila is too young to be reliable, and the two from his first marriage aren't going to be very excited about speculating as to whether daddy murdered his hot young wife. Adams' widow, Monica, may have some insight into the financial items, but I doubt she'll talk to me about it. So that leaves who? No one."

"What do you mean, no one? There's Orville. Lila might have mentioned it to him."

"Maybe the payoff from Kevin Adams' death, but not the details from her own or Harlan's."

"Shoot, you're right." She placed a delicate finger to her lips then pointed it at Tate. "That's still not a dead end. You could talk to the men who work at A & B Construction. And the night of her accident, Lila was at the Lumberjack tavern in Big Bay. Wouldn't you want to interview the people who were there?"

"That's a lot of work, Gayla. All for what? Just to verify what we already know. And even if Barzoon *did* do it, what possible difference could it make now? All this just so Orville Dorian can say 'I told you so' to the good citizens of Marquette? Who's going to care?"

A rain cloud hovered over Gayla's head. "Orville will."

Tate made a series of faces expressing his emotions better than words ever could. Then they sat in silence for three long minutes. Then he broke. "Oh, geez, don't look at me like that. Oh, all right! I'll do some more digging. The construction company and the tavern. But that's it. Deal?"

"Deal."

# Ain't No Reason

ADAMS AND BARZOON Construction was located six miles west of town on US 41, up the long grade leading inland toward the iron-mining town of Negaunee. There was an eight-by-twelve plywood sign bolted to sturdy posts next to a driveway leading back to second-tier property. No road frontage. That was probably Adams being frugal, thought Tate, assuming he'd bought the land before Barzoon wormed his way in. The driveway was covered with snow; it appeared the death of Barzoon had meant the end of the business.

He wheeled the Lincoln into the parking lot of the appliance store next to A & B's drive and got out. Crystalline flakes drifted from a slate sky. He had his Sorels on, but the drifts on the driveway would be higher than the tops of his boots and that meant snow down his boots. He scowled then trudged over the crusty bank and tromped up the tree-lined road. Two hundred feet later he arrived at a locked gate and a high chain link fence topped by razor wire. The fence enclosed an area Tate guessed to be five acres. Inside and to the left was a tall metal warehouse with an office door and a lonely window. Around the perimeter of the yard sat an assortment of construction vehicles and equipment, all neatly lined up. The assortment included an end loader. Snow was melting in Tate's boots, soaking through his socks. There was nothing to see. Waste of time, he thought, as he turned and began slogging back to his car.

"Hey! You want something?"

The voice was from the open back door of the appliance store. Tate struggled through a drift separating A&B's drive from the rear of the store then walked to the doorway, stomping the snow off his trousers and boots as he arrived. "I was looking for A & B Construction. They shut down?"

"Ever since the owner died."

"Wouldn't happen to know any of the people who worked there, would you?"

"You're talkin' to one."

"My name's Tate. I'm checking into . . . ah . . . a late payment on the gas account. And you are?"

"Jim Satterfield."

"Working here now?"

"Yeah. Gotta eat." He gestured toward A&B. "Day after Barzoon died, his kid came over and told us he was shuttin' the place down and we should go collect unemployment. No notice, no severance, nothing. Eight years I worked there and he says, 'Hit the road, asshole.' Not exactly like that, but that's the way it felt."

"Barzoon's kid?"

"Yeah, Earl. Snotty little pissbucket."

"What about the jobs in progress? Did you just stop doing them?"

"Weren't any. We were down to a skeleton crew, just me and three others. Barzoon had bids out, but wasn't nothing happening."

"When did you finish up the last project?"

Satterfield rubbed his chin. "'Umm . . . round the end

of December, I guess. There's always residual work, stuff you have to do even after the client moves in, so the end of a job isn't real clear cut. Not like you'd think. Anyway, it ended 'round the end of December and we were doing residual work till sometime in January."

"Then nothing?"

"Maintenance and a few small jobs. A shed, a garage, stuff like that."

"Anything on the horizon?"

"There was always talk. Barzoon would tell us about this or that he figured was about to break loose. I think he was just trying to keep his core people from jumping ship. He'd let a lot of guys go and had the rest of us down to half time. That didn't sit well with some. They'd make noise about looking elsewhere, but they never did."

"Was Barzoon a good boss?"

"Kevin Adams was a good boss. Barzoon was a dipshit."

"At the time Kevin died, was the company busy?"

Satterfield shook his head. "Uh-uh, slow. That was three years ago. Tail end of the recession. No one was building anything."

"What about now? The economy's healthy. Seems there's building going on all around Marquette County."

"Yeah, there is. But we weren't doing any of it."

Tate was about to ask another question when Satterfield said, "Nice talkin' to you. I better get back to work." He turned to go.

"One last question."

Door half open: "Sure.".

"Who was next in command under Barzoon? Who was the ramrod after Adams died?"

"Ardell Wagaman. He lives in Ishpeming."

Tate trekked back to his car, jotted some notes, then departed west toward Ishpeming.

Late-thirties, hard-muscled, and weather-beaten, Ardell Wagaman looked every inch the construction foreman. They were seated at the kitchen table in his sixties-era split-level.

"Harlan Barzoon, huh! Stupid shit to go get himself lost. How the hell do you do that when you're on a road? Just follow the goddamn road and get where you're goin'. No surprise though. Dumb sonsabitch."

Tate imagined Wagaman stranded in the middle of nowhere with a balky snowmobile, first growling, then kicking ugly dents in the cowl, then tying a rope to the skids and dragging the hulk to his destination, all the while cursing a blue streak.

"Why do you say no surprise?"

"The guy thought he knew everything 'bout everything. Goddamn Einstein. Get halfway through something and it'd be all fouled up, then me or one of the boys would have to clean up after him. Always took more time than it woulda if we'd done it ourself. Plus, he'd come 'round and buttonhole you and talk you half to death 'bout one of his concepts. *Concepts* don't get foundations dug, footings poured, or walls framed. I used to tell him, 'Just gimme the goddamn plans and get the hell outta the way.' He didn't like that none, but wasn't a damn thing he could do about it."

"He'd take it?"

"Darn right he'd take it. After Kevin died, wasn't anyone 'round knew which way was up 'cept me." Wagaman emitted a coarse laugh. "Barzoon had his punk kid try to foreman a job out in Chocolay Township. Goddamn garage for chrissake. Don't get no easier 'n that. Stupid shit did the transit work himself and had the boys set the forms wrong. After the 'crete was poured and set up and the forms came off, the crew saw the pad was sloping toward the back wall." Ardell laughed again.

Tate said, "What I know about construction you could fit in a glove and still have room for your hand. What do you mean? Is it supposed to be flat?"

Ardell said, "No," as in, 'No, you fool.' "Got to have it sloped *out* a couple degrees so when there's snow melt or rain water coming off the car it runs downhill toward the garage door. Now, if you want, you can have a drain in the center with a dry sump or plumbed to the system and have the 'crete tapered in toward it. But that weren't in the blueprints. So if you don't have a center drain, then you gotta slope the pad a little so it drains out the garage door, or at the very least, pour it flat. Understand?"

"Yeah. Straightforward the way you tell it. Seems anyone who'd been in construction for a while would know."

"Damn right! First day. What the heck ya got a house and garage for? To keep the water *out*, not *in!*"

"So, junior screwed up the concrete work and it cost time and money."

"Sure did. Jimmy, the guy you talked to at Range Appliance, told him straight out he had to fix it before they started framing the walls, but the stupid shit said they could take care of it later. Huh! How you gonna do that?"

Tate didn't have the slightest idea.

Wagaman went on. "Night before they put the roof on,

it rained. Next morning there was an inch of water sittin' in there like a lake. Coulda put some bass in and had a fishpond. Meathead had the crew tryin' to push it out with brooms when the owner came out and saw. An' you better believe he was pissed."

"So what'd they do?"

"Wasn't nothin' they could do. Owner calls Barzoon and tells him he ain't gonna pay less they redo the floor. I was in the office and heard it. Barzoon's tryin' to sweet talk him out of it, but it don't do no good. After he gets off the phone, he blows a gasket and blames everybody 'cept his numbnuts kid. But there weren't nothing he could do 'cept tear it down and start from scratch."

"Tear the entire garage down?"

"Yeah. Ain't no other way. We had to jackhammer out the old pad and pour a new one with the right slope."

"Couldn't you just lift up the building and pour a new pad underneath?"

"You don't know nothing 'bout construction, do you?"

Tate shook his head.

"I guess you seen people moving houses. That's because those houses got floor joists. A garage don't have no floor joists. The walls sit on a sill on a concrete slab. Can't get nothing under to jack it up. If you tried, everything would be all twisted and busted apart by the time you got done. Better to just tear it down and start over again."

"There couldn't have been much profit left in the job after that."

"Profit? Hell no! Build it, tear it down, build it again. Probably cost five grand over the bid. Stupid fucking kid. It was all his fault, but Barzoon blamed everyone else."

"So was the kid, Earl, that's his name, isn't it?"

"Yeah, Earl the Pearl."

"Was Earl out there on the job all the time?"

"Just in the summer's all. Went to college the rest of the year. It was like a challenge for him, though, to see how much stuff he could fuck up in three months." Ardell gave a hearty laugh.

"Tell me about when Kevin Adams died. How exactly did it happen?"

"That was another Earl the Pearl screw up."

Tate's eyebrows rose. "Huh! How so?"

"Like everyone else, we use gravel when there's a new driveway been cut into a construction site. Otherwise, if it rains and you run trucks in, the ground turns to mush and pretty soon you got trucks gettin' stuck. So, before we start we order a couple loads of gravel and have it spread along the driveway to make the ground stable enough for our equipment."

"I see."

"Yeah, well, we used to call up Conrad, that's Conrad Aggregate, and have 'em haul out a load or two and spread it. That's what they do and it makes sense to use them. Doesn't pay to try to do everything yourself, just what you're good at."

"Sure," agreed Tate. "Gotta specialize."

"Yeah, specialize. Anyway, junior finds what he thinks is this fantastic deal on road gravel from a company finishing up some roadwork on 41. He buys their surplus, 'bout twenty loads, and has 'em dump it in the yard during the weekend, and we get there Monday morning to find it's all been dumped right in the middle. Kevin pops his cork and tells the kid off. All the while, junior's saying what a great price he got on the gravel and what's the big deal? They have to move it, so what?"

"Moving it was a problem?"

"Damn right. Gravel's cheap, see, but labor and machinery are expensive. Got to figure seventy an hour or better to run an end loader, machine and operator."

"Seventy seems like a lot."

"Think about it. You got an expensive piece of gear there. You can't have some minimum-wage doofus pounding the piss out of it. You treat 'em right, they'll work a long time, but if you don't know what you're doin', you can break 'em in a heartbeat. So you're payin' the operator twenty-five an hour, and that don't count social security and workman's comp and all that other stuff. Top of that you're paying for diesel and the clock is running and the machine is wearing out and it's gotta be paid for. And believe me, you go out and buy one o' those things and you'll find out they ain't cheap. And you gotta have a mechanic maintain 'em all the time—grease, oil, bearings, hoses, seals, tires—it ain't no picnic. And people beef about paying ninety an hour for loader work, it's a goddamn bargain when you think about it."

"I'm starting to get the picture."

"Yeah. So by having to pay for five years' worth of gravel up front and then having to move it around the yard and have it take up valuable space till we used it, and then having to fire up the loader, load it up, and truck it to the site and spread it ourself, using our truck and our manpower, well, anyone can see that it added so much to the cost that it was going to be way more expensive than having Conrad do it. But that was typical Earl the Pearl.

Big college boy, thought he was a genius but dumb as a beer fart."

"What about the accident. How'd it happen?"

Wagaman became somber as the memory came back. "Jimmy tell you I was the one who found him?"

"No."

"Yeah. I was the first one there that Saturday morning. Had some things to take care of. Anyway, I get there and the gate's unlocked, Kevin's truck is in its spot, and right away I see the loader on its side. I drive over to it, and that's when I seen him. He was half underneath. I guess he was there all night."

"What do you figure happened?"

The rough man wiped a calloused hand across his face. Kevin had obviously been a friend. "Don't know. Kevin was careful with stuff. Not prissy, you understand, but careful not to waste time or energy or break things. Way it looked, he drove the loader up the side of the gravel pile till it tilted sideways and tipped. Then he musta fallen outta the seat and the loader rolled on top of him." Wagaman shook his head in frustration. "I still can't figure out why he'd do that? Ain't no reason."

"What do you mean, no reason?"

"Listen, Tate. It's gravel, see, loose gravel. You don't drive up on it. Ain't no need. You just drop the bucket down flat and drive it *into* the pile until the bucket's full. Then you raise it up and back away. You don't drive up on the pile. Ain't no reason for it!"

# The Lumberjack

AFTER HIS TALK with Wagaman, Tate's next stop was the Lumberjack Tavern in Big Bay. He decided to take County Road 510 and along the way hoped to find the place where Lila had her accident. As he motored eastbound on US 41 toward the turnoff, Ardell Wagaman's words kept running through his mind: *You don't drive up on the pile. Ain't no reason for it.* Tate couldn't imagine any reason why Kevin Adams would drive up the side of a gravel pile until the ten-ton end loader toppled over. It really *didn't* make any sense. Maybe the police report would have an answer. But he wasn't on the inside anymore. He didn't have a badge. He'd have to ask. And he'd have to ask politely.

He turned off 41 at the sign, pulled over, and used his map to inspect the twisting trail of County Road 510. Pavement for the first few miles then nearly twenty of gravel between Negaunee Township and Big Bay. Pulling the articles copied at the library from his pocket, he leafed through them until he found the one describing Lila's accident. *It occurred approximately midway between Big Bay and Negaunee Township.* Hmm, about halfway, not very exact. Tate punched the trip odometer and dropped the gearshift into drive. Soon the pavement ended and the road changed to a frozen washboard, bouncing the car wildly until he slowed to a modest thirty-five.

Two miles short of the halfway point, Tate began paying attention to the trees lining the road for signs of damage from Lila's Jeep. The snow was deep, it was a long shot, but he had to look. Two miles after the midway point, with nothing to show for his effort, he called it quits. Between the high banks and plow-thrown snow stuck to trees, there was no way to identify the accident site. Maybe after the snow melted there'd be signs—scars on trees, gouges in the earth, parts from the Jeep—but there was no hope of finding them now.

After forty-five minutes of driving, Tate neared the end of 510, where it meets County Road 550 south of Big Bay. Arriving, he turned left at the junction, toward the village, grateful to be back on pavement.

The Lumberjack Tavern was on the left just before the town. A few minutes past four. Too early for a crowd. One car and one pickup in front. As the door squawked shut, Tate stomped the snow off his boots then ambled to the worn bar. The bartender, a husky man with a florid face and thin hair lacquered with a petroleum product, was in casual conversation with a professional drinker planted at the far end of the bar. After Tate was seated, the bartender turned to him. "What can I get for you?"

"Beam, straight up."

"Out," said the bartender, shaking his head. "Got bourbon, but it's bar stock."

"Sure," said Tate.

When it arrived, he took a sip. The taste was corrosive and made his eyes water.

"Startin' to snow," said the bartender, offering to pull him into conversation.

"I just drove up on 510. With all those curves and the snow coming down, had to watch my speed."

"Gotta be careful," offered the drinker.

"Yeah," said Tate. "Occurred to me that if I had an accident along there, it could be some time before anyone would be along."

The bartender said, "Gets a few dozen cars every day, even when there's no logging going on."

"Kids with their jacked up four-wheelers out for a cruise," added the drinker.

"Probably wouldn't have to wait more than a couple hours at the most," opined the bartender.

Tate asked, "Many accidents along there?"

The bartender pulled the corners of his mouth down, shook his head. "Uh-uh. Time to time, but not many. Too bumpy to go fast. Hard to get in an accident when you're going slow." He began to chuckle. "Not impossible, mind you. Last weekend Wally Rintala backed outta here all the way across 550 and into the ditch on the other side." He and the drinker laughed at the telling. "So speed ain't always the issue."

"What about that accident last year with Lila Barzoon? What's the story on that?"

Both the bartender and drinker stopped laughing.

"What do you mean, *the story*?" asked the bartender, suspicious.

"Well, I read about it and didn't think anything of it. But now that I've driven the road, like you said, it's so bumpy you can't go fast. So I'm wondering how it was that she was going so fast that her Jeep rolls over? Just seems odd."

"Damn shame," said the drinker, genuine sorrow in his

voice. "Lila was good people."

"You knew her?"

"Yeah, sure. Everybody knew Lila. Damn shame if you ask me."

The bartender gave Tate a hard once-over. "You from the Alcohol Commission?"

"No," said Tate, shaking his head. "Nothing like that. Actually, Lila's father, Orville Dorian, asked me to do some checking into her death. He just can't believe she'd roll her Jeep like that. Look, I don't have any axe to grind, I'm just doing a favor for a friend. Told Orville I'd poke around and see if there was anything more to it."

"If you're trying to pin it on us, you can hit the road, pal. She had a couple drinks here, this is a bar, it's what people do, but it ain't our fault she died."

Tate held up his hands in a gesture of peace. "Not saying it is. I'm telling you straight. I'm not a cop. I'm not a lawyer. I'm not from any commission. I'm not out to lay blame on you or anyone else. I'm just a guy doing a favor for a friend. When I go to a bar, I drink. That's what bars are for. She was an adult. Far as I know, nobody forced her to come here and nobody forced her to drink. So if drinking was part of the cause of her accident, way I see it, it was her own fault, certainly not yours."

Some of the tension left the bartender's face. "Damn right. Can't baby-sit everyone. Adults gotta take care of themself. Now-a-days, no one's got personal responsibility anymore. No matter what happens, it's always someone else's fault."

"Maybe we just think it's now, but it's always been," said the drinker.

Tate thought he might be right. "So what do you figure

happened to Lila?"

The bartender spoke first. "Going too fast, missed a turn, rolled. Guess she wasn't wearing her seatbelt 'cause she got tossed and the Jeep rolled on top of her."

"I was here that night," offered the drinker. "She was in a grand mood, dancing and whoopin' it up. 'Course, she was pretty much always that way. Life of the party, that one. Damn shame."

"What time did she leave?" asked Tate.

"Closing time. Same as everyone else."

"Two o'clock?"

"Yeah."

"Do you know if she was going straight home?"

"It's not like she'd be confiding in me if she weren't."

"Do you recall if she left alone?"

"I remember she was outside talking to some people when I left. I don't recollect who, but Steve and Cheryl Girard were here that night. Maybe they'd know."

"Where can I find them?"

The drinker gave directions. Tate jotted them in his pad.

The bartender said, "Everybody here liked her, mister, but accidents happen."

"How many people have died in auto accidents on 510 in the middle of the winter with four-foot high snowbanks on both sides of the road to soak up the impact of a skid?"

The bartender didn't answer.

Tate stepped out of the bar into the increasing snowstorm. Pulling the door closed, he stood in the crisp air absorbing the sparkling vision of millions of snowflakes falling. It's like life, he thought, beautiful and fragile. The door opened behind him and the drinker, who was quite a bit shorter than he'd appeared while warming a throne, strolled up to his side. He wasn't wearing a coat and he didn't seem bothered by the cold, or by the snowflakes collecting on his shoulders and head.

"Don't seem right," he said. "Lila was wild and took life head on, but she wasn't stupid. She'd been up and down that road dozens of times in that blue Jeep o' hers. I agree with you, mister. Seems mighty odd she'd wind up dead there."

"What about her husband, Harlan Barzoon? He come up often?"

The drinker shook his head.

"She came alone?"

"Yup."

"Anybody special she was coming up to see?"

The drinker's face shut down. "That wouldn't be for me to say. But as for the accident, I never did think it passed the smell test." He touched the tip of his nose for emphasis. "You oughta go see Steve and Cheryl."

"I will."

The drinker gave a firm nod then turned and ambled back inside.

The air was thick with snowflakes. He tilted his head back and stared straight up, figured he could see two hundred feet, then gazed down the road and revised his estimate to a hundred. Dangerous for driving. Was it like this the night Lila Barzoon died? With that question in mind, Tate opted for the comfort of the Town Car, checked the directions to the Girard residence, and pulled onto the highway.

# Everyone Knows

THREE MILES AND six turns later he was knocking on a door of a small well-kept home with a freshly snowblown drive. A tall, thin man with large features on a friendly face answered. Tate explained his mission and was invited inside. An ample woman with a more suspicious demeanor was drawn from something cooking to find out what was going on. Tate didn't see any reason to be coy.

"Lila Barzoon's father asked me to look into her death. I know it's been a year and the cops did an investigation, but Mr. Dorian wants to make sure no stone has been left unturned in finding the truth about what happened that night. So, if it isn't too much trouble, perhaps you could tell me what you told the police and we can start from there."

Mr. Girard's eyes went to his wife. She scrunched her lips. "Didn't tell the police anything."

"Why not?"

Mr. Girard answered. "They didn't ask."

Tate's eyebrows knitted. "You mean no one interviewed you?"

They shook their heads. "Nope."

"There was a short guy at the Lumberjack. I didn't get his name. About fifty. Short gray hair—"

Before Tate could finish describing the drinker, Mr. and Mrs. Girard said, "Gordy," in unison, then laughed at the symmetry of their response.

"Yeah, that's probably him. Anyway, he told me he was at the bar the night Lila died. Said at closing time she was talking to some people outside. He couldn't remember who, but thought you two might."

"What does Mr. Dorian plan on doing with this information?" asked Mrs. Girard.

There was no point in beating around the bush. "He thinks Lila's husband, Harlan Barzoon, was somehow involved in her death. He wants to find out if it's true. I don't think it's about anything other than the truth. His only daughter is dead and he can't rest until he knows how it happened, one way or the other."

"Guess I can understand that," said Mr. Girard.

Mrs. Girard said, "Okay. We remember that night real well. Talked about it many times, but no cops ever came and asked us about it." She shrugged. "No big surprise though."

"Why not?"

"Wasn't important enough. You see, some people thought Lila was trash. So she dies in a car crash, big deal."

"That what you thought?"

"Heck no. But if you live here or hang with people around here, you're, well, maybe not as cool as if you're partying downtown."

"We're just a bunch of rubes to them," said Mr. Girard.

"So you think the cops blew it off? Figured she was drinking, going too fast and, *bam*, end of story?"

"Yeah, what's to investigate?"

"What do *you* think? Were you there that night? Did you see her leave?"

"We were there," said Mr. Girard.

"Did you see her leave?"

There was an uncomfortable silence.

"Ah . . . yeah, I suppose so," said Mrs. Girard.

"Let me guess. She was with someone."

No one spoke, finally she nodded.

"Who?"

"We don't want to get anyone in trouble."

"Mrs. Girard, Lila Barzoon died that night. No one can get in any more trouble than that." He paused then added, "I am not here to pass moral judgment on Lila or anyone else. She was an adult and made her own decisions. I respect that. I just want to know the truth about what happened."

She rubbed the tips of her fingers together, giving her time to think. "All right. Yes, she was with someone."

"Someone who wasn't her husband?"

"Yes."

"More than a friend?"

"Um . . . you could say that."

"Do the cops know about it?"

"Uh-uh. Don't think so. From what I heard, they only talked to Carl. He was bartending that night, and he didn't see her leave."

"This guy who was more than a friend, was it new or had it been going on for a while?"

"Going on a while."

"Think her husband knew about it?"

She sucked in a breath, let it out slow. "Hard to say. Wasn't any secret around here. It's a small town and people talk. Especially about stuff like that."

"So, who was the lucky guy?"

"Oh god! Do I have to tell?"

"If anyone asks, I'll say I heard it someplace else. Lots of people knew, so it wouldn't be a stretch."

She gave it another moment of thought and then shrugged in resignation. "All right. Johnny Nolen."

"Johnny Nolen. Tell me about him."

"Johnny's a nice guy. He's an artist."

"I take it he lives around here."

"Yeah. He's got a place on Lake Independence. You oughta see it. Real nice. Built it himself."

"So Lila left with Johnny. Do you know if they went to his house?"

"Couldn't say."

"Did Lila take her Jeep?"

"Nope, they went in Johnny's pickup."

"Was that the last time you saw her?"

She nodded.

"Had she had a lot to drink?"

"I wasn't counting."

"Hmm . . . Lila and Johnny, so were they a thing?"

"Kinda."

"How long?"

"Month or two, maybe longer."

"How often did you see her up here?"

"It's not like we're at the Lumberjack twenty-four seven. Steve and I may stop in on Friday and Saturday night and have a drink or two. Lila was there I guess at least one of those nights, sometimes both."

"With Johnny?"

"After they met, always."

"Do you think her husband knew about it?"

"Wasn't any of my business."

"I'm just asking your opinion."

"You married, Mr. Tate?"

"No."

"Let's say you were. And let's say your wife left home a couple nights a week and drove to a bar twenty miles away and didn't come home until the early hours of the morning. What would you think?"

Tate nodded. "I get your point. You ever see them up here together? Lila and Harlan?"

"No."

"But you know who he is?"

"Yeah. Don't know him personally, but I know who he is."

"Ever see him up here alone?"

She shook her head. "Can't recall."

"Last question. How do I find Johnny Nolen's house?"

# No Question At All

DAYLIGHT WAS FADING as Tate followed the Girards' directions to Johnny Nolen's home on the north shore of frozen Lake Independence. Not large, yet very appealing, the house had rough-cut siding and interesting lines and glasswork. Taste on a budget. There were no vehicles in the drive and the windows were dark. Fine, thought Tate. His infallible stomach clock reminded him it was nearing dinnertime. Enough for one day. Executing a three-point turn, he aimed the Lincoln toward home.

Driving south out of Big Bay, he slowed as he approached the turnoff from paved and recently plowed 550 to unpaved, unplowed 510. The snow was three to four inches deep. Visibility was down to a hundred feet, zero when the wind picked up and swirled the snow into a whiteout. Even on 550 the driving would be slow and dangerous. And he'd have cars coming at him. What the heck, he thought, I have chains in the trunk. Gotta do it to know what it was like that night. He made the turn.

Darkness, snowstorm, the same conditions Lila Barzoon had been driving in the night of her death, except Tate hadn't been partying, and it was six-thirty, not four in the morning.

He was carrying too much speed into the first turn, and the rear end of the Lincoln broke loose. He pulled his foot off the gas, the rear tires slowed, grabbed, and the car straightened out. Too fast already. He backed off to thirty. The skid was a rude reminder that it would be an hour-long drive requiring sustained concentration. He knew Lila's Jeep would've handled the road better and easier than his Lincoln. The extra traction of four-wheel drive plus snow tires, if she had them, would have been safer. But the bumps were still there to limit top speed. How fast could a person go and still keep control? Tate didn't want to find out. From time to time there were straight stretches with barely a pothole and Tate sped up, anxious to make miles. Was it that way for Lila? A straight stretch. Tired. Wanting to get home. Needing sleep. Her foot pressing harder on the gas. A curve. Some ruts. The tail end skids away, slams into a bank, causing the Jeep to roll. Tate checked the mounds of snow on either side of the road: Four feet high, higher in places. Seemed that if the Lincoln skidded it would hit a bank and bounce off, not roll up over it. But maybe a Jeep, being narrower and higher off the ground, would have had a tendency to roll. Hard to say. The accident report would be helpful. Pictures too, if they had any.

As Tate neared the halfway point he was wishing he'd taken paved 550. The darkness, snow billowing against his windshield, jarring potholes, and never-ending series of curves had him hypnotized. His eyelids became heavy, his muscles relaxed, and he nodded. Jerking upright, he powered the driver's side window down and stuck his head out, face to the oncoming snow. Fluffy globs smacked against his cheeks, melting clots of cold drawing him back from the edge. Then he was awake again and thinking.

Lila Barzoon's accident was probably just that, an accident. Tough road, late at night, drinks, snowstorm, it would be easy to run off the road, real easy. Yet, there were loose ends that made him uncomfortable. The cops hadn't been thorough. You can't call an investigation thorough if you haven't interviewed the last person to see the victim alive. Big Bay is a small community and word gets around. If Johnny Nolen had been interviewed, the Girards would have known about it. And bolstering Orville's theory, Lila's affair with Nolen would give Harlan Barzoon even more reason to kill her than money alone. If she'd been spending as much time in Big Bay as the Girards claimed and coming home well after the bar closed, he'd have to have been suspicious. Any man would be.

Tate was two miles from the end of the gravel, deep in thought, driving in the center of the road as he rounded a curve and faced the glaring headlights of a raised four-wheeler barreling at him. Adrenalin surged through his body. Yanking the wheel to the right, he swerved to miss it. The Lincoln fishtailed, right rear quarter-panel slamming against the snowbank before the car straightened out. The four-wheeler swerved too. They passed without touching.

*Whew!* thought Tate, close call. He hadn't been going fast, but with the thick snow cutting visibility and the washboard road lulling him into a stupor, he'd almost had a head-on collision. No longer was there any question of whether Lila Barzoon could have had an accident on this road. No question at all.

# Johnny Nolen

AT 9:30 THE next morning Tate was in his regular booth at the Omelet Eggspress, Gayla standing next to him. He gazed up at her. "We on for dinner tonight?"

"You bet, big boy." She gave him a wink. "Hope you belong to the clean plate club."

"I'm a founding member."

She leaned forward. "Sooo, what'd you find out about Lila?"

"I'll tell you tonight."

"You rat!" She gave him a swat with her order pad, "Tell me now."

"No way. The only thing I'm getting out of all this legwork is a home-cooked meal. I want food on the table before I talk."

Her hands went to her hips. "Fine, I'll wait. But it'd better be good."

"I don't know about good, but it's complicated."

Gayla edged to his side, brushed against him, cooed, "Tell me now."

"I'll have the Ore Boat."

Her face compressed into the scowl of an angry butterfly. "Darn you! Okay, but you'd better have some hunger on when you arrive."

"Count on it."

After breakfast Tate used the phone in the diner to call Johnny Nolen. He was in. Tate asked if he'd mind talking about Lila. After a hesitation, Nolen said, "Sure, we can talk about Lila." Tate said he'd be there in forty-five minutes and hung up. Once you've sold it, don't buy it back. He'd gotten the interview; no sense in staying on the phone and giving Nolen a chance to change his mind. He dreaded the drive, but there was no choice. He'd take paved 550 this time, not bumpy 510.

The sky was still overcast, but only scattered flakes fell. The snowplows had done their job, the road was clear but icy, so it took Tate nearly an hour to get from the O.E. to Nolen's. Arriving, he found a forest-green pickup parked in a freshly shoveled drive. Tate pulled in next to it, climbed out of the Lincoln, and rambled to the wooden porch. A pair of cross-country skis leaned next to the door. There was an ornate knocker. He used it. A moment later it opened.

Early-thirties, tall, lean, and handsome, with long sandy-brown hair, an angular, sculpted face, brown eyes flecked with gold and an engaging smile, Johnny Nolen was friendly and easygoing even to Tate, a complete stranger. He was wearing a tan cotton work shirt with paint stains on it, jeans faded to a pale blue, and deck shoes with no socks. Tate thought if artists had a look, Nolen was the personification.

"Come on in."

"Thanks," said Tate, kicking the snow off his boots and stepping inside. He gazed around. "Nice place." He meant it. The main room was long and open: a living room in the middle, kitchen to the right, Nolen's studio on the left. The living room portion had tall windows divided in the center by a stone fireplace, the windows offering an excellent view of frozen Lake Independence, ice-fishing shanties dotting its surface. Nolen's artwork was all around. Attractive and functional woodwork, colorful ceramics, and moody, engaging oils. The man had talent.

Nolen invited him to have a seat. A couch and two chairs were grouped near the fireplace. The couch was covered with books in the process of being sorted. That left a handsome maple rocker and a complex ergonomic number made of alternating strips of light and dark wood. After a critical appraisal, Tate chose the rocker.

After they were seated, Nolen said, "You said you wanted to talk about Lila. What would you like to know?"

"I'll get to the point. Her father thinks her death might not have been an accident. Any thoughts on that?"

Nolen's eyes drifted away from Tate and his smile vanished. "I think he's right."

Lulled into relaxation by the heat from the fireplace, Tate became alert. "You do?"

"Never seemed right to me," slowly shaking his head. "Lila had driven that road many times. She was a good driver. Skid and roll?" He again shook his head. "No way. And it doesn't make sense her being thrown from the Jeep. She would have been wearing her seatbelt. Especially that night, storm and all. No, Mr. Tate, it never seemed right."

"Nolen, I'm not here to pry into your private life, but like I said, I told Lila's father I'd look into this, so there are questions I need to ask."

"Like what?"

"Were you with her that evening?"

Nolen hesitated. "Yeah. I . . . ah, saw her at the Lumberjack. We had a couple beers and talked."

"And when the bar closed, you left together."

"Somebody tell you that?"

"Yes."

Nolen became thoughtful. "Okay, it's true, we left together."

"Mind if I ask where you went?"

"We came here. I wanted to show her a piece I'd been working on. We came here and talked for a while. Then I drove her back to her Jeep."

"About what time was that?"

"Umm . . . time kind of got away from us. It was pretty late. Maybe three or four, sometime around then."

"Did she have anything to drink while she was here?"

"We shared a bottle of wine."

"And she'd been drinking earlier at the Lumberjack?"

"Yes," quickly adding, "but she wasn't drunk. Lila had maybe two or three drinks at the bar and some wine here, but she was clear-headed, she could drive. If I hadn't thought so, I wouldn't have let her go. I . . . ." He didn't finish the sentence.

"But it was late, though, when she left. I drove 510 last night. It's a long, hard drive in the dark with snow coming down. I can understand how someone could have an accident if they weren't fully alert. It almost happened to me."

Nolen shook his head. "Uh-uh. Lila? In her Jeep? Can't see it. Never could. Like I said, she wasn't drunk. She was wide awake."

"At four in the morning?"

Nolen twisted in his chair. "You're not a cop?"

"No. Whatever we talk about is strictly between us." It was a white lie, maybe even a black one, but Nolen had something to tell and Tate needed to hear it.

Nolen sucked on his lower lip while collecting his thoughts. "There was some coke floating around. She did a couple lines. I did too."

"And that was enough to keep her awake?"

"Yeah. Big Bay is about thirty miles past the end of the road. By the time anything gets up here it's been stepped on so many times it's mainly speed and baby powder. She was buzzing pretty good. Wasn't about to go to sleep on the drive home."

"So, Mr. Nolen, here's the sixty-four thousand dollar question. If Lila was wide awake and a good driver and was wearing her seatbelt and it wasn't an accident, what happened?"

Nolen stood up and wandered to one of the tall windows overlooking the ice-covered lake. "Her husband, Harlan Barzoon, she was going to leave him. She said he wasn't taking it well. Why don't you ask him?"

"He's missing and presumed dead."

"What?" said Nolen, turning to Tate in surprise.

"You hadn't heard?"

He shook his head.

"His snowmobile quit on his way to his camp at Echo Lake. It's about a mile—"

"I know where it is."

"Friday before last, nighttime, snowing. He abandoned the machine and began walking. His tracks veered off the road and petered out in the woods. The cops figure he became disoriented in the darkness, least that's what the paper said. It's been eleven days now and no sign of him. They've been searching, but last I heard, no luck."

"He's not out there," said Nolen, disgusted.

"No?"

"Lila said he was always scamming. It's probably just another in a long line. Keep looking, Tate, you'll find out she was right. The guy's a real sleazebag." Nolen's face was tight with anger. Then it passed. "Lila . . . Lila was going to leave him and move in with me. I think what happened was he couldn't handle it, so he killed her and found a way to make it look like an accident. That's what I think now, and that's what I've thought since the day she died."

Tate remained silent hoping Nolen would continue.

"Follow me," he said, turning toward the studio end of the house. Tate followed. Nolen stopped in front of a canvas on an easel. It was facing away from the living room so Tate hadn't see it from where he'd been sitting. On it was an oil painting of a woman in shades of blue. A nude, reclining on a couch, his couch, reading a book. Relaxed and sturdy, yet very feminine and extremely seductive, the woman was Lila Barzoon.

"Lila said it was her color," said Nolen, struggling to hold back emotion. "I told her I saw her in earth tones, gold and cinnamon, but she said no, paint me in blue."

Johnny Nolen was still staring at his painting when Tate let himself out. What now, he wondered as he cruised back toward Marquette? So Nolen was her lover and doesn't believe Lila's death was an accident. Orville and Johnny, the two men who loved her most, both feel the same, and the common denominator is Harlan Barzoon.

Both of them believe he's capable of murder. Or *was* capable, since it's likely he's dead too. But *is* Barzoon really dead? Hmm . . . the Sheriff's Department would be the logical place to go for more information, but the last thing Tate wanted to do was talk to cops. He sighed. There was no choice.

# Deputy Fugman

DRIVING TO THE courthouse on Baraga Avenue in the center of Marquette, Tate parked the Lincoln on the street, dropped a quarter in the meter, and reluctantly shuffled across the street to the Sheriff's Department.

"How's it hangin'," said Tate as he entered.

Deputy Logan Fugman was on duty at the desk. "Tate! What a surprise. Stop in to report some missing intelligence?"

"Oooo . . . that's funny, Deputy."

Fugman beamed a satisfied smile. "So, what could possibly bring an ex feeb into a place where real cops work?"

I'm hating this, thought Tate. "Missing person, Deputy. Harlan Barzoon in particular. He get found yet?"

Fugman shook his head. "Uh-uh."

"Search and Rescue still out at the lake?"

"Nope. Called it off day before yesterday. Already been over a week. Barzoon left on a Friday and wasn't reported missing till Sunday. Days have been in the twenties, nights in the teens and single digits. That means there's about a zero percent chance of finding him alive."

"That's not good."

"Not good at all. And with the amount of snow we've had lately, there's probably a foot or more covering the body. My guess is he won't get found till the melt. Maybe not even then, animals and all."

"Comforting," said Tate. "You sure he's out there?"

Fugman screwed up his face. "What do you mean by that?"

"I'm just asking what it is that leads you to believe he's there?"

He scratched his chin. "Well, let's see. He told people he was going to his camp. He left home with his snowmobile. His pickup was parked at the camp road, and his snowmobile was found halfway to the camp, cowl up and tool kit out. Pretty funny, though, since the machine wasn't broke. He just thought it was because it quit."

"If it wasn't broke, why'd it quit?"

Fugman grinned. "Outta gas."

Tate shook his head. "Any tracks?" He already knew there were. He'd read it in the newspaper.

"Yeah. They went toward Echo Lake. The machine was only about halfway in, so he had a good half-mile yet to walk. Problem was, it was around six-thirty when he left the house. Seven-thirty by the time he unloaded the machine and started in to his camp. That's o-dark-hundred. So when the machine quit, he probably couldn't see in the tank to know if it was out of gas, or maybe he thought it was a fouled plug or something else and didn't think to check. He used the electric start till he ran the battery down, then most likely pulled on the rope until his arm wore out. After that, he started walking toward his camp. Probably didn't have a flashlight or what he had went dead, because his tracks followed the road for a while then angled into the woods and tailed off in a brushy, swampy area. Searchers weren't able to pick 'em up again. What he shoulda done is followed the snowmobile track back to his truck. Would have been easy. Even in the dark. Out there alone at night, snowstorm, once he got off the road he was screwed. Dumb shit."

"Bad luck to speak ill of the dead, Fugman."

"Bad luck to get lost in the woods at night in a snowstorm in the middle of the winter."

It was after 1:00 when Tate left the Sheriff's Office. Predictably, he was hungry, so he made a beeline to the O.E.

"Mike! Do I have news for you!" bubbled Gayla as he walked in the door. "Grab a seat. I'll be with you in a minute."

Tate took his usual end booth with its view of Third Street's quaint shops, locals and university students, businessmen and housewives, young and old of every type, braving the cold, trudged up and down the sloping street, a Rockwellesque slice of American life. Tate realized he was beginning to feel a proprietary interest in the town. A feeling that Marquette was more than just a place on the way to somewhere. A feeling that it was where he wanted to be. Gayla slid in across from him, breaking his chain of thought. She leaned forward conspiratorially. "Guess what I found."

Smiling. "Tell me quick or let me order first. I'm starved."

"Okay, Mr. Smart Guy, just for that I won't tell."

He went into full-grin mode to mollify her. "I'm kidding, okay? Please, please tell me or I won't be able to eat a bite."

Her lips compressed. "Hmm, I shouldn't, but . . . ."

She leaned across the table and whispered, "I found out about the insurance money, and you won't believe how much there was."

"Mega-bucks?"

"I'll say. Harlan had a quarter-million dollar policy on Lila. And that's exactly what he collected."

Tate's eyebrows went up. "A quarter-million. That's a lot of reasons."

"That's right," said Gayla, confident in her logic. "Well, Mr. P.I., doesn't it seem a bit odd that Barzoon would have a quarter-million dollar life insurance policy on his young wife? He was the breadwinner, not her. That's not normal."

He nodded. "It would be interesting to know what percentage of married thirty-something stay-at-home wives have quarter-million dollar insurance policies on them. Probably some, but not many."

"Heck no. The only reason you'd do that is to collect."

Tate frowned. "Or maybe to help with extra expenses if you were raising a kid alone. Not everyone who takes out an insurance policy is planning on bumping off their spouse, you know."

"Of course not. But you have to admit it's unusual."

He conceded the point then asked, "So, how'd you find out?"

A sly smile. "I have connections all over town."

"In particular?"

"Janet Mayweather, a friend of mine, she works at New Century Insurance. They wrote the policy. Janet swore me to secrecy, so don't mention her name, okay?"

"Who would I tell?"

"Just don't tell anyone."

"Fine with me. Did she know anything about the pay-off on the Adams policy?"

"She said she'd look it up when she gets a chance."

"Good work. Orville's going to have to pay you professional rates."

She laughed. Tate loved her laugh. "Come on, Mike, it's your turn. What'd you find?"

"Found out Lila had a boyfriend in Big Bay."

Gayla's expression changed to interest. "Oooh, juicy."

"Told him she was going to leave Barzoon for him."

"Wow."

Tate nodded.

"Anything else?"

"Just a couple of odds and ends. I'll fill you in tonight. I told Orville I'd spend two days on this and I only have five hours left, so I'd better chow down and get hustling."

After a buttery, greasy, extremely satisfying lunch, Tate paged through the O.E.'s phonebook for the phone number and address of Earl Barzoon. As it turned out, Earl the Pearl was living in a house on Hewitt Street, a short five blocks from the O.E. With a wave of his hand and a "Later, hon," Tate was out the door.

After a three minute drive, he parked in front of a dilapidated mud-brown two-story Victorian that matched the address from the phonebook then trod a snow-crusted path to the porch and rang the bell. A mangy twenty-something with greasy hair, multiple tattoos, and a discolored stud snared through an angry hole in his eyebrow answered the door, irritated, as if he'd been interrupted from something important, the sound of a television game show droning in the background.

"Yeah?"

"I'm looking for Earl Barzoon. He around?"

"Who's askin'?"

"Name's Tate."

"What'd ya what with him?"

Tate's eyes narrowed. "What are you, his mother? Tell him I want to see him."

"He ain't here, asshole."

Tate's first reaction was to take it. Then a pleasant thought occurred, he wasn't in law enforcement anymore and didn't have to. Maybe Gayla was right; maybe he needed to change his style. He smiled, then his fist blasted through the rotting screen door and into the solar plexus of the crudsack on the other side. The sack crumpled to his knees. Tate pulled the door open and stood over him as he recovered and then hoisted him to his feet.

"Think of me as Miss Manners and that as a free lesson. Now, *where* did you say Earl was?"

The sack promptly told him. "On campus, playing racquetball at the gym."

Tate keyed the Brontocarus and drove east to Front Street then hung a left, motoring north to Fair Avenue and the parking lot of Northern Michigan University's gymnasium. After asking directions from a gaggle of young ladies who didn't seem the least bit interested in exercise but whose shapes suggested they never missed a day, he found his way to the racquetball courts and watched through a second floor viewing window as the game progressed. First Earl would be up, then his partner, then Earl again. He resembled the photo of his father that Tate saw at Monica Adams' house. Six feet, strong build, solid jaw, dark-brown hair, stylish cut, rows of white teeth. They ran, sweated, and stroked, shoes squawking on the lacquered wooden floor. When the game was over, struggling to breathe, they laughed and glad-handed each other. Tate guessed the mourning period for daddy was over and quickly took the staircase to the first floor. The door to the racquetball court opened. The two men came out. "Gotta go, Earl," said his partner, jogging away. Earl was waving a goodbye as Tate walked up.

"Earl Barzoon?"

"Yeah?"

"Name's Tate. I'm a private investigator." It was the first time he'd said it, and it felt odd. He wondered if it sounded odd too. "I've been hired to look into the death of your stepmother, Lila. If you have a minute to talk, I'd appreciate it."

"Looking into Lila's death? What for? It was an accident."

"Certainly seems that way. I'm just trying to get a handle on the details."

"So, ah, like what do you want?" And 'so, ah, like make it fast' was implied.

"There someplace we can go to talk?"

"No time. Got a class in twenty minutes. You have questions, ask 'em now. Otherwise, I'm gone."

"Sure," said Tate, frustrated. He looked directly into Earl's eyes. "So why is it that a young mother in excellent health has a quarter-million dollar insurance policy on her?"

Earl scowled and stepped forward, well into Tate's personal space. "You got a problem with that? Take it up with the insurance company. Otherwise, stay the fuck away from me. Understand?" He glared at Tate.

"Sounds like little Earl's got an anger management problem."

Earl reached out to grab Tate's shirt. Tate's hand was already moving, grabbing him by the thumb, twisting it back, forcing him to his knees to keep it from breaking. Earl used his other hand to try to free himself, but to no avail.

"Listen, sonny, you're a lot like your roommate, no manners. Funny thing. Today was going to be the last day of my investigation. But now I'm not so sure. What do you think, Earl? Should I keep digging?"

Earl glared upward at him but didn't answer him. A crowd was gathering, staring.

"You don't seem too broken up over the disappearance of you father, Earl. Could it be because you think you're in for a nice, fat payday? Too bad for you. My bet's on the insurance company opening an investigation, and if they find what I think they'll find, they won't be paying a cent."

Tate let go of Barzoon's thumb then turned and walked away.

Kneading his sore hand, Barzoon yelled after him. "I'll remember you, Tate! You're gonna be sorry!"

After the incident with Earl, Tate decided to drive back to the Sheriff's Department. Deputy Fugman was still at the desk.

"The scent of law enforcement is a powerful aphrodisiac. Brings them back every time."

Tate wrinkled his nose. "Is that what I'm smelling? Anyway, Fugman, although being insulted is immensely entertaining, that's not what I came for. I was thinking more along the lines of seeing the accident report on Lila Barzoon."

"Harlan Barzoon's wife? Died in an auto accident last year. What else you wanna know?"

"I'd like to read the report."

Fugman worked his tongue around the inside of his mouth. "Yeah, I suppose. But you gotta read it here." He led Tate to an empty interview room, returning a minute later with a manila folder, the name Lila Barzoon printed on the tab. "Nothing leaves the room, right?"

"No problem," said Tate.

Fugman returned to his station and Tate took his time reading through the report, jotting notes as he went. Afterward, he put the papers neatly in order and carried the folder to the front desk.

"Thanks, Deputy."

"Professional courtesy," said Fugman, scanning the documents to make sure they were all there. Tate grimaced at the insult.

"One last thing. It was Barzoon's son who reported him missing, right?"

"Believe it was the son," said Fugman, not looking up from the paperwork.

"Did the lad spend much time searching for his father?"

"Couldn't say. You might want to ask Mel LaChance, our Search and Rescue coordinator."

"He around?"

"Nope, day off."

"Got his number?"

Fugman scribbled it down, shoved the slip across the counter. "You really think there's something hinky here, or are you just fishing?"

"Had a chat with Earl Barzoon. He didn't seem too broken up. Let's say your dad went missing in the woods. Do you suppose you'd be out looking for him? Or would you be hanging around Northern's gym playing racquetball with your buds?"

Tate made the call. LaChance answered on the third ring and invited him to stop by if he wanted to talk.

Average size but sturdy, with a military brush cut and a relaxed demeanor, LaChance invited Tate into the garage of his immaculately kept ranch home on ten acres of rolling land a few miles south of Marquette. He was replacing a broken belt on his snowblower. "They never go in the summer," he joked.

Tate wasn't good with machines and hoped his own snowblower would not break a belt. At least not until summer.

"Fugman said you got the call from dispatch and put together a search team."

"Yup. We were at the camp road within an hour. Wasn't fifteen minutes later we found his sled."

"Was it his son, Earl, who reported him missing?"

LaChance nodded. "Yeah. Called it in on Sunday afternoon. I didn't take the call, of course, but I talked to him at the scene. He told me he was supposed to meet Harlan at two that afternoon at Barzoon's place on Nash Lake. When he arrived, Harlan wasn't there. He said he hung around for a couple hours waiting, then became concerned. At four he left Barzoon's and drove to the road leading to Echo Lake. It's not plowed, so they use snowmobiles during the winter. Harlan's truck was parked on the side of the road. Earl assumed he was still at camp and he said it worried him, so he decided to hike in on the snowmobile trail. It's about a mile from 550 to the lake. Earl found the machine about halfway in and then followed what he figured were Barzoon's tracks until they disappeared in the woods. After that he thought he might have been wrong about the tracks, because it'd been snowing and it was hard to tell, so he walked the rest of the way to camp. When he arrived the place was cold and it didn't seem his father had been there, so he used his cell to call 911. The dispatcher patched him through to the Sheriff's Department, and I got a call from them around six.

"It was already dark by the time we had a search team with machines out to the camp road. We went in anyway, of course, and searched until midnight." He made an apologetic gesture with his hands. "Needless to say, with all the snow that'd fallen and a dozen men and machines tearing up the ground, that pretty much messed up any tracks that might have been there. So, when we went back the next morning, there wasn't any chance of tracking him. We had an airplane sweep the area. No luck. Then we set up a grid search and over the next couple of days covered everything within a half mile radius. I know that doesn't sound like much, but it's so darned thick and hilly that a half mile through the woods is a damn hard slog on snowshoes. Hell of a lot harder without 'em, so it's doubtful Barzoon could have strayed farther. That poor soul was out there two days and nights before the search even got started. Probably died of hypothermia Friday night or early Saturday morning and the body got covered by snow. Musta had nearly a foot since then. My guess is he's taking a long nap under a cold white blanket."

"Was Earl out searching with you?"

"We met him at Barzoon's snowmobile and he showed us the tracks he'd followed, thinking they were his father's. After that, there wasn't any point in him staying and I told him so. He'd already been outside for several hours, it was dark and getting colder, and he really wasn't dressed for it."

"He come out the next day?"

"Monday? Yeah, he was there maybe four hours. By the end of that time our search party had thoroughly covered a quarter-mile radius with no trace of Harlan. Later we widened it to a half-mile, but at the time, conditions being what they were, we didn't think a normal man could walk more than a quarter mile through deep March snow in that hilly, heavily-forested terrain and not be totally exhausted. Anyway, around that time Earl was pretty discouraged and there wasn't any point in him staying, so I told him he ought to go home and be with his family. To tell you the truth, he was just getting in the way. You know how it is."

Tate nodded. "So, he didn't come back out after that?"

"Not that I recall. Why?"

"Just curious. How about Barzoon's trail of footprints when he left the snowmobile? Did you see them?"

"Fragments, maybe. Earl had walked over his father's tracks to where they petered out, and then once more on his way back from the camp. So, with Earl's tracks covering up the ones Barzoon supposedly made, plus all the snow that had fallen between Friday and Sunday, it was impossible to tell. And at the place where Earl said he stopped following them, there wasn't anything to see. If Barzoon went that way, the wind and snow had erased his tracks completely."

Tate finished talking to LaChance shortly after four. Six o'clock was his self-imposed deadline to end his preliminary investigation and he still needed to shower and change before driving to Gayla's for dinner. He was tired of restaurant food, and his own cooking skills—charitably described as modest—were only used as a last resort. A home-cooked meal was something he did not want to be late for. Though there were several tantalizing investigative avenues he would have pursued had there been more time, he thought the best course would be to go home, sift through the information he had, and listen to what the facts were telling him.

# Pressure

HE LIT A fire in the fireplace, sat on the couch, and gazed through his picture window at Lake Superior, a dark and melancholy blue now that the last cold front had passed. The huge lake wasn't frozen over, but after months of cold, the shore was a massive bulwark of craggy spray-ice, twenty-feet high in places and extending a hundred feet into the water. It was snowing again, thick flakes drifting past his window, the glow and the warmth from his fireplace made him feel enclosed and comfortable. He was home. Home from work. But was he really working? Or was he just playing a game, a charade, going through the motions to placate Gayla? Was he really a private investigator now? Or was he, as Fugman had implied, an ex feeb, a retiree pretending to have some value left in his existence? Tate pondered this for a few moments and then thought it best to leave the navel-gazing for later. He'd analyze the information he had, come to a conclusion, then clean up and get to Gayla's. At this stage in his life, food always took precedence over philosophy.

Tate knew Orville wanted to believe his daughter was the image of innocence and purity. Obviously, she wasn't. Married and with a young child at home, she spent nights in a bar and had an affair with Johnny Nolen. And if Barzoon didn't know about it, he was about the only one who didn't. No, a man's wife stays out till all hours, he knows what's going on. And what man would relish that? Not someone like Barzoon, filled with ego and bluster, someone accustomed to being the Alpha dog. Would it be a motive for murder? If the sordid history of mankind is any indicator, the answer is an unqualified yes. And there's also the matter of the insurance money. A quarter of a million dollars seems an unusually large sum to have on a young wife and mother. Many families don't have any life insurance, and the ones that do have most or all on the breadwinner. Even absent hard statistics, in Tate's eyes the high-dollar policy on Lila made Harlan a suspect. But whether he had the opportunity was still in question. Tate knew if he continued with the case, he'd need to determine if Harlan had an alibi. Probably not, since the murder, if there was one, took place in the early hours of the morning, at a time when most people are home asleep and no one can vouch for them. Hmm, the daughter he and Lila had, was she in the house with him? She'd be too young to be a credible alibi, but would he leave her there alone to go searching for his wayward wife?

Kevin Adams was another issue. The men he'd spoken with said Adams knew what he was doing and was careful. Tate once again recalled what Ardell Wagaman said about moving gravel: *"You don't drive up on the pile. Ain't no reason."* Of course, Adams could have had a heart attack or some other debilitating medical event while operating the machine. But he was reasonably young and in top shape from hard work, so it seemed unlikely. And again the insurance angle paying off to Barzoon. And business was slow. And Barzoon was a spender. Tate knew if he stayed on the case, he'd have to look into the Adams accident too. If Barzoon was involved, it would establish the base of a pattern that could easily extend to Lila. He needed to get a look at the police report on the Adams accident to know the details, and he'd need to establish Barzoon's whereabouts the evening Adams died.

And now Barzoon himself is missing and presumed dead. But, conveniently, there's no body, and no evidence, other than circumstantial, that he's even missing. Perhaps Gayla could have her contact at the insurance company find out if Barzoon had a policy on himself. No insurance would suggest a real accident. A hefty payoff to Earl or Monica would call it into question. Tate could easily imagine Earl being involved in a scheme that promised easy money, and he didn't seem overly concerned about his father's disappearance. Maybe that's because he knows daddy isn't really missing. A tail and phone tap would likely uncover the truth. But Tate knew his days of going to a judge for a wiretap had ended when he handed in his resignation. And for a tail to be successful, he'd need one or two people willing to sit in a car, bored stiff, for hours and days on end.

And there was Monica Adams. She certainly didn't fit the part of the grieving widow. But it had already been three years since her husband's death. How long should the woman grieve? Still, she hadn't mention her dear departed even once during their conversation, only what a wonderful man Harlan Barzoon was. There's a strong possibility she and Barzoon had a thing going. And Monica seems to be doing okay financially. The insurance angle again? If so, how much did she get? And how much from Barzoon for her half of the business? Was she sleeping with him after her husband died? Before? Tate knew that if he took the case, he'd need to find out. The

Bureau would handle it by dredging up every scrap of information on her that ever existed, with an emphasis on finances, and then sifting through it with a fine-toothed comb. And while that was going on, they'd interview everyone who ever knew her. It would be tough going for a lone private investigator, very tough.

But the one thing he didn't need the resources of the Bureau for, the one thing that nearly always forced a reaction from the sleazebags, is pressure, the in-your-face type of pressure. Subjected to it, the innocent go to lengths to convince you of their innocence while the guilty become incensed, tell lies, hide, and lawyer up. If he stayed on the case, that's the tactic he'd take. Pressure. Relentless pressure.

# Dinner at Seven

"HEY YOU BEAUTIFUL thing!"

"Hey to you too, handsome. You're right on time."

"You said dinner at 7:00, not 7:01."

"I'll bet I could tie a steak to the bumper of my car and lead you anywhere I want."

He chuckled. "Please don't, it's hard on my shoes." Then, sniffing the air, "Speaking of food, whatever's cooking smells great!"

"Hope you like pot roast. I've had it in the crock pot all day."

Tate groaned with pleasure.

"Want a beer?"

He slid onto a bar stool in front of a gray Formica counter. "Your mind reading skills are extraordinary."

Gayla's apartment was small but well laid out. Situated on a hill near the middle of town, she had a view of city lights at night and a peek at Superior during the day. Fetching two frosty Labatts from the fridge, she opened both and handed one to Tate. "Glass?"

"Not necessary." He sloshed down a dose.

She took a measured sip then asked, "So, Mr. P.I., what'd you find out?"

Tate filled her in on his activities.

"Come to any conclusions?"

He shrugged. "Shoot, I don't know. The picture's out of

whack. Three people dead—well, two for sure and maybe a third—and all within three years. And there's a business that isn't working, Barzoon with financial problems, an unfaithful wife, and a truckload of insurance money. Could be something. Barzoon could be dirty. But I still need more information."

"Well . . ." she said, drawing out the last consonant, a coquettish smile on her face.

Tate's eyebrows went up. "Yes?"

"*I* took the afternoon off and did some shopping at the Wave."

"You did?"

"Yes, I did. And after that, I stopped at Faces Spa."

Tate gave his cheek a pat. "I'm jealous."

"I'll bet you are. Then I had coffee at Graziano's."

"Hmm."

"And then I came home."

"I hope there's more."

"Oh, there is. As I'm sure you know, the Wave is the most exclusive women's store in town."

Tate feigned thought. "Umm . . . that may have slipped my mind."

"Right. Anyway, a friend of mine, Carla Larsen, is a sales clerk there and she gave me the lowdown on Monica Adams."

"Do tell," said Tate, interested.

"Regular customer, expensive taste, *and* sexy lingerie."

"Ooo-la-la! Did your friend have any idea of who might be assisting her in removing that sexy lingerie?"

Gayla's smile widened. "Why yes, as a matter of fact she did . . . because he came in with her . . . more than once."

"Wouldn't happen to be our pal, Harlan Barzoon, would it?"

"Got it on your first guess."

"Did she say how long this had been going on?"

"As long as she's been there. About a year and a half."

"Any idea about before? What I'm getting at is—"

"I know. Were they special friends before her husband was, ah, how shall I put it? . . . accidented?"

"Has anyone ever mentioned that you have a way with words?"

"Thanks for noticing, and the answer to your question is, I don't know. But I got something, don't you think?"

"Sure. That's good detective work."

"And that's not all."

"There's more? Spill it."

"I talked to Janet again at the insurance company. She said Kevin Adams' death *was* covered by their firm. Their underwriter paid out a quarter million to Harlan and another quarter to Monica. *And,* Harlan has a policy on himself for a cool million that'll pay off to, drum roll please—"

"His son, Earl."

Gayla frowned. "How'd you know?"

"I'm a good guesser."

"So, what do you think now?"

"It's a mess, that's what I think." Tate took another swig of his brew. "Yesterday, when Orville told me his story, it seemed so farfetched. But now," he shrugged, "hard to say. Maybe he's right. Maybe Barzoon did do it. Everything we uncover puts him in a worse light. Nothing exculpatory. Everything pointing to him being a sleaze, at best, and possibly a murderer. He'd have plenty of motive, Lila's infidelity and his financial problems in particular. So, all things considered, I'm beginning to seriously question whether his disappearance is real. He may have staged it. He could be alive. Maybe he knew his business was a payroll or two from being belly up and thought that one more insurance scam was his best, or only, alternative. For a man like Barzoon in a small town like this, business failure and bankruptcy would be tantamount to death from a thousand cuts. He'd be a pariah in the business community and *persona non grata* at social gatherings. For an extrovert with a big ego, that really would be worse than death. Or at least worse than a fake death. Better to engineer one last payday and reinvent himself on a sunny tropical beach."

"What about the daughter he had with Lila?"

"If he staged his disappearance, he's decided to abandon her."

"That's cold," said Gayla, drawing her arms around herself as though the temperature had dropped.

Tate had rubbed elbows with enough sociopaths over his past twenty years to know they were incapable of any love or empathy for other human beings, and that included their own offspring.

"What happens to her?" she asked.

"I guess Orville's next of kin."

"Geez, I can't imagine Orville raising a little girl."

"There's Earl . . . and the sister. She's what? Twenty-one maybe? That might work."

Gayla frowned. "All that insurance money going to Earl and none to the girls, it doesn't seem right."

"I'm with you on that. But unless Barzoon left a will stating otherwise, I imagine the rest of his estate will be split evenly between the three children."

She shook her head. "Still doesn't seem right."

"If Barzoon's alive, I'm thinking the money from the insurance policy will be funneled back to him via Earl, with a rake for the house along the way. If Barzoon's not frozen in the woods near Echo Lake, it almost certainly means he worked everything out in advance. It's not a plan that would pop up spontaneously after running out of gas. He'd need a way to get out of town, or at least a place to hide, and enough money to sustain himself for a few months, if not longer, because once the scam was running there'd be no going to an ATM for a withdrawal. It's likely he'd have made other arrangements too, such as stocking up on cash or having a spare car to drive off in or—"

"Or," interrupted Gayla, "having a partner to help him get away."

"Yeah, a partner. Earl's the logical choice because of the insurance money, and because he set up the lost-in-the-woods story with his tale about tracks leading into the forest."

"There were nearly two full days between when Barzoon left the snowmobile on the road to Echo Lake and when Earl called 911, that's enough time to drive halfway across the country."

"Or fly anywhere in the world."

"Even so, seems he'd need a partner to pull it off."

"Agreed," said Tate. "And Earl is at the top of my list. Monica Adams second."

Gayla smiled. "Sooo . . . you've decided we should take the case?" Her smile changed to a grin.

Tate sniffed the air. "How's that pot roast coming?"

# Jackson and Tate

"ANOTHER GLASS OF port?"

Tate was stuffed. "Just a drop. That's the best meal I've ever eaten."

"Un-huh," said Gayla, adding two fingers to his glass. "I've seen your refrigerator and understand why you'd think so."

"No, really, it was fabulous."

"Thanks, Mike, glad you enjoyed it."

"All right, back to the case."

"So you've decided to do it?"

Tate squirmed. "Well . . . yes and no."

"What does that mean?"

He sighed. "I suppose yes. I'm in too deep to quit. But at the same time, I can't see taking money from Orville Dorian. The guy looks like he's barely scraping by. I can't go charging him three or four hundred a day plus expenses. Wouldn't be right."

"You're a big softie." She leaned over the table and gave him a peck.

"If you tell, I'll deny it."

"Your secret's safe."

"On the other hand, I do need him as a client, if only for credibility. No one, especially the cops, would appreciate me running around, stirring up muck without a reason."

"So, we're on the case?"

His eyebrows went up. "We?"

"Didn't I get the client?"

He had to admit she did.

"And haven't I been a help?"

He had to admit she had.

"And wouldn't you say I have, um, how shall I put it? . . . a unique set of skills advantageous to unraveling this mystery?"

He sucked in a breath and then grudgingly replied, "Oh, all right." Quickly adding, "But I want you to remember something. It's an established fact that if a person commits one murder and doesn't find it repugnant, the second is easier and takes far less provocation, the third even less."

Gayla forced herself to become serious. "Point taken. I should be careful, right?"

"Right."

"So we're a team?"

Tate slumped. "Right."

She beamed a thousand-watt smile. "Well then, I guess the only question remaining is whether we should call ourselves Tate and Jackson or Jackson and Tate?"

His eyes moved upward to the heavens and he clasped his hands in mock prayer. "Lord save me!"

"We need a plan," said Gayla.

Tate's gaze fell back to earth. "A plan?"

"Yes, of course. That's how it's done. We need a plan to trap Earl into showing us where his father is hiding. Then we need to get Harlan to confess to murdering his partner and his wife and faking his death for insurance money."

Tate's mouth fell open. "If Barzoon did all the things you're accusing him of, we could staple him to the side of a barn and shoot flaming arrows at him and he'd still never confess. There's no death penalty in Michigan, but admitting to premeditated murder would mean life without parole. He's never going to do it. That means we need hard evidence to make the case. First, we need evidence he's still alive. Then we need to show he intentionally faked his death to collect insurance money. That's insurance fraud, and that alone would be hard enough to prove. Heck, he could ramble into town tomorrow and spew some cockamamie story about running out of gas on the camp road and becoming so upset that he hitched into town, hopped a bus to Green Bay, and spent the last eleven days at the Marriott, but now he's back because time away gave him an opportunity to reflect on his situation and see that, yes, he did have some problems, but they weren't as intractable as he'd thought, and with hard work, faith in God, and the help of his loved ones he'd be able to get through it and . . . . See what I mean? What we need is proof. Concrete proof. Means, motive and opportunity. DNA, fingerprints, a weapon, bloodstains, tape recordings of incriminating conversations, confessions of associates, film footage of the crime in progress, things like that."

"That's it," she said, undaunted. "Get Earl to confess. Or put pressure on Monica. One of them is bound to talk."

"No, they're not. They are *not* going to talk. Criminals confessing is what happens on television. In real life, criminals take the lie to their grave. Go on over to Marquette Branch Prison and ask around. Every one of those guys will swear he's innocent. For them, admitting guilt is the same as admitting they're the dirtbags they really are. They *can't* admit it. It would be ego crushing. Nope," he shook his head, "a criminal will blame everyone except himself."

"You mean, no one ever confesses?"

"Not often, unless it's part of a plea deal or so a family member can get a lighter sentence. What usually happens is they lie, run, hide, lawyer up, or all of the above."

"So, what do we do?"

It was a damn good question, and one that Tate hadn't worked out yet. With the Bureau, most cases were handled by a team, with each investigator covering a different aspect and an administrator sifting through the results until there was sufficient evidence for an arrest. The case was then presented to a district attorney, and it was his or her job to prosecute. But now everything was on him. He'd have to gather as much evidence as possible, build a strong case, and then hand it over to the cops, who'd have to buy into it one hundred percent before it ever got near the DA's office. It wasn't going to be easy. Even the Bureau, with all its resources and personnel, only made arrests leading to convictions on a fraction of the perps they went after. No, it was not going to be easy.

"Gayla, the first thing we need to do is establish that a crime has been committed. Kevin and Lila's deaths are ancient history. It's likely most of the physical evidence has long since disappeared or been tainted. But Harlan Barzoon's presumed death is fresh. That's where we should begin."

# Crossing the Line

THE NEXT MORNING Tate was up early. Months had gone by since he'd done any exercise. Years since serious exercise. But for reasons he couldn't wrap his mind around, he felt the need to do some today. He'd always been strong and reasonably agile, but the long Northern Michigan winter kept him inside more than he preferred. And, before meeting Gayla, he'd spent more time doing one-arm curls at the local watering holes than he'd care to admit. Damned retirement. Hell, he was too young to retire. Not even fifty yet. Sure, he was burned out on the bureaucratic grind of the Bureau, but he wasn't burned out on life.

Eighty pushups. Not all at once like when he was in shape, but two sets of forty. Then two sets of fifty sit-ups, weights in the basement and a few rounds on the heavy bag. Finish it off with a couple miles of roadwork on Lakewood Lane. Once he got his motor warmed up it was okay. Not easy, but okay. And when he was done, the shower and coffee felt earned.

He'd worn a suit to work for so many years that it hardly seemed right not to put one on. But this was a different life. He was private now. A private investigator. Magnum P.I. in a parka and Sorels. Time to walk on the wild side. Jeans and a blue polar-fleece shirt, that's what he'd be wearing.

Second cup of coffee in hand, he found Orville Dorian's phone number in the book, jotted it in his pocket-pad, then dialed. Ten rings later, he hung up. Dorian said he worked, that's probably where he was. Have to try him in the evening. Then his thinking took a tangent and he wondered about the young Barzoon girl, the real victim of this tragedy. Who was taking care of her? Orville? Earl? He couldn't imagine the latter doing it. But what about when Barzoon was spending the night at his camp at Echo Lake? Obviously, she wasn't with him. Where was she? Tate checked his notebook then dialed Monica Adams.

"Hello, Ms. Adams. This is—"

"I know your voice, Mr. Tate. What do you want?"

"I was wondering if you could tell me who was taking care of Harlan Barzoon's daughter the weekend he disappeared?"

"Why?"

"Call it curiosity."

"Why ask me?"

"Thought you might know."

"Sorry, she's not my responsibility."

"How about if you give it your best guess? You knew Harlan as well as anyone. Who would he leave his daughter with when he went out to camp?"

He heard a click and dial tone.

Damn! he thought. People didn't hang up when I said I was from the FBI. But private investigator, screw you.

Tate's next call was to Laura Fields, a reporter at the Peninsula Journal. He'd met her while working on a Bureau case, saved her bacon so to speak, and he'd seen her in social situations since.

"Laura, it's Mike. How's it hangin'?"

"How's it hanging? Were there any women in the FBI, Tate?"

"Okay, okay. Just trying to be conversational."

"Bet you're living the easy life now that you're retired."

"Not exactly." Hmm, how was he going to say it without sounding like an idiot. "I'm . . . ah . . . self-employed."

"Like what?"

"Private investigation."

"You're a P.I.!" she exclaimed. "I've never known a P.I. There's never been a P.I. in Marquette before, at least none who advertised. Do you have an office now or what?"

"Nah, just starting, working out of the house."

"Got a case?"

"Sort of. A fellow named Orville Dorian asked me to look into his daughter's death. Happened last winter. Late March."

"I remember. She left a husband and daughter behind. Darned shame. Now the husband, Harlan Barzoon, is missing and presumed dead."

"Yeah. Anyway, you being a professional busybody and all, I was wondering what you might be able tell me about the family. You know, things that might not be printable but would be interesting."

"Gossip?"

"Yeah, that's what I'm talking about, and some other stuff too. In particular, who's taking care of the young Barzoon girl now, and who was taking care of her the night Barzoon went missing? That, along with anything else that might be of interest regarding Harlan Barzoon, his dead wife, Lila, his dead business partner, Kevin Adams, or their finances."

"Oooo. You on to something?"

"Just fishing."

"If you hook something, you'll tell me first, won't you?"

"Of course, Laura. Who else?"

"Hmm, well then I guess I could ask around."

"Thanks. I appreciate it."

"What's your cell number?"

"Don't have a cell. It's like being on a leash. How about if I give you a call later. How much time do you need?"

She assessed the complexities of the task. "Couple of hours should be enough."

"Great. I'll call around noon. Or better yet, why don't we meet for lunch at the O.E.? I'll buy."

"You sure?"

"What do you mean, sure?"

"Well . . . you are on a fixed income now."

"Thanks, you've made my day."

"Just trying to be considerate."

Feeling older, Tate dialed the number for Theresa Barzoon. A machine answered. He left a message and called Orville again. Still no one home. Then he called the Bureau in Marquette and asked for his former partner, Bill Noon, only to be told Noon was at a conference in Detroit and wouldn't be back till tomorrow. Stymied, Tate drummed his fingers on the kitchen table. Then he rifled through the phonebook until he found Barzoon's name, jotted the address in his pad, gulped the last of his coffee, donned his parka, and made for the Lincoln.

The beach lots were narrow and deep where Tate lived. Because of it, his garage was forty feet up the drive from the house. Walking toward it he sensed a movement along the edge and became alert, then a chook-covered head with eyes hidden behind plastic sunglasses gave a surreptitious glance around the corner.

"Hi, Greg. Doing some surveillance work?" asked Tate as he ambled toward him.

The boy stepped from behind the garage and marched through the snow to Tate, mittens stuffed in his pockets, a pencil and a piece of folded paper in his hands. "Yeah. I'm practicing spying. That's what FBI agents do sometimes."

"Oh, sure. But you have to be careful. You don't want the bad guys to see you watching them."

Greg nodded, recording this sage advice. Then, saturated with new knowledge, he bolted back through the snow, around the garage, and was gone.

Twenty minutes later Tate was pulling into the freshly plowed drive leading to Harlan Barzoon's stone and log palace overlooking Nash Lake. Braking to a stop in front of a three-car garage, he stepped from the warmth of the Town Car into the cold, dry air. The sky was brittle blue frosted with wispy clouds of ice crystals, and his boots made a crunching sound on the snow as he strode toward the front door. As he neared it, he could hear a stereo inside blaring rap music. Tate hated rap music. He rang the bell. Nothing. Again. Nothing. He pounded on the door. Nothing. There was a vertical glass panel next to the door, the inside covered by a semi-opaque drape. Tate squinted to see through it. Thought he saw a shape moving. He pounded again. The shape came near, pulled the curtain aside, peered out. Damn! thought Tate, scowling, it's the crudsack from Earl's house on Hewitt Street. The sack squinted, puckered with recognition, mouthed an expletive, then gave Tate the finger and let the curtain fall closed. Tate pounded on the door again. The stereo volume went up in response. Giving up, he trudged back to his car, but rather than get in and drive away, he thought he'd take a moment to look around.

Stepping over to one of the garage doors, he peered in a window. The glare from the sun and darkness inside the building made seeing difficult, but by pressing his nose flat to the glass and cupping his hands around his eyes, he was able to identify a gray Ford pickup and a dark-blue Jeep Wrangler. If Earl wasn't home, what was he driving, wondered Tate? And what's the crudsack driving? The pickup maybe?

Unlike with investigations undertaken by the Bureau—where the make, model, year, color, plate number, and ownership of all significant vehicles is easily ascertained—Tate knew the state and federal databases would be off limits to him and he'd have to chronicle and research every vehicle, every address, every phone number, and every detail of every aspect of the inquiry. Strangely, the idea of doing these routine, and at times noxious, administrative chores didn't seem to bother him. At the Bureau he was just a cog in the wheel, now he was the whole machine, and it would be up to him to take care of everything.

Because of his poor vantage and the darkness in the garage, he couldn't see the license plate numbers on the cars. He debated stepping inside to get them. Uninvited, it would be felony breaking and entering. He wasn't anxious to cross that line. So, pulling out his notebook, he jotted down what he had then strolled back to the house, rambled to a side window and gazed in. The crudsack was nowhere to be seen, but playing on the living room floor was a young dark-haired girl. Tate guessed she was four or five and the product of the Barzoon-Dorian union. Great, he thought, the crudsack is blasting her with rap music, there oughta be a law. Well, at least now I know where the girl is and who's taking care of her, if you can call it that.

With nothing left to see, he began trudging back to the Lincoln but stopped twenty feet short. The walkway to the side door of the garage had been recently shoveled. It was like an invitation saying step in and take a look. Should he or shouldn't he? He glanced left, then right, then curiosity overcame caution and he walked to it. Trying the handle, it turned easily. He pushed. The door opened. A moment later he was inside, striding around the pickup to the far stall where the blue Jeep sat. Soon, his eyes adjusted to the darkness and his vision improved. An eagle feather and multi-colored Indian beads hanging from the rearview mirror said girl car, Lila's car. Tate noted a few slight scratches on the right-hand side, the right front fender showed a crease where paint was cracked, and the right-side mirror was missing. There was a coating of dust over the entire car. It was Lila's Jeep, and it didn't seem to have been used since the accident. How did it get here? Towed? Driven? He made a mental note to find out.

Tate saw that the Jeep was fitted with a sturdy metal hardtop, removable in the summer, its center concave from the rollover. He looked carefully but couldn't see any signs of dried blood. He walked to the driver's side, opened the door, and stuck his head in. Glancing around the interior, he could see nothing unusual, nothing of interest. Pulling his head out, he grabbed the top of the door frame for balance, then stuck his leg in and pushed down on the brake. It was firm. Quietly closing the door, he walked to the back of the vehicle and memorized the plate number. Having seen all there was to see and edgy from the illegal nature of his activity, he decided it was time to go. Slipping out of the garage, he hustled to the Lincoln, pulled out of Barzoon's yard, and motored back toward Marquette.

Passing Range Appliance along the way, a thought occurred to him and he hung a U-turn. He parked in front, entered, and asked a salesman if Jim Satterfield was around. He was directed to a storeroom and found him unboxing a refrigerator.

"Got a minute?"

"Sure," said Satterfield, flicking a box cutter closed and sliding it into his pocket. "What's up?"

"First, when we spoke earlier, I wasn't being straight with you. I'm not with the gas company."

Satterfield laughed. "Since A&B used propane and I'm personal friends with the folks who sell it, I didn't really figure you for the gas man."

Tate nodded. "It was lame."

"What are you really doing?"

"I've been asked to look into the death of Lila Barzoon. I assume you knew her."

"Sure, kind of. Barzoon's wife."

"Mind if I ask a few questions about her?"

"Don't mind at all."

"Was Lila around the business much?"

Satterfield shook his head. "Not really. She'd stop in every now and then, but not often. Why?"

"Just curious. You recall what kind of car she drove?"

"Jeep Wrangler. Always wanted one myself. Still do."

"Recall the color?"

"Dark blue."

"She ever come out with any of her pals? You know, girlfriends?"

"Yeah, there was this super-hot chick. Dark hair. Sun-browned skin. Had a body that wouldn't quit."

"Know her name?"

"Un-uh. Wish I did. Way out of my league, but I wouldn't mind stepping up to the plate and taking a swing." He was grinning ear to ear.

"Anyone else?"

"Umm . . . there was some guy with her a couple times. Tall and nerdy looking, you know, not the type who'd be a threat to Barzoon, so it'd be okay for her to hang with him. Wouldn't want your ol' lady cruisin' around with some big stud. Know what I mean?"

Tate did. "Anyone else you can think of?"

Satterfield strained to remember. "Nah, that's about it."

"How about Barzoon? Did he have any pals stop by on a regular basis?"

"You mean buddies? Yeah, sure."

"Got any names?"

"Pug Halliwell and another guy."

"Know anything about Halliwell?"

"He's a plumbing contractor. His crew worked some of our jobs."

"How about the other guy?"

"Don't know him, but he didn't look like he was in construction."

"How about ladies?"

"You mean like something on the side?"

Tate nodded.

Satterfield worked his jaw, trying to decide whether he should say her name. Then he shrugged. "Guess you'll hear it sooner or later. Yeah, he had a friend. She was always coming out and hanging around. Actually, I think it got so it bothered him. But not so much that he told her to stay away."

"Let me guess. Monica Adams?"

"Oh," said Satterfield, disappointed, "you already heard."

"I'm a good guesser."

"Kind of rubbed the guys the wrong way. It was like Kevin was barely in the ground and she was there hanging all over Barzoon like he was the captain of the football team and she was the head cheerleader, if you know what I mean." Tate did. "It was, well, let's just say it didn't look good. The men on the crew would talk about it. We all liked Kevin, respected him. He was a regular guy. Told you the way it was. Worked harder than anyone else and expected you to work hard too. But he wasn't a jerk about it. You know. Like if you needed something, all you had to do was ask. If he could help you, he would. Guy like that, when you're working for him, it's not all about the money. Heck, I woulda turned down more just to stay with him. Most of the other guys felt the same. So, with him still warm in his grave, to see his wife crawling all over Barzoon, well that didn't sit right with most of us."

"How soon after Adams died did his wife begin coming on to Barzoon?"

Satterfield sighed. "Like I told you before, I was the yardbird. Took care of the warehouse and a lotta other stuff. When that was done, I'd go out to the job site and work. Anyway, I was around the warehouse more than anyone else, even Kevin or Harlan, so I saw pretty much everything that was going on."

"And what *was* going on?"

"The kind of stuff you do behind closed doors . . . and it started before Kevin died."

By the time Tate was finished talking to Satterfield and back in his car, the interior had cooled to the outside ambient temperature of 27 degrees. It would be another month before the weather warmed, and Tate was three levels beyond tired of winter. Cranking up the Brontocarus, he rammed the heater control to high and checked his watch, 11:50. He'd have to violate some speed laws to make it to the O.E. in time for his appointment with Laura Fields.

# Fields and Dunlevy

TATE SHED HIS parka and slid into the booth across from the reporter. Mid-twenties, five-five, boyish figure, light brown hair that fell casually over her shoulders, questioning green eyes, no makeup on a face that didn't need any, and a demeanor that said 'You might as well tell me what I want to know because I'll find out anyway'. Tate figured if anyone was ever born to be a reporter, it was Laura Fields.

He asked, "Am I late?"

"Nope, just got here."

A skinny brunette named Samantha appeared with a steaming pot of coffee. "You're not as smart as I thought, Tate, bringing your dates here."

"Gayla's off and I knew you wouldn't tell."

"Hi, Sam," said Fields, smiling.

"Hi to you, too," said the waitress with a wink. She poured their coffee, took lunch orders, and disappeared into the kitchen.

Tate turned to Fields. "Come up with anything?"

"Maybe," she said coyly. "But first, let's review the rules."

"Sure. Anything that comes up, you're the first to know. Is that the rule you're talking about?"

"Yup."

"So, what'd you find out?"

"Who would you like to start with?"

"Barzoon."

"Local heavyweight. Business and social connections. Made his money buying and selling houses and apartment buildings during the boom. About six years ago he went into business with a guy named Kevin Adams doing construction. They built an apartment complex on Lake Shore Boulevard for some investment group. Did a bunch of other contract work too. Then they built some large custom homes out east on M-28, on the rock beach past the public access. All on spec, if you're familiar with the term?"

"I am. Means they used their own money to build 'em."

"That's right. They were speculating there would be a market for the homes when they were done."

"Got it," he said, nodding. "You're pretty up on the real estate biz."

"Had a chat with Floyd Woodridge. He's our business reporter."

"I see."

"Floyd said since the real estate market is cyclical, building on spec is a crap shoot. If you catch the buying wave when the market's hot, you can make a bundle. But if you start building too late and the market cools, you can get stuck holding properties and be forced to liquidate at a loss to pay your construction loans. Floyd said that's what happened to Adams and Barzoon. They ended up having to sell a couple of expensive homes for less than they had into them."

"Ouch!"

"Darn right, ouch. Floyd said in a deal like that, everyone gets paid except the principals. The bank, the employees, the creditors, they all come out fine, it's the business owners who take the beating. But no one's crying crocodile tears for them. If the market had been hot, they'd have made a huge profit."

"When did they take the hit on the spec homes?"

"About four years ago."

"Before the accident that killed Kevin Adams."

"Yes." She paused, eyeing him. "So . . . are you thinking maybe it wasn't an accident?"

"Seems convenient. The business takes a loss on the spec homes and the construction business is slow, but the bills don't stop and there's payroll to be made and Barzoon has alimony, kids in college, new wife, new baby, new home to pay off and other expenses. That's a hell of a lot of financial pressure."

"Yeah," said Fields. "And Barzoon was supposed to be the rainmaker, the guy with the sales ability and contacts who brings in business. Floyd said that's why he and Adams hooked up in the first place. Adams was small but profitable and teamed up with Barzoon to grow the company."

"Doesn't seem to have worked."

"Guess not. What a mess." She eyed him. "So, you're thinking maybe there's more to Kevin Adams' death that just an accident?"

"Not sure. Quite a coincidence though. One day Barzoon has financial problems and the next his partner has an accident and the problems are solved. At least for the time being."

Laura's eyes grew large. "You think he killed both of them! His partner *and* his wife!"

"They say after the first, it's easy."

The Omelet Eggspress was comfortably warm but Laura gave a shiver. "Maximum creep out."

Tate nodded. "Not saying he did, you understand. I'm saying the timing and circumstances raise questions."

"But . . . how do you kill someone by auto accident?"

"If a killer is rational, he'll try to deflect suspicion from himself. What could possibly be better than a car accident?"

She tilted her head. "Sure. But how do you do it? Lila Barzoon's car accident is one thing, but Adams was crushed under an end loader. Barzoon couldn't just say, 'Hey, Kevin, lie down while I roll this machine over you.' And then a couple years later say 'By the way, Lila, I want you to lie right here while I roll—' "

"Yeah," said Tate. "Roll. People are creatures of habit. They almost always take the path of least resistance. When something works, there's a natural tendency to do it again rather than develop a new plan. It's human nature.

"Laura, what we have are two deaths that for all intents and purposes appear to be accidental. Adams made a mistake, rolled the loader, wasn't wearing the seatbelt, falls out, ends up with the machine on top of him. Lila is in her Jeep, misses a corner, rolled the vehicle, wasn't wearing her seatbelt, gets thrown, ends up with the Jeep on top of her. Let's count the similarities. Number one, vehicle rollover. Two, occupant not wearing a seatbelt. Three, victim ejected from the vehicle. Four, lands where vehicle will roll on them. Five, ends up underneath. Six, died. Seven, no one around to witness the event. Eight, both accidents occurred when Barzoon was in financial difficulty. Nine, both victims had hefty insurance policies paying off to Harlan Barzoon."

"That's a lot."

"Damn right, it's a lot. And vehicle accidents resulting in death are so common that people tend not to look for irregularities. Forty thousand people a year die in auto accidents. That's one out of every eighty people. It's a mountain of mayhem, and it dulls the senses. People hear auto accident, driver died, and they don't question it. Cops too. They see it more than anyone. It's possible an intelligent murderer would realize a vehicle accident wouldn't be scrutinized nearly as much as say a shooting or drowning. And unless there was something out of the ordinary that caught their eye, the cops would draw the easiest and most obvious conclusion, operator error, and not look any further. And, since cops and rescue workers will always try to help the victim if there's even the remotest hope of life, that means people crawling all over the accident scene, trampling on tracks, and destroying evidence. So, by the time the forensics people get there, if they're even called, the crime scene is compromised. Fingerprints, footprints, tire marks, and other telltale evidence that would indicate a crime had been committed has been erased."

"But *how* did he do it?"

Tate made a helpless gesture. "Don't know. But just because I don't doesn't mean it didn't happen. Barzoon's history says he's bright. If he did do it—and that's still a big if—I doubt it was spur of the moment. My guess is he thought out every detail in advance, and that's why it worked."

"You're talking about Harlan Barzoon as though he's still alive. Is that what you believe?"

"Yeah. They find a body, I'll change my mind. Till

then, I gotta believe he's scamming the insurance company for one last paycheck before he disappears for good."

"Who's the beneficiary this time?"

"His son, Earl."

"Big dollars?"

"A million sound big to you?"

She gave a breathy whistle.

He asked, "What'd you find out about Lila?"

"Party girl. Got married just out of high school to a guy named David Tucker. Divorced less than a year later. No children from the union. Nothing noteworthy. Barmaid on and off for a few years. Moved to Houston for a year with a couple girlfriends. They stayed, she came back. Hooked up with Barzoon a few years later. He was still married but they didn't do much to hide what was going on, so it was just a matter of time until his wife filed for divorce. After that, Lila and Harlan got hitched. They had a child named Jenna. Then Lila starts getting bored with the domestic scene and, from what I hear, begins driving up to the Lumberjack Tavern in Big Bay on a regular basis. Guess she wasn't getting enough attention at home. It's always easy for a girl to get attention in a bar, especially if she's the flirty type, like I hear Lila was."

Tate nodded. "Hear any names attached to that attention?"

"A couple."

"Busy girl."

"Larry Hollender is one, and Johnny Nolen."

"Think there were others?"

"If so, just one night stands."

Tate worked his jaw. "That'd have to grind on Barzoon."

Fields crinkled her lips. "Women can be stupid."

"Is Hollander from Big Bay?"

"Was. Moved away to Florida, I think."

"What about the first husband? Where's he at?"

"He's still around. Got remarried."

"How about Barzoon's first wife, Theresa? What's her story?"

"Socialite. Involved in the arts. Had some money from her parents. Has a nice home on the East Side she kept in the divorce. Drinks too much and has been known to make a scene, especially when Barzoon was sneaking around behind her back. *And* I heard she has a young boyfriend."

"How about Harlan and Lila's girl, Jenna? Who's taking care of her?" Though he already knew.

"Barzoon's son, Earl. He was living in town and going to Northern, but I understand he's moved into Barzoon's house on Nash Lake to look after the child. Poor thing."

"Yeah. Raw deal for her."

"So, you think Harlan Barzoon murdered two people for insurance money and faked his own death for more? If that's true, his son would have to be involved."

"Yup, that's the way it seems."

"If that's the case, Barzoon must be long gone by now."

Tate nodded. "If he's as smart as I think he is, he had clothes, money, and transportation set up in advance. Like I said, none of this seems spur of the moment."

"He's probably on a beach in the Caribbean waiting for Earl to call and tell him the check's in the bank."

"Yeah, maybe. But maybe not."

"Why do you say that?"

"Control. A guy like Barzoon would want to be in control of the situation in case anything unexpected came up. He'd need to stay in touch with Earl, but phone calls from Brazil or Mexico would raise a red flag for anyone looking."

"Earl could be calling his father from a pay phone."

"Could be. They'd have to be rock stupid to use Earl's home phone or his cell."

"So, what are you going to do, keep an eye on Earl?"

"No other way. It'll be tough, though, because he knows what I look like."

"Want help?"

Experience told him using a non-professional was a mistake, but Tate knew Fields was relentless and would work hard just to get the scoop. "Maybe. I'll let you know."

Samantha brought their food. They ate in silence.

After lunch Tate stopped by Gayla's apartment. She was home. Kicking off his boots at the door, he tossed his parka on a chair.

"Coffee?"

"No thanks, just had lunch at the O.E. Any luck?"

"Some. Jason Seaberg and Associates is, or was, the accountant for A & B Construction. The office manager is a friend of a friend. She couldn't say anything outright because she was afraid Seaberg would find out and fire her, but she did hint there were problems."

"Like what?"

"Like the firm hadn't been paid in a while. That's the sort of thing you *can* say and not get fired."

"Another indication A & B was in trouble. Was Seaberg the accountant Adams' used before Barzoon climbed on board?"

"Nope, he was Barzoon's accountant. A & B switched to Seaberg after Barzoon bought in."

"Who did it before?"

"Willard Dunlevy. Adams stayed with him for his personal finances even after moving the business accounting to Seaberg."

"I'd be willing to bet you know someone who works there."

She grinned. "You'd be right. Lonnie Portola eats at the O.E. all the time. She's one of his bookkeepers. She's a big gal and I give her extra. We're pals. She's really nice, but with the weight and all, lonely. Why can't men be more understanding?"

He shrugged. "Gayla, there's a huge herd of desperate and imperfect guys out there who aren't going to squabble over a few extra pounds, but most of them draw the line at serious tonnage."

"Tonnage! She's a *person*, Tate. She has *feelings*."

"Yeah, you're right. No one's perfect. Present company excluded."

"Sweet talker."

"So, what'd she say?"

"Said Kevin Adams was doing fine until he hooked up with Barzoon. After that, it was always a struggle."

"Interesting."

"And did you know that Monica Adams used to have a job but quit working after Barzoon bought into the business?"

"No, I didn't."

"She was a clerk or salesperson or whatever at Morgan and Company, the woman's clothing store in the mall."

"Lonnie tell you that?"

"That's right. She was the one who did their tax prep. Said their personal income went way down after that, with her not working and the business not spinning off enough cash with Barzoon's salary added to the overhead. She also said Kevin and Monica began spending more too. Including buying an expensive cottage on Shag Lake near Gwinn. And there were new cars and expensive vacations. Said it was a real turnaround from the way they used to be."

"And how was that?"

"Frugal. Frugal and hard working. Big change, is what she said."

"And Adams let it happen."

"Or didn't have any choice."

"How about now? Is Monica still with Dunlevy, or need I ask?"

"Quit him after Kevin died."

"Let me guess. She moved her personal business to Seaberg."

# The Numbers

WILLARD DUNLEVY OCCUPIED a modest suite on the third floor of the ancient Harlow Building on the northwest corner of Washington and Front. Three bookkeepers, a receptionist, and Dunlevy shared two creaky rooms that had already given a century of faithful service. There were files everywhere, and the bookkeepers were in deep mind melds with their computers. A large woman with an intelligent face and immaculate hair toiled in front of one. She had to be Lonnie, and Tate felt a pang of remorse for his unkind words. The receptionist showed him into the only space with a door.

Dunlevy sat in a dangerously old swivel chair behind a desk too filled with files and papers to be truly efficient. A thin man whose most captivating feature was the top of his head—a fringe of white fuzz ringed a polished dome highlighted by a wispy comb-over that mimicked thin snow blowing over barren soil. Wire-rimmed glasses and a sunlight-intolerant complexion completed the picture. Yes, thought Tate, he's an accountant.

"Thanks for seeing me, Mr. Dunlevy."

"Don't mention it," said Dunlevy, happy for the break from routine. "What can I do for you?"

"Name's Tate. I'm a private investigator looking into some irregularities regarding A & B Construction. I understand you handled the account for Kevin Adams, but when he partnered with Harlan Barzoon they moved to another firm. I was wondering if you could tell me anything about that?"

He rubbed his chin with a questioning fingertip. "Irregularities? Like what? You're not suggesting—"

"No sir, nothing that reaches back to when you were handling the account. It seems both his business and personal finances prospered while Kevin Adams had you for an accountant, but after he took on Harlan Barzoon and moved his business to another firm, well . . . ."

"I was surprised," said Dunlevy, opening up. "I'd been doing his work for years. You do good work for someone and you think they'll stick with you. Doesn't always turn out that way."

"But he kept his personal accounting here."

"Sure, and I appreciated it. He trusted me. But the business accounting was the moneymaker. Two or three billable hours per week. Sometimes more. His personal accounting was only an hour or two at tax time."

"I see. So it was a big hit when he decided to move the business."

"Darn right, and I told him so."

"What reason did he give?"

Dunlevy screwed up his face. "It was Barzoon. He was the one pushing the buttons. He'd convinced Kevin that another firm could give them better tax advice and save them money. But there was more to it. Barzoon wanted to build some spec homes. Kevin asked me what I thought about it and I told him. Mr. Tate, I've been doing this for forty years, and I've seen a trainload of contractors go out of business in that time. The real estate market is cyclical. Build on spec and time it wrong, you can get hurt. Hurt bad. Kevin didn't need it. He was doing fine. I told him it was a risk he shouldn't take. Guess he told Barzoon what I said, because the next thing I know, they're moving their work to Seaberg." He paused for air, then went on, but less forcefully. "It took 'em a while to get the construction loans, but they eventually managed to build three houses. It was the tail end of the boom and they began too late and ended up taking a real beating. At the time, I was still upset about losing the account, but I didn't take any pleasure in seeing Kevin get hurt."

"Why Seaberg in particular?"

"It's a small accounting community here in Marquette. It doesn't pay to make enemies."

"I'm a retired FBI agent, Mr. Dunlevy. I know how to keep a secret."

Dunlevy hesitated. "They don't seem to mind being creative."

"You mean like fudge the numbers?"

He shook his head. "No, nothing like that. Ah, well . . . for instance, there are gray areas where a particular item can be either thought of as an expense or as a capitalized item. Expenses hurt your balance sheet; capitalized items are listed as assets and help the balance sheet. So, depending on how you claim things, one versus the other, you can make the company appear to be more profitable than it really is. The classic example is marketing and goodwill. You can spend marketing dollars and increase the name recognition of a firm and its goodwill, and then, with some creativity, call those marketing dollars a capital expenditure and show them on the asset side of the balance sheet. But go to the supermarket and try to buy a pound of bacon with some of that goodwill and see how much it gets you.

In my book, marketing dollars are always expensed. It's the most conservative way to do it, and the correct way. I always advised Kevin to take the most conservative approach. And he did, until Barzoon came along."

"But why jigger the balance sheet?"

"Bank loans. A bank wants to see a healthy balance sheet before they'll loan you money. Especially if that money is being used to finance something speculative."

"Do you think Harlan Barzoon was a crook?"

"I'm not going to answer that, Mr. Tate. The man's dead. What good would it serve?"

"Let me put it another way. If he were alive, would you want to be his accountant?"

"That I can answer, and the answer is no."

Sitting in the Lincoln on Washington Street, Tate added Dunlevy's negative assessment of Barzoon's character to the growing stack of circumstantial evidence against him, each piece weighing in on the side of guilt. He realized that if his suspicions about Barzoon were correct—that he was still alive and had committed two murders and was presently seeking to defraud the insurance company with a faked death—time was of the essence. Earl Barzoon's comings and goings, and most particularly any calls made from a payphone rather than his home phone or cell, had to be chronicled. There was also a chance Barzoon was still in the area and Earl would meet with him. Witnessing such a meeting would be a bonanza making any amount of stakeout time worthwhile. But there were costs involved: time, money, and manpower. He wasn't comfortable with the idea of using amateurs like Laura for a stakeout. He'd need pros who could handle themselves if things went sour. But first things first, he needed a client. Tate drove until he found a pay phone.

"Orville."
"Yeah, who's this?"
"It's Mike Tate. I've been trying to reach you."
"You have?"
Huh? Thought Tate. "Wanted to let you know I've decided to take your case."
Dorian responded with a flat. "Oh."
Tate's antenna went up. Something was wrong. "Yeah. I've done some checking like you asked. Looks like there might be something to it."
Tate waited for a response. None came.
"You still there?"
"Yeah," said Dorian.
"So, I'm calling to set up an appointment for us to talk about how to proceed."
There was an uncomfortable pause. "Well, I'm not sure I want to go any farther with this."
Tate was flabbergasted. "What? The other day you were ready to crawl over broken glass to find justice. What's changed since then?"
Hesitation. "I . . . I just don't want to do it, that's all. Barzoon's dead. Jenna's coming to live with me. I don't want to rock the boat. I'm quits on this. If I owe you anything, send me a bill, I'll pay, but I don't want any . . . I don't want to rock the boat."
Tate was upset, but he understood. "Let's see if I have this right. Earl called and said you could have custody of Jenna. He'd make it happen. But you had to call off the investigation in exchange. That about sum it up?"

"Listen, Tate. You got no business poking your nose in where it's not wanted. I hired you. I can fire you. And that's just what I'm doing."

Before Tate could respond, Dorian hung up.

Damn! thought Tate, Orville got bought off. He went back to his car and sat stewing for several minutes before driving home. The phone was ringing as he stepped inside.

"Yeah?"

"It's me," said Gayla, excitement uncontained. "Big news."

"Yeah, I have big news too."

"You do? What?"

"I just talked to Orville Dorian. He said to call off the investigation."

"What! He can't do that!"

"It's his money."

"But . . .but . . ." she stammered, "but Barzoon will get away! He did it, Mike. I know he did. I can feel it. We can't just let him get away!"

"Sometimes the bad guys win."

"I can't believe you're saying that! You *know* he's guilty. You *know* he's still alive and out there laughing at everyone. And you're the only one who can prove it. No one else seems to care."

Tate sighed. He'd been down this path many times with the Bureau. Good people getting hurt, bad people living large, no one giving a damn. "Gayla, a serious investigation takes time and money. I don't mind spending some time, but I'm not in a position to finance justice for dead people."

"Then *I'll* pay you."

"You know I can't do that."

"What? My money's not good enough?"

"You know it's not that. We're friends. I can't take money from you." Exasperated. "Listen, it's easy to get emotionally involved in a situation like this. It's human nature for conscientious people to be revolted by injustice and seek to make things right. But it's not our responsibility. The cops and DA should be looking into this. Maybe empanel a Grand Jury."

"Do you think it'll happen?"

He couldn't lie. "No."

"Then I'll pay."

"Gayla, I told you, I can't take your money. It wouldn't be right."

She was silent.

This is exactly what I was afraid of, thought Tate. Gayla's in a snit and that means the O.E. is off limits. Then a thought occurred. "How about this? I'll talk to the insurance company and see if they're offering a recovery fee that would take care of expenses. I'm not making any promises, but I'll check and see. Okay?"

"Fine," she said, her tone signaling he'd entered into a binding contract. "You'll call and let me know?"

"Yeah, sure."

"When?"

Oh geez, pressure. "I'll call them today and see if I can get an indication and then I'll get back to you. And . . . ah . . . are we still on for Friday night?"

"Of course," she replied. "This Barzoon thing won't affect us."

Tate's eyes went to the ceiling. "And was there something you were going to tell me?"

"Oh, I almost forgot. Earl Barzoon contacted a real estate agent about selling Harlan's house."

"A little premature, isn't it?"

"That's what my friend at Peninsula Real Estate thought. She said Earl wanted an agent to appraise the place and have the paperwork ready so they could begin marketing it as soon as the court declares his father deceased and the will is read."

"Hmm . . . if he's moving on the house, he's probably liquidating everything else as well."

"Does he have a right to do that?"

"Maybe, maybe not, but who's going to contest it? With the exception of Orville, all of the interested parties are in the family. And it's likely Orville's been co-opted as well by the promise of raising his granddaughter. Maybe with some cash thrown in as a sweetener."

"So you think everyone's hunky-dory with this?"

"Probably."

"Hmm . . . makes me wonder about something."

"What?"

"Is Monica Adams liquidating, too?"

"Tell you what. Why don't you check that angle and I'll work the insurance company. I'm not committing to anything long term. I'll work this till Friday, and then we'll take another look and see if it makes sense to keep going. All right?"

"That's three days. You'll probably have it solved in three days."

Tate's posture sagged. "Gayla, that stuff only happens on TV. In real life these things drag on for months. Years even. Especially if the perp is sophisticated. So, I wouldn't hope for a quick resolution."

"Don't sell yourself short, big guy. I have faith in you."

"That makes one of us."

# Nicole

GRABBING A PHONEBOOK from the kitchen counter, Tate thumbed through pages until he found the number for New Century Life and Casualty. He called, explained what he wanted, and was told he'd need to speak to Dale Mickens. But Mickens was out for the day. Tate took it in stride. He'd met Mickens before and knew he wouldn't get the runaround, so it was worth the wait.

After the insurance company call, he dialed Johnny Nolen's number, reaching him on the second ring. Tate asked if he'd be home for a while and could he stop by with a few more questions? Nolen said he was working but, yes, it'd be fine. Tate stopped at a gas station along the way to fill up, then, sixty dollars lighter, motored toward Big Bay.

When he arrived at Nolan's there were two cars in the drive. One the green pickup he assumed was Nolen's, and the other a red Mustang convertible, sporty and fun, but not the most practical car in a Northern Michigan winter.

He knocked. Nolen answered and led him into the living room. Directly in front of Tate, lounging on a fur rug and a scattering of colorful pillows in front of the fireplace, was a remarkably beautiful and completely nude young woman. She was facing the fire, yellow and orange tongues of flame dancing for her pleasure, rejoicing at her being. Long dark hair flowed over her shoulders and fanned across her back. Her skin was a golden brown, as though from sunning on a tropical isle—a stunning contrast to the translucent white of the local Scandinavian stock. She'd been gazing at the fire but did a half roll toward them. Upon seeing her face, Tate thought that any man would consider her attractive in the extreme: large dark eyes accented by eyebrows darker than her hair, high cheekbones, a straight nose, defined jaw line, and exciting, expressive lips. Her breasts, which Tate could not seem to ignore, were round and firm, her stomach was flat, and her hips said 'woman' in a thousand languages. She did not smile or frown or show any emotion at all, and seemed totally unconcerned that she was completely naked in front of a stranger. Tate tried not to stare, failed, then set his eyes roaming about the room so as not to embarrass himself any further than he already had. He belatedly noticed there was an easel set up with a large canvas clamped to it. A painting was in progress. He looked at the painting. He looked at the woman. Words failed him. He nodded. She nodded back.

"Why don't we sit in the kitchen," said Nolen.

Oddly grateful, Tate followed him into the kitchen area, which was open to the living room, and purposely took a chair facing away from the woman.

"Beautiful, don't you think?"

Tate gave a solid nod. "Absolutely."

"Would you like something to drink? Coffee? Tea? The water's hot. It's no trouble."

"No thanks. I can see you're busy, so I don't want to take up any more of your time than necessary. I just have a few questions."

"Fire away."

"Did Lila ever express any fear of her husband?"

Nolen glanced toward the living room, then his eyes returned to Tate. "No. She said he would at times become angry, but if there was more, she never mentioned it."

"But the marriage was coming to an end."

"Yes."

"She was going to leave him for you."

A slight hesitation. "Yes."

"Did she ever mention that Harlan had an insurance policy on her?"

His eyebrows went up. "No."

"How about friends? Other than yourself, who did she consider a friend?"

"I was her friend." It was the young woman in the living room. She'd pulled on a sweater and jeans and was strolling toward the kitchen.

"Mr. Tate, this is Nicole," said Nolen. Then to the woman, "Nicole, Mr. Tate is a private investigator. He's looking into Lila's death."

"And what are you finding, Mr. Tate?"

"Nothing yet, I'm still trying to get the big picture. Did you know her well?"

She crossed the kitchen and stood, barefoot, leaning against the counter by the sink, one long leg crossed over the other. "Yes, I think so."

"Friends for a long time?"

"Actually, just a year or so."

"Was she reckless? I mean, with her driving?"

"She was, um . . . adventurous. But reckless?" She gave her head a shake. "No, I wouldn't say that. Lila knew what she wanted and went after it. She loved life. She didn't get off on danger just for the sake of danger.

But she wasn't afraid of it either. I mean, she'd take a risk if it was coupled with a reward."

"Did you and she ever do anything risky together?"

Her facial expression slowly changed to a smile, giving rise to any number of thoughts. "Sometimes."

"Care to tell me about them?"

The smile grew wider. She gently shook her head no.

"Was there some guy she was pals with who might be described as, um, academic looking or nerdy?"

She laughed. "You must be thinking of Clyde."

"Clyde?"

"Her brother."

"Didn't know she had one." She had the most penetrating stare of anyone he'd ever met.

"Is this your first case, Mr. Tate?"

"Yes," he said, not bothering to explain.

"He lives in Marquette, 229 Hewitt Street. You can probably find his number in the book."

"Hmm . . . clever idea."

She smiled again. "Just trying to be helpful."

"Did Lila ever mention anything to you about insurance or insurance money?"

"That's not the sort of thing we would have talked about."

"What about her relationship with her husband, Harlan? Did you ever talk about that?"

"Yes, we did. She said he wasn't . . . satisfying her." Her lips parted as though she were going to continue, but instead she asked, "Do I need to explain?"

"Yes," said Tate.

Pushing herself from the counter, she moved toward him, slowly, one long leg in front of the other, the smooth movements of a jungle cat stalking its prey. "Something new, Mr. Tate. Something exciting. The promise of . . . forbidden pleasure." She moved closer, leaning in. "That's what she wanted. That's what *all* women want." Her voice was husky with desire. "You see a man who attracts you, he's sexy, you want him." She was within Tate's personal space and he felt his internal thermostat shoot up a hundred degrees. "You try to stop thinking about him, but you can't. So you lie in bed at night dreaming . . . longing . . . aching . . . for him."

Judas Priest! thought Tate.

"And when the desire overwhelms you, you go to him and make your confession, asking, no, *begging* for him to give you what want, what you long for, what you need to fulfill your wildest desire. Then he takes you until you pant and claw while he brings you to the edge and holds you there, longer and longer until you can't wait anymore and explode into white hot plasma."

She was within inches of Tate's face. He was having trouble breathing.

"That's what she wanted, Mr. Tate. That's what all women want." Then she slowly moved away.

She's good, thought Tate, really good. There wouldn't be many men who could handle her. "And she found that in Johnny?" He used his thumb in a rather comical gesture toward Nolen.

Nicole turned to face the artist. "Oh, yes. Johnny knows how to please a woman, don't you, Johnny?"

Nolen gave a dismissive laugh. "Don't take any of this seriously, Mr. Tate. I asked Nicole to read a chapter from an erotic novel to get in the mood for the painting. Those lines are straight from the book."

Tate wondered if there was sweat on his face. "Maybe I should spend more time at the library."

Nicole grinned mischievously, brushing by him as she strolled back to her station by the fire, peeling off clothes as she went.

It took Tate an extraordinary amount of willpower to turn his attention back to Nolen. "Did you ever meet Barzoon?"

Nolen shook his head no.

"How about his son, Earl?"

"No."

"Kevin or Monica Adams?"

"No."

Tate knew he had more questions, but for the life of him couldn't think of a damned one. "Thanks for your time, Mr. Nolen. I'll let you get back to your . . . ah . . . work."

Nolen smiled and showed him to the door.

# Door Number Three

TATE KEYED THE ignition of the Lincoln and pulled out of Nolen's drive thinking that a night with Nicole would just about ruin a man . . . but would undoubtedly be worth it. Needless to say, he gave the subject considerable thought as he drove through the village of Big Bay and southeast on County Road 550 toward Marquette.

Ten miles later he was back on track and thinking about the case. Nicole was almost certainly the woman Jim Satterfield saw with Lila. But why? She was barely in her twenties, and Lila was enough older that it wasn't a natural match. Maybe Lila's brother, Clyde, could shed some light on their relationship. Or maybe it could be coaxed out of the tightlipped Johnny Nolen: artist, lover of beautiful and married women, and man of few words. Tate knew he'd looked foolish for not knowing Clyde was Lila's brother. It was the beautiful woman factor that made it embarrassing. Absent that, who would have cared?

It was after 6:00 when he rolled into Marquette. Driving through town, he went directly to 229 Hewitt Street. It was the same house he'd visited earlier in search of Earl Barzoon. Could it be that Clyde and the crudsack were the same person? The sack was obviously a loser, not a nerdy intellectual. But perhaps Satterfield, not being all that intellectual himself and maybe not getting a good look at him, got the description mixed up. Or was there someone else living in the house? A third person who was Clyde Dorian. Only one way to find out.

Tate trudged up the slippery path to the door and knocked. Nothing. No sounds or signs of life. He pounded again with the same result. As he stood waiting for a response that would not come, an ethereal devil in a crimson leotard materialized on his left shoulder and whispered, *"Do it!"* Tate gave it a brief moment of reflection, glanced left then right then tried the knob. It was locked. He chewed on his lip, took another look around, then walked back down the snowy path to where it met the driveway and hustled up the sloping drive, around the house to the back door.

Peering around once more and seeing no one, Tate tried the door. The knob turned. He pushed it open and stepped into a small porch that led into a kitchen. "Anyone home?" When there was no response, he took another step inside and closed the door. The lights were off and the interior of the house lay in a hazy darkness so thick that it seemed to have texture. *"Keep going,"* said the devil.

Entering the kitchen, Tate saw evidence of a bachelor lifestyle: dishes and pans stacked in the sink, an overflowing garbage can, and an overall grunginess that strongly implied hordes of predatory bacteria. It was easy to understand why Earl and the sack would take up digs at Harlan's rather than stay here. He moved forward into the adjoining living room. Drab gray walls. Old overstuffed couch and chairs. Coffee table filled with empty beer bottles and an overflowing ashtray. A set of weights against one wall, massive flat-screen on another, speakers on either side. What was he looking for? Find it and get out.

His eyes searched for a phone. He saw one on an end table, scraps next to it with messages and numbers. Local prefixes, girl names, no point in copying them. He went through an archway leading to what was once a dining room but was currently fitted with nothing but a scarred metal desk for studying. Based on the clutter, it didn't appear any scholastic activity had taken place on it in the recent past. There was nothing else to see. Walking back into the living room he found himself at the base of a staircase leading to upstairs bedrooms. If he went upstairs and someone came home, he'd trapped. Felony breaking and entering all the way. *"Do it!"* said the tiny devil. *"Do it quick and get out."*

Hurrying up the steps, he arrived at the landing to find a dark, windowless hallway with one door to the right and two on the left. All were closed. He silently stepped to the first door on the left and pressed his ear to it. No sound. Gently turning the handle, he pushed it open. If there was someone sleeping, he did not want to wake them. Peering inside, he saw an unmade mattress on the floor and men's clothing and sundry items scattered about. The acrid odor of old sweat mixed with the stale residue from cheap weed was almost overpowering. There was no phone—at least none he could see amid the chaos—and there was no evidence the inhabitant could read or write. Crudsack, thought Tate. He moved on.

Opening door number two, he found the room better kept. The bed, though unmade, was at least on a frame, and the room, though messy, did not seem a bio-hazard. There was an end table with a phone. Tate went to it, checked for messages, found none. There was a drawer in the end table, he pulled it open. Inside were a few loose bills, some change, several condoms, and a small flip-top box. He opened it. Weed, pills, and a gram vial of cocaine attached to an automatic dispenser for on-the-go snorting. He closed the box and the drawer. Clyde or Earl. Nothing left to see, he moved on.

The third room was probably the original master bedroom. Based on his personality, he guessed it would be Earl's. He tried the door. It was locked. Tate noted it was a simple interior lock with a child safety override that could be opened from the outside with any hard, straight object by pushing it into a hole and applying pressure while turning the knob. A stout paperclip would do. Tate checked one bedroom and then the other but found none. Taking two stairs at a time to the first floor, he hurried into the room with the desk and rummaged through three drawers before finding one.

Back in the living room, he stopped. He'd already been inside the house too long. What the hell was he thinking? It was getting dark outside. Through the front windows he could see lights on inside the house across the street. A car cruised slowly by, didn't stop. Tate desperately wanted to get out, but he couldn't, so he turned and charged back up the stairs. Then he was crouching at the door, pushing the straightened paperclip into the lock release, applying force to the knob. He heard a click. The knob turned. The door inched open. Tate stood up. The hallway was in semi-darkness, the room darker, curtains drawn tight. He squinted to see. It wasn't enough. He was reluctant to turn on the light for fear of it being seen from the outside, but he didn't have a flashlight and there was no other way to search the room. Reaching around the doorjamb to where a light switch would be, his fingers searched. Just as they found it, he felt something touch the back of his hand and an instant later fell to the floor writhing in pain. His muscles were in spasms and he couldn't breathe. He groaned in agony. As soon as his limbs stopped shaking and the misery began to subside, he felt the prongs of the stun gun again and another 40,000 volts shot through him. He had no control over his body. He couldn't fight, he couldn't speak, he couldn't even crawl away! Then his attacker began mercilessly kicking him in the ribs and stomach, then in the head and face. He was powerless to do anything about it, powerless to defend himself or even roll out of the way. Then the stun gun again followed by more kicks to the body and head. Then he felt nothing.

# Abandoned

HE WAS COLD, colder than he'd ever been. Or was it hot? Was he on fire? It couldn't be fire, because he couldn't see it. It had to be cold. His face, the side that was up, hurt beyond belief. The side that was down was numb. His chest and gut were weak with sickness. He tried to move his arms. The left one wouldn't move, but he felt the right one stir. Ever so slowly he brought his hand to his face, touching himself but barely sensing the touch. There was something wrong with his hand. Oh, god, he was cold! He was going to die of cold. With his thumb, he wiped at his right eye, brushing away a clod of snow. Blinking, he was able to open it. As it focused, he looked upward and saw stars in the night sky. It was cold, so cold.

His body was wracked with pain, consumed with pain. He prayed someone would see him, help him, or simply put him out of his misery. He listened, but there was no sound other than the hollow whisper of artic wind as it coursed through the pine boughs. No voices, no cars, nothing.

He was on his left side in the snow, and he was freezing to death. If he didn't get up and move, he'd be dead by morning. He sucked in a half breath for energy. The hard, cold air made him cough. When he did, the sky exploded into fireworks, blazing stars of every color. He felt the ground moving, the trees swaying, the Earth rotating, tumbling, then it began to slow. Paralyzed with pain, he thought he'd been stunned again, but over time the anguish ebbed to a level where he realized it was the cough that had brought on the pain. He must not cough again! Shallow breaths. Shallow breaths.

Ever so slowly, Tate began to get up. First rolling to his stomach, then using his right arm to push himself to his knees, the other dangling limp and useless. With infinite care, he rocked himself into a crouch, then stopped, light-headed, drifting into a dream of a cold, frozen hell, and in semi-lucid moments, terrified he would pass out. To pass out was to die.

As the dizziness abated it was replaced by the brutal, agonizing pain. Tate knew he must stand, but it was as if gravity had tripled. His legs were weak, rubbery, but he pushed and pushed and then he was up. Don't fall! he thought. Please, please don't fall!

He could only see out of his right eye, but the sky was clear and a there was a three-quarter moon, its florescence reflecting off the snow. The temperature was in the single digits, maybe lower. Had to be. It was hard cold. Crackling cold. Brittle cold. The kind of cold that freezes spit before it hits the ground. He was on the side of a plowed rural road. Get out of the snow, he thought. Get out before your feet freeze and you can't walk. A body will freeze if precautions aren't taken. Precautions? Were his boots still on? He looked down. Yes, and his feet seemed to have feeling. What about his hands? His left arm hung lifelessly at his side, fist in a ball, but his right arm worked. He lifted his hand to look at it. There was something wrong. His ring finger was bent backward, a break or dislocation, but it didn't seem to hurt. Perhaps he was in shock. Or maybe that particular hurt was masked by the overall agony he was in. Or could it be that the hand is frozen and dead and will never hurt again? He tried flexing his fingers, saw them move, except the one. He was thankful his parka was still on. It was open, just as it had been while picking the lock on the bedroom door. Then his thoughts returned to the hand with the wild finger. If he didn't keep it warm, it would freeze. He did not want to lose his finger, he did not want to lose his hands. Slowly, carefully, he reached over and took his left hand and pulled it up and inside his coat, tucking it under his right arm pit. It was as though he was pulling on a rubber arm strapped to his shoulder. He took care to keep the hand pinned by applying pressure with his right arm. Then he took his right hand and carefully slid it inside his jacket on the left. He couldn't put it under the armpit because he couldn't raise his left arm, and the dislocated finger would have been a problem, but at least his hands were secure. It was time to find shelter and warmth.

Using his good eye, he looked one way and then the other along the road, but there was nothing except the moonlit trees and snow and darkness beyond. How far would he need to walk to find a house? How long would it be before a car came by? And most importantly, which way should he go? The road was rural, tree-lined, narrow, seemingly running from nowhere to frigid nowhere. Which way? It could mean his hands. It could mean his life. There was a light breeze blowing right to left. The prevailing wind was from the northwest. That meant right was probably northwest, left southeast, or something close to it. Lake Superior is north. Marquette is on the lake. The busiest roads are east, west, and south. Then he realized all of it meant nothing. He could be anywhere in relation to the roads and city, and they could be many miles away. Nevertheless, he had to decide. So, since he didn't want to walk into the wind and have wind chill add to his misery, he turned left and began dragging one foot forward and then the other, vowing to walk until he could walk no more, then he would lay down on the road and die. He could not know that he was only two miles east of US 41 and was walking in the wrong direction on a road that tailed off into nothingness six miles farther on.

# Victim

THE YOUNG LOVERS had been there before. Only one long driveway at the end of the road, old people living in a farmhouse. Lights off. No one would bother them. On their way back to the highway, they saw him, curled in a ball, lying in the middle of the frozen road, dead, they thought. The boy was strong, and between the two of them they were able to hoist Tate's bulk into the back seat of the car. Turning the heater up full blast, they sped in the direction of Marquette. As Tate regained consciousness, the pain in his thawing hands and face, broken ribs, dislocated shoulder and finger, and battered face and head was so intense that all they heard from the back seat were moans as they raced toward town.

The teenagers drove him to the emergency room at Marquette General where he was hoisted on a gurney, rushed inside, and immediately attended to by a doctor who ordered morphine and warm blankets. Later, heavily sedated, they worked his shoulder back into its socket and his finger back into its joint and threaded fifty stitches to close his wounds. There was concern of him losing several fingers and his left ear, which had been against the snow as he lay unconscious after being beaten and dumped, but time would tell.

The duty nurse found his wallet in his pocket. Checking the driver's license and consulting a directory, she called his house. No answer. Since it was obvious he'd been beaten, as per regulations, she called the police department and reported it. The dispatcher logged Tate's name and the circumstances of the call. Then, since it had interrupted an engrossing conversation with a handsome deputy, she promptly forgot about it.

The next morning when Laura Fields made her cop-beat visit to the station, along with one DUI arrest and the report of an attempted B & E at Midas Muffler, Tate's name was on the incident log as the victim of an assault.

"Mike Tate! Are you sure?"

The clerk at the duty desk nodded in the affirmative.

"Oh my god!"

She wrote down the relevant information then called Bill Noon at the FBI office.

Tall and slim with blond hair that resisted combing and a boyish face gashed by a pencil mustache grown to make himself appear older, and hopefully debonair, William Noon was back from Detroit writing a boring summary of the boring seminar he'd attended. When he understood what Laura was saying, he dashed out of the building and raced to the hospital where he met her in the parking lot. They went in together. Inquiring at the desk, they were told Tate was under sedation. Since neither was a relative, under normal protocol they wouldn't be allowed to visit, but Noon's badge made him a first cousin. Taking the elevator to the fourth floor, home of the intensive care unit, they trod a long, hard hall that amplified every step with a slapping echo. Tate's room was second to the last. Stepping inside, Laura gasped and grabbed Noon's arm. The man in the bed was unrecognizable. "Oh my god!"

Noon swallowed hard as he stared at his friend. Tate

was unconscious. There was a tube to a needle in his arm, fluid from a bag dripping into it. His face was swollen and discolored, a line of stitches crawled like a thin caterpillar down his left temple. There was another along the jawline and more under the bandages that swathed his head. His right hand was bandaged, his left invisible under the covers.

"He's been seeing Gayla Jackson," said Laura. "She'll want to know. Does he have any family we should contact?"

"I don't think so. He's pretty much a loner."

"He's going to need someone."

"Oh, no!" said Gayla, sinking into a booth at the O.E. "Is he going to be all right?"

Noon shrugged. "The doctors say they don't know. He's been beat up pretty bad. A couple of kids found him lying on a road east of Skandia. No telling how long he'd been there."

"It's all my fault," said Gayla, tears welling in her eyes, fingers worrying a napkin into shreds. "It's all my fault!"

"What's your fault?" asked Laura.

Between sobs: "It's this Barzoon thing. I talked him into doing it. He didn't want to, but I . . . I pushed him. And now they've hurt him. Oh, god! I'm so sorry. He's never going to forgive me. Ever."

# The Road Back

MUMBLING FROM THE side of his mouth that wasn't swollen shut, "I don't remember."

"Anything?" asked Noon, standing at the end of the bed and stunned by the sight in front of him. It was the day after the beating. He was at the hospital with Laura and Gayla. Laura to his right. Gayla at Tate's side, tears on her cheeks, gently stroking the back of his bandaged right hand.

"Not after I left Nolen's."

"Tate, how can you not remember getting beaten up?"

"I don't know. Maybe a blow to the head. Whatever it is, I don't remember."

It was a lie. He did remember. He remembered every incredibly painful detail until the last kick knocked him out. And he desperately wished he could forget. *Damn!* But what could he say? Yeah, I went over to Clyde Dorian's place—you know, the same house Earl Barzoon lives in—and since nobody was home, I thought I'd break in and take a look around. But, dang, when I went upstairs, one of the bedroom doors was locked. So, naturally, I picked it and was about to enter it when I got zapped and beaten up by the occupant. Nope, can't say that. Better to play dumb.

"Laura told me you've been investigating the death of a woman named Lila Barzoon. Think it had anything to do with that?"

"Maybe. Don't know." Why was he lying? It wasn't as though the phone company had assaulted him over a late bill. These were his friends, or at least as close anyone came to that, and he felt bad about lying to them. "Guys," he haltingly mumbled, "I appreciate your concern. More than you can imagine. But there's nothing to be done about it. I'm okay."

Between sobs, Gayla said, "Okay? You're *not* okay. This is *not* okay. It's this Barzoon thing. Mike, *tell us!* We need to know so we can protect you. They tried to kill you! *You have to help us!*"

Tate slowly rolled his head toward Gayla. He gazed up at her with his good eye and pulled the corner of his mouth that wasn't swollen into what he thought might pass for a smile. "Don't worry, hon, everything will be fine. But . . . right now . . . I'm a little tired, so . . . ."

Gayla bent over and kissed him on a section of forehead that wasn't bandaged.

"Sure," said Noon. "Get some rest. Don't worry about anything."

"Yeah . . . sounds good," replied Tate. Then he closed his good eye, feigning sleep, and soon heard their footsteps as they left.

He hated being needy. He hated having people take care of him. A couple months of convalescence is what the doctor said. A couple of weeks is what he was thinking. A couple days was more than he could stand. But there was nothing to be done about it, bodies take time to mend.

The second day in the hospital was worse than the first. He spent most of it, and the next, in a drugged stupor. On the fourth, he was able to sit up. On the fifth, he demanded to be discharged and had Gayla drive him to the beach house. She begged him to stay with her so she could take care of him. He politely but firmly refused. Like an old bear lucky enough to have pulled his leg from a trap, he needed to heal in his own cave, alone. But food trumped independence and he did agree to her coming by each evening with a hot meal and doing his shopping. Tate was grateful, but withdrawn. There were wounds, and not just physical ones. For him, that meant retreating into his shell until the hurt went away. Gayla didn't understand and blamed herself for his dark mood. Noon did and left him alone. Tate would talk when he was ready.

At first he was overjoyed just to be alive. Someone had tried to kill him, without even a pretense of an accident. But he hadn't succeeded. To be alive was a victory. Good enough for now. But later, as his body healed, he vacillated between fear and anger. Fear because he was so weak a child could whip him in a fight. One tap on the ribs and he'd be down. But as time passed, torn tissue knitted, and the pain changed from constant to intermittent to occasional, he had other thoughts, dark thoughts, satisfying thoughts, and they all coalesced around revenge.

He could not ignore what had happened to him, and there were only two paths he could take. One was to quit, cower, hide, buy extra locks, avoid everyone, and never again speak the name of Harlan Barzoon. The other was to face it head on, the fear and its root cause. Deal with it, bring it to a head, and dig, dig, dig into every aspect of Barzoon's life and the lives of everyone involved until it brought him into the open. It *must* have been Barzoon in that dark bedroom at Hewitt Street. No, Tate hadn't seen him. Hadn't seen anyone. But he was certain it was Barzoon and no one else. That's where the facts pointed. Who else would have left him on the side of the road to die? No one, not even Earl or his sleazy pal. He was in their house, uninvited. They were within their rights to confront him. They could have beaten him senseless and then called the cops and had him arrested, or simply tossed him out the front door onto the street. But they didn't. And that was all the proof Tate needed. It had to be Barzoon. He couldn't call the cops, he couldn't risk being seen, not with the insurance scam in progress. And he absolutely would have the motivation—a very strong motivation—to eliminate anyone turning over stones, digging through dirt, sifting out facts, and getting too close to the truth. Earl and the crudsack would love to give him a beating. But they would've shown their faces. They would *want* him to know who was dishing out the punishment. For them, it would be revenge. And not being killers, they wouldn't have left him to die. What would be the point? It would change their legal status from citizens defending their home to first-degree murderers. That's a game-show question even the crudsack could get right. No, it was Barzoon. Harlan Barzoon. But why was he there? Why is he still in Marquette, where he's so well-known and the risk of being recognized so great? Why not get as far away as possible as soon as possible? Was he so unsure of his accomplice, his own son, Earl? Or, were there others he had to keep on a leash, someone like Monica Adams? Were there details to iron out that couldn't be handled over the phone? Like what? What would be worth the risk of discovery? Or was it simply bad planning? Was the disappearance a spur of the moment decision after all?

Was he short of money? No transportation? Nowhere to go? What? These questions and more haunted Tate during the long days that passed while his body recovered to a point where he could breathe, talk, stand, and walk around the house, albeit slowly, without any serious pain.

Five weeks after he was left on a deserted road to die in the snow, Tate showered, shaved, dressed, ate a hearty breakfast, then donned a light jacket—spring had arrived—and carefully walked out to his garage. His Lincoln had been found at the airport several days after the beating. Noon had driven it to the house. The Brontocarus started on the first crank. Tate backed out and then cautiously motored toward Marquette and the offices of New Century Life and Casualty. He had a ten o'clock appointment with Dale Mickens.

# Mickens

NEW CENTURY LIFE and Casualty was housed in the ancient Savings Bank Building on the southeast corner of Front and Washington in downtown Marquette. The brick five-story structure with its distinctive copper clock tower was once a bank but now hosted professional offices.

Tate parked on Lake Shore Boulevard by the Lower Harbor, and after climbing the steep half-block to the building entrance, gratefully took the elevator to the third floor. He arrived on time and wasn't kept waiting. As he hobbled into the office, Mickens rose to greet him.

Early forties and five-seven with a runner's frame, Dale Mickens had the vitality that regular exercise brings and the easy disposition of a man at peace with himself. Though his eyebrows were off balance and his nose was large, he was blessed with an appearance of honesty that made people like him at first sight.

Mickens shook his hand. "Heard you had a slip and fall. Damn glad your policy wasn't with us."

Tate eased himself into a chair. "Wasn't watching my step."

Mickens sat back down. Gave him a sideways glance. "Heard through the grapevine what you've been up to. Must have rubbed somebody the wrong way."

"I forgot to say please."

"Find anything?"

"Found out people aren't always as friendly as they could be."

"There's a surprise."

Anxious to change the subject. "Anything new on Harlan Barzoon?"

"Nope. The Sheriff's Department's been looking—searchers, dogs, the works—but his body hasn't turned up. Kinda makes you wonder."

"Yes, it does."

Neither of them spoke. Mickens broke the silence. "Don't bullshit me, Tate. You know something or you wouldn't be here."

"I know your firm paid off twice on Kevin Adams, once to Barzoon and once to the grieving widow. Then Barzoon hit triple sevens again when his wife died. And now you're on the hook for a cool mil based on his own disappearance."

Mickens' brow furrowed. "How do you know all that?"

"I read the paper."

"It wasn't in the paper."

"Oh . . . then I musta guessed."

"Yeah, right. So what are you here for?"

"You paying on recoveries?"

The insurance man's eyebrows went up. "Think you're going to recover something for us?"

"Could be."

"Is that how you got hurt, poking around in this Barzoon business?"

"They're kind of touchy."

"I see. Well, for what it's worth, the company's delaying payment on the Barzoon policy. Snows melting, almost gone, we'd like to see a body turn up."

"It won't."

"You seem sure."

"Told you, I'm a good guesser."

"We can hold off paying until the court declares him legally dead. That won't happen as long as there's an active search effort taking place. So, needless to say, we've encouraged the Sheriff's Department to be thorough. But the payee has an attorney and he's putting pressure on us. Pretty soon we're going to start racking up legal bills. That's not good."

"Rock and a hard place."

"Yup, that's where we're at. So, yeah, you find Barzoon before anyone else does, alive that is, and I'm sure we can reimburse you for your trouble."

"How much?"

Mickens rubbed an imaginary itch on the back of his hand. "I'll have to get it cleared with the mucky-mucks, but how does two thousand sound?"

Tate laughed. "Two grand? That won't even cover my dental. Tell the mucks it's gonna cost 'em five percent."

"Five percent! That's fifty thousand dollars! They won't go for it."

"Hell of a lot cheaper than paying the whole million."

"If he's still alive, we'll probably find him ourselves."

"Sure you will."

Mickens hesitated. "So you think you know where he's at?"

"Let's just say I fell down while I was looking, so I know where to start."

"Two percent."

"Five's a bargain. It's that or nothing. Plus, I want

twenty-five percent of anything you recover on the Kevin Adams and Lila Barzoon payouts."

Mickens' eyes grew wide. "The hell you talkin' 'bout?"

"Murder."

Mickens gave a low whistle. "Yeah . . . sure . . . that's something wouldn't take much priming. Twenty-five percent if you can prove murder for insurance fraud."

"Five and twenty-five, I want to see it in writing." Tate brushed his fingers over a fresh scar on his temple, "As you can see, I already have some sunk costs."

Mickens nodded knowingly. "All right, I'll call you as soon as it's approved. After that it'll probably take a day or two to get it all written up and signed. I'll let you know." Mickens watched him grimace as he rose to his feet. "Tate, you sure you know what you're doing?"

"I'm sure," he said, hoping he sounded more confident than he was. He turned and began shuffling out of the office.

"Tate, one last thing."

He stopped. "Yeah?"

"Try to be careful, because if you get killed, we're gonna have to pay off the whole claim."

A smile tugged at the corner of his mouth. "Thanks for your concern."

# On the Trail

HOME AFTER A hearty lunch at the O.E., Tate took a two-hour nap then lay on the couch contemplating his next move. Except for his resolve, which was stronger, it was like starting over. But time had passed. It was the late May. Over a month had been lost. The element of surprise was gone. And Barzoon knew—or damn well should know—he'd be coming. Tate hoped the pressure of being pursued would cause Barzoon to act rash, make a mistake, leave a clue that would provide a way to find him. Time would tell. But for now, Tate needed leads, and the place to begin was with Orville Dorian.

A hazy yellow sun hung low in the west, and still air added warmth to the late afternoon. A light jacket was all he needed. Tate didn't miss the parka and Sorels ritual of winter, and barring an unseasonably late snowstorm, he wouldn't pull them out again until November. With Dorian's address paper-clipped to a map on the seat, he pulled out of his driveway, windows down, with the scent of springtime wafting through the car.

Dorian lived on Cherry Creek Road south of Marquette, less than a fifteen minute drive from Tate's place on the Lane. His house was a square one-story with a covered porch and detached one-car garage. Easily a half-century old, its green composition siding had long since lost its sparkle. Since it was Wednesday, a workday, Tate had waited until 5:30 to drop by. When Dorian opened the door, Tate heard the sound of a girl inside.

Dorian's face registered surprised. "You here for money?"

"No, Mr. Dorian. Rather than money, I'd like to ask you a couple of questions."

"Told you, don't want no investigation."

"This isn't about you, it's about me. A month ago somebody tried to kill me. Did it because I was asking about Barzoon."

"I heard," said Dorian. "Felt bad about it, but there's nothing I can do. Just stay away from it. That'd be best for all."

"Can't do that. Could before. Can't now."

"You want money? Okay, I guess I owe you that much. I'll give you a thousand bucks, but no questions."

"How about if I trade you the thousand for one question. Just one. Think about it. You're not young. Raising a child is an expensive proposition. You're better off putting the money in a college fund for your granddaughter than giving it to me."

Dorian stared at his hands, calloused and tired from decades of labor. "What you say makes sense, so maybe. Ask your question."

Tate nodded. "Who was the person who contacted you about the deal: Lay off and you can have custody of your granddaughter; keep stirring up trouble and face a custody fight. I know that was the threat. Probably delivered by a lawyer. I just want to know who. I'll find out anyway, but this would save me time." He sensed Dorian pulling away. "I'll go out of my way to make it seem as though I found out on my own."

"And if I don't tell, I suppose you'll let on that I did. Is that what you're gettin' at?"

"I'm not like that, Dorian. I want your granddaughter to have a good home. It's obvious you care about her. Do you think Earl would care as much? I sure as hell don't. I promise you, I won't do anything to disturb your situation here. Whichever way you decide, your name will never be mentioned."

Dorian cocked his head in the direction of the girl sounds inside. "I'm scared, Tate. Not for me, but for her. You think I don't want justice?" He gritted his teeth. "You goddamn better well believe I do. But I gotta think straight. Lila's gone. Jenna's all that's left. I gotta think straight. I gotta do what's right for her."

Tate didn't speak.

"Even if he *did* do it, and I sure as hell believe he did, what good would it do to bring it up now, drag it all over town? Like you said yourself, better she grows up thinkin' her momma and daddy died in accidents than knowing daddy killed momma and ran off with insurance money, leaving her behind like she wasn't worth nothing." He pulled himself up straight. "I got a mirror, Tate, and sometimes I look into it. I know who I am. An' though I ain't much, I got a heart full of love for that girl. An' that's real important. And it's more than any of them others have. So, you see, Tate, my thinking's changed. It ain't about Lila anymore, and it ain't about me, it's about Jenna."

Tate drove away from Dorian's with a higher regard for the man than when he'd arrived. He didn't get a name and he didn't take Dorian's money, which he hadn't planned on taking anyway, but one part of his question was implicitly answered: Someone *had* put pressure on Orville and made him an offer he couldn't refuse. Tate guessed it would be through an attorney. But who would have been the one to contact him? Not Barzoon, of course, he's playing dead, so it was probably Earl. Hmm . . . since Earl seems the lazy type, left to his own devices he'd probably use his father's attorney. Dunlevy might have a name.

# Cullen Anderson

AT 9:30 THE next morning Tate was sitting in a chair across the desk from the accountant.

"Mr. Dunlevy, thanks for seeing me again."

"Not a problem. Say, I read about what happened. Are you okay?"

"Yeah, as long as I don't laugh."

Dunlevy smiled. "I promise I won't tell any jokes."

"I'll hold you to it."

He straightened his glasses. "What can I do for you?"

"I'm still looking into A & B Construction. Barzoon in particular."

Dunlevy's face registered concern. "That how you had your accident?"

"Could be."

He nodded.

"What I'd like to know is this: Who was Barzoon's attorney? Thought you might know."

"Hmm . . . let me think." He picked up a pencil, twirling it in his fingers like a miniature baton. Tate watched the ferrule strobe reflected light. Then it stopped. "Cullen Anderson. He has an office on South Front."

"Got a read on him?"

Dunlevy set the pencil on his desk then rubbed his thumb and forefinger together. "Money, my friend. Handles high rollers."

"Ethics?"

Dunlevy grinned. "He's a lawyer. Ethical is whatever works."

Tate began to get up, stopped, then asked, "How about Pug Halliwell? Know him?"

"Sure," said Dunlevy. "Plumbing contractor."

"I understand he and Barzoon were good friends."

"Could be. I've seen them together."

"Got a read on Halliwell?"

"Hard worker, smart businessman, has a good business. I hear he does good work. That's about it."

"Not walking the edge like Barzoon?"

Dunlevy shook his head. "Can't be sure, but I don't think so."

"Anyone else you can think of who was friends with Barzoon?"

Dunlevy's face creased in thought. "Hmm . . . try Jeff Kent. He's a dentist."

Tate found Cullen Anderson's firm stabled in a modern two-story on the west side of South Front. An impeccably dressed receptionist with arresting eyes and a demeanor that heralded 'I'm more important than you are,' said, "I'll see if he's in. May I tell him what it's about?"

"Fraud charges, jail time, disbarment for attorneys, you know, the usual stuff. And tell him I'm not speaking in general terms."

The receptionist rose and casually strolled down a carpeted hall and through a closed door, reappearing a moment later to say in her friendliest voice, "Mr. Anderson will see you."

Tate expected someone older and less well kept. The man behind the desk was about thirty-five and had the chiseled good looks of an actor. As Tate walked toward him, Anderson smiled, showing off perfect teeth.

"Mr. Tate, have a seat. What can I do for you?"

Tate settled into a comfortable leather wingchair in front of Anderson's desk. "I'm investigating an insurance fraud case for New Century Life and Casualty. Harlan Barzoon. Name ring a bell?"

"Harlan? Of course. He was my client before he disappeared."

"Disappeared, yes, that's the operative word. Dead would be a misnomer."

Anderson leaned forward. "You don't believe he's dead? Why not? That doesn't square with what's in the paper."

"Don't believe everything you read. The body hasn't been found, he was having marital problems, he was having financial problems, and he had a million dollar life insurance policy, not paying off to *all* of his children, as would be expected, but specifically to his son, Earl. And, strangely, Earl doesn't seem too broken up over his daddy's death, because he immediately began liquidating Harlan's assets." Tate shrugged. "If it walks like a duck and quacks like a duck . . . ."

"All circumstantial," said Anderson, relaxing. "Problems in Mr. Barzoon's life, unusual beneficiaries, or insensitivity by his son isn't the same as criminal behavior."

"How about when you called Orville Dorian and told him sonny boy wouldn't contest custody of Barzoon's daughter if Dorian stops making waves about Harlan's previous crimes?"

That got Anderson's attention. "Previous crimes?" He caught himself and smiled. "Like what?"

"Oh, insurance fraud times two. And, um, what's that other one? Oh yes, murder."

Anderson's smile vanished. "Murder!"

"That's the word. And not just once."

The attorney studied Tate's face. "What is it you want from me?"

"Is Earl Barzoon a client of yours?"

"There's such a thing as attorney-client privilege."

"Acknowledging he's a client isn't a breach of that privilege."

"I think it is."

"I think that you may be abetting fraud."

"Mr. Tate, this conversation is over."

Tate didn't move. "Over, hmm, yes. What do you think your other clients will do when they find you pressured an old man, threatened to have his granddaughter taken away so your sleazebag clients could skip town with insurance money? Do you think they'll say 'Oh that's fine, that's what lawyers do?' This is a small town, Mr. Anderson, no respectable businessman can afford to be associated with an attorney of questionable ethics. They don't want the stink to rub off on them. When word gets out, doors will close. So keep your clients' names to yourself. Won't be long before you can list them on a business card." Tate rose to leave.

"Wait," said Anderson. "You have the wrong impression. I don't condone law-breaking. And I certainly don't want my name dragged through the mud. I can't divulge privileged information, but I will give you this much: Earl Barzoon is a client. That's it. That's all."

"Mr. Anderson, no amount of money can repair a tarnished reputation. If I were you, I'd sever my relationship with Earl Barzoon, immediately. It'll save you a truckload of grief."

Anderson nodded. "I'll take that under advisement."

# Ruffling Feathers

TATE'S NEXT STOP was the Sheriff's Department. As usual, Deputy Fugman was on duty.

"Fugman, still riding the desk?"

"Like a cowboy without a home. Say, I heard about you gettin' beat up. Shoulda left before the husband got off work."

Tate made a helpless gesture. "Lost track of the time. Anything new on the Barzoon disappearance?"

"Uh-uh. Nada. You probably heard, Search and Rescue went back out. Snow's almost gone. Figured they'd find him sticking out of what's left."

"Nothing, right?"

"You got it."

"What's the thinking?"

Fugman shrugged. "Hard to say. Maybe he's there and they didn't see him, or maybe he wandered farther than they figured and he's out of the search radius."

"Or?"

"Yeah, I know, or maybe he isn't out there at all."

"Anyone working that angle?"

"What's to work? People up and take off all the time. No crime in that. Word is, Barzoon had his share of problems. Wife died and business going down the crapper. Can't say I'd want to stick around either."

"The son, Earl, has he petitioned the court to declare his daddy dead?"

"That's what I hear. The judge hasn't ruled on it, though."

"What's the holdup?"

"He doesn't think the delay would impose a financial hardship on the petitioner, and he'd like to see a body. Or, at the very least, more searching."

Tate smiled.

\* \* \*

The snow was gone from Monica Adams' yard. The grass was green and there were fresh buds on the front yard maples. A silver late-model Mercedes sport coupe was parked in front of the garage. Tate rang the bell. Monica Adams opened the door with a smile, as though she were expecting someone else. Seeing it was him, the corners of her mouth drooped into a frown.

"You! What do you want?"

"Harlan Barzoon. Is he in?"

Her expression changed to disgust. "Is that some kind of sick joke?"

"No joke at all, Mrs. Adams."

"Harlan's dead, Tate. What don't you understand about that?"

"Oh? Then where's the body? But you know all about that, don't you, Mrs. Adams. Harlan is alive and well and biding his time until he gets his hands on the insurance money. Then he really will be gone. My bet is that's the last time you'll ever see him."

"You'd better leave right now or I'll call the police."

"Good idea. And while they're here, maybe they can poke around for evidence of Barzoon."

"You don't know what you're talking about."

"When Search and Rescue went back after the snowmelt and couldn't find him, the case went from missing person to possible insurance fraud. That means instead of looking for him near Echo Lake, they're going to be looking for him in places he might be staying, both in town and elsewhere, and one of those places would certainly be at the home of his long time paramour, Monica Adams."

"You're crazy. We were friends, nothing more."

"Sure. But you won't be for much longer."

"What are you talking about?"

"You think Barzoon is going to take you with him when he leaves? He's not that stupid. There's too much risk. Everyone knows about the two of you. If you leave, the cops will follow you. He knows it, and he can't take the chance. Oh, sure, he'll lead you along for now, but once he gets the money, *poof*, he's gone. You'll never hear from him again."

Monica Adams slammed the door in his face.

Tate had already upset two people and it was only noon. With a little more work, it could be a record-setting day. Right now, though, it was time for lunch, and the Omelet Eggspress was his destination. Gayla took a break and joined him in his booth.

"How's the weather, big boy?"

"Your attention is a raging storm and my heart a frail ship foundering on the rocks of love."

Gayla burst out laughing. "You read that somewhere."

"I didn't. I just made it up."

"Keep going and I'll let you talk dirty to me."

"I'll do my best."

She leaned forward. "Sooo, what'd you find out?" She knew he was back on the prowl, didn't approve, but didn't try to stop him. He was still weak, she didn't want him hurt, but she knew better than to interfere.

"Talked to Orville again. Nothing much there. The guy's scared silly his granddaughter will be taken away by Earl. That's understandable. I put the squeeze on Earl's lawyer, Cullen Anderson, and I think there'll be some backwash. Anderson may drop him as a client. At least that's what I'm hoping. That should get things stirred up. Checked with the Sheriff's Department too. Search and Rescue went out to Echo Lake again. Didn't find anything. Dropped a couple hints about insurance fraud. We'll see what comes of it. Then I paid a visit to my favorite widow, Monica Adams. She was less than cordial. Told her I knew Barzoon was alive and she was helping him. Told her he'd dump her the minute he had the insurance money. She dropped me from her party list, but at least I planted a seed of doubt, that is, if she really does know he's alive and really is helping him with the expectation they'll run off and live happily ever after."

"You've ruffled a lot of feathers."

"Yeah, and feather ruffling makes me hungry."

Tate ordered two quarter-pound cheeseburgers and a double order of fries.

"Healthy choice," said Gayla. She watched in awe as he ate. It was like a traffic accident involving food and a mouth. As he stuffed down the last trio of fries, she slid a small piece of paper across the table. "I found an address for Clyde Dorian and Earl's sister, Nicole."

"So that's her name. I forgot to get it when I interviewed her mother."

Tate glanced at the paper. "I see Clyde's moved. He and Nicole have the same address."

"Yup. Lakewood Lane, out by you."

"Handy," said Tate, pulling some bills from his wallet and placing them on the table. He rose to leave. "See you tonight?"

"What are you hungry for?"

"Other than you, hard to say." He tried to suppress a smile. "But since you've been feeding me for the past month, how about if I cook?"

Her brow crinkled. "Oooo, risky. But, okay, surprise me."

"I'll surprise both of us."

Before stopping to see Clyde and Nicole, Tate drove home, went to his bedroom closet, and pulled a shoebox from the shelf. Inside was a Smith and Wesson snub-nosed .38 with a clip-on belt holster. After checking to make sure all of the chambers were loaded, he clipped it to his belt behind his back. He'd applied for his private investigator's license, but the application hadn't yet been approved. He'd also applied for a concealed weapons permit, which he'd given up when he left the Bureau, and which also had not been approved. If he were caught with the gun, both the license and permit would be denied, but he knew he couldn't endure another beating, not now while he was still on the mend. It could have been Clyde in that room. Better safe than sorry.

Tate's home was near the east end of Lakewood Lane, the address in the high numbers, 705. The number Gayla gave him for the cottage Clyde and Nicole were sharing was in the low numbers, 367, at the other end of the lane, nearer US 41. Like his, it was an odd number, so he knew it was on the beach.

After a serene two-mile cruise along the tree-shaded lane, he arrived. A dirt drive led to an old but well-kept bungalow tucked among the jack pines on the edge of the wide, sandy shore of Lake Superior. There were two cars in the parking area, a rust-on-brown Plymouth and a red Mustang convertible.

He knocked. A muffled woman's voice on the other side of the door said, "I'll get it," and a moment later he was face to face with the dark-haired beauty from Nolen's.

"Mr. Tate, what a surprise!"

He was disappointed she was wearing clothes. "You're Nicole Barzoon?"

"In the flesh."

The imagery caused Tate problems. "Does Clyde Dorian live here too?"

"Yes, would you like to speak with him?"

"Both of you, actually, if you have a minute?"

"Sure, come on in." She opened the door wide, stepped aside to let him pass, then announced, "Clyde, someone's here to see us!"

The cottage was furnished in beach-rental casual, a mish-mash of styles and colors that somehow worked in harmony. Clyde Dorian strode from a dimly lit hallway into an over-furnished living room that was bathed in the cool afternoon light from a picture window facing Lake Superior. Tall, average build, soft, academic, curly auburn hair and a scraggly goatee on a face that could use more sun and fewer chips, bushy eyebrows and horn-rimmed glasses completed the picture. Satterfield was right, he was a nerd, no threat, Tate relaxed.

"Hi, can I help you?"

"My name's Mike Tate. A while back, your father hired me to look into your sister's death. Later, he called it off. But circumstances prevailed and I'm still involved. Mind if I ask a few questions?"

His face, already serious, became more so. "Not at all. Have a seat." He gestured toward a fat couch covered by a blue floral throw. Clyde sat in an easy chair to the right, Nicole on the left, cross-legged on a thick weave rug. After everyone was comfortable, Clyde said, "My dad never accepted Lila's death. He blames himself for not being a better father."

"Actually, I think he blames Nicole's father, Harlan." Tate glanced at Nicole but couldn't read her expression.

"My dad's just mixed up. It was an accident, that's all."

"There may be more to it."

"What more could there be?"

Tate turned to Nicole. "What do you think?"

"I think it was an accident."

"Nicole, the problem I have is there are a number of common themes running through incidents connected to your father."

"Themes? And what might they be?"

"Vehicle roll-overs, dead people, insurance money. Each time someone died, your father collected."

"Except the last."

"Who's to say he's dead? Do *you* think he is? Sorry, but I don't."

That got to her. "What? You think Harlan's still alive?"

"Yes, I do. The missing-in-a-blizzard routine was cheap theater he and your brother wrote and directed to collect on his million-dollar life insurance policy." Tate paused a beat to let it sink in, then added, "That's what the police are beginning to think too. And if it's true, anyone involved will be charged with insurance fraud or as an accessory. Both are felonies punishable by prison time." He paused again, glancing from one to the other. "If either of you has any information about it, now would be the time to start talking, while your cooperation will still make a difference. Later, the cops won't care what you say. Anyone involved, even on the periphery, will be arrested and charged."

Clyde said, "This is a joke, right? Somebody put you up to this."

"I don't think he's joking," said Nicole.

Tate said, "Nicole, don't you find it odd that the insurance policy names Earl as the sole beneficiary?"

Her face opened in surprise. "What? Earl's been handling it. He told me it was for all of us."

"Nope. Talked to the insurance company myself. Just Earl. Maybe he didn't feel comfortable mentioning it."

"Why should I believe you?"

"You shouldn't. Check with the insurance company. That's the only way to be sure. Or call Earl."

Her dark eyebrows knitted. "I can't. He's gone on a trip."

"A trip?" responded Tate, discouraged.

"He emailed me a couple of weeks ago saying he needed to get away for a while."

"Did he say where he was going?"

"No."

"When he'd be back?"

"No."

"And he never mentioned he was the only beneficiary on the insurance policy?"

"No, he didn't." She frowned. "I can't understand why Harlan would do that?"

"I can. It's because your father's not really dead. It's part of an act he and your brother are putting on for a payday . . . a million-dollar payday."

"But why? Harlan had a successful business."

"Unfortunately, that's not the case. The business was failing. Kevin Adams, the guy who made it work, was gone. The insurance money from Kevin's death was gone. The money from Lila's policy gone too. There was nothing left. He probably saw this as his only way out."

"Hold on," said Clyde. "Are you suggesting Harlan killed Kevin Adams? And my sister? That's obscene!"

"You're right. It is."

"But they were accidents. How can you prove otherwise?"

"Same way it's always done. With evidence." Tate rose to leave. "One more question, Clyde. When did you move out of the Hewitt Street house?"

"Two days after Harlan went missing."

"Why?"

He shifted uncomfortably, glancing at Nicole, then he held his hands out as though trying to explain something difficult. "Earl . . . ah . . . he was under a lot of pressure. We had an argument, and I just thought it would be best if I moved out, that's all."

"When you were living there, which bedroom was yours?"

"Upstairs and to the right. Why?"
"Just curious."

Tate left Nicole and Clyde in the living room, each in their own world of thought. Back in the Brontocarus and rolling eastbound on Lakewood Lane, Tate pondered the transaction. Clyde had resisted the notion that Harlan Barzoon could have done the things Tate claimed, but the seed of doubt had been planted. And Nicole seemed genuinely shocked to hear her father's business was failing, and that the insurance money was going entirely to Earl. Apparently, he'd told her otherwise, and Tate found himself wishing he could be a fly on the wall during their next conversation. He found it interesting that she seemed more concerned about the money than the possibility of her father still being alive. And she never referred to him as father or dad, only Harlan. He wondered what there was to that? Only one way to find out. Tate turned around and pointed the Lincoln toward Marquette and the residence of Theresa Barzoon.

# A Woman's Scorn

CIGARETTE IN ONE hand, glass of red wine in the other, Theresa Barzoon again led Tate into the kitchen and took up the same posture, leaning against the counter, one leg crossed over the other, that she'd had during his first visit. Tate took a familiar barstool next to the island. Now, as he gazed at her, he saw the resemblance between Theresa and Nicole: the facial structure along with the dark eyes and hair. But where Theresa was thin and elegant, Nicole was fuller and sexier.

"Back again, Mr. Tate? I'm beginning to think you like me."

"I'll try to subdue my passion long enough to ask a few questions, Ms. Barzoon."

"Still trying to get the dirt on my wayward ex?"

"Trying to find him."

"Check the woods near camp. Look for a spot where nothing grows."

The vitriol of ex-wives never ceased to amaze him. "I don't think he's out there."

"No? Where then?"

"Hard to tell, but I don't think he's dead."

Theresa's smile vanished. Bad news can sour the best of days.

"Sorry to say this, Ms. Barzoon, but I think Harlan and

your son are involved in an insurance scam to collect on Harlan's policy."

Her face tightened in anger. "Damn him! If that shit got Earl involved in something illegal, I'll kill him myself."

"Were Earl and Harlan close?"

"Unfortunately, yes. But Earl wouldn't do anything like that. He can be irresponsible, but he's never done anything illegal. Damn that Harlan! I told him to stay away from Earl, but no, he had to have him working for him during the summer so he could brag about him to his friends at Rotary. Up and coming businessman and all that crap."

"If Harlan asked, would Earl go along with insurance fraud?"

"I sure as hell hope not." She paused. "But Earl's never been very motivated to work. Have you met him?"

Tate nodded.

"He's a good looking kid. Strong, healthy, intelligent. He could have it all, if only he'd apply himself. Damn that son of a bitch! If he's gotten Earl mixed up in something . . . ."

"Let's say Harlan's alive. Any guess as to where he might be?"

Theresa Barzoon took a long drag from her cigarette, blowing the smoke upward in a thin stream. "Hard to tell. Probably skipped town."

"Does he have another house or cottage somewhere?"

She shook her head. "Not that I know of."

"Just his house and the camp at Echo Lake?"

She nodded. "Unless he bought something after we split."

"How about Monica Adams? Do you think she'd be a

willing party to his scam? Maybe put him up for a while?"

"That tramp? Sure, she'd do it. Harlan could talk her into a blow job on Main Street."

The saying 'Hell hath no fury like a woman scorned' seemed woefully inadequate when applied to Theresa Barzoon. "So I take it that would be a yes."

She didn't respond. The look on her face said she could dish out more. Time to switch gears. "Did Harlan and your daughter, Nicole, get along?"

"Uh-uh. She was daddy's girl when she was young, but after she became a teenager she barely acknowledged his existence. He was upset about it, thought she should show more respect, but she was a strong, bright kid, very independent, and there was nothing he could do to make her change."

"How about after she left home? Did they see each other often?"

"Couldn't say for sure, but I doubt it. She just didn't care about him."

"Got any idea why?"

"She lived here and knew who he was, not the facade he put on in public. That's reason enough."

"Do you think she'd ever get mixed up in any of his schemes?"

She coughed a laugh. "Not a chance."

"Were she and her brother close?"

"Um, so-so. The usual sibling rivalry. Plus, she was a worker, straight A student, and Earl was content to get by on his looks and athletics. That grated on her. And Harlan used to give him a pass on everything. Bought him a new Corvette, gave him spending money, the works. But since she didn't kowtow to him, he rarely gave her a thing. I was angry at the time, but it's all worked out for the best. Nicole's about to graduate from Northern with a degree in psychology. She's already been accepted into the graduate program at Cornell."

Tate was surprised but kept it in. "I spoke with Nicole earlier. She said she and Lila were good friends."

Theresa's eyebrows went up. "You're joking?"

"Uh-uh. They have a mutual acquaintance in Big Bay, Johnny Nolen. Know him?"

Her posture closed up. "Yes, I know him." Implying more.

Geez, thought Tate, suddenly envious, that guy gets around. "Seems Nicole and Johnny and Lila used to party together up at Johnny's place in Big Bay."

"News to me," she said, clearly upset at the prospect. "Like I said, Nicole and Harlan weren't close. She despised him for having an affair and leaving me. I can't believe she'd chum up with that slut he married."

"Going back to the insurance. Can you think of any reason why he'd leave Nicole and his daughter by Lila off of his policy?"

"He was an asshole. That's reason enough."

# Dinner and a Plan

"HE COULDN'T BE dumb enough to stay at Monica Adam's house. That'd be the first place anyone would look," said Gayla, critically eyeing Tate as he struggled to assemble a meal. "You sure you don't want me to do that?"

"No, no. It's been a while since my gold-medal days as an award-winning chef in Paris, but I think I can still manage chili."

Gayla was skeptical, but it was a price she was willing to pay.

The chili didn't turn out half bad. Tate complemented it with a loaf of warm Italian bread dripping with garlic butter, and topped it off with a bottle of decent Chianti. Afterward, they lounged on the couch in front of the fireplace, Tate's arm wrapped around Gayla as she snuggled into him.

"That was wonderful, thanks."

Thinking of how she'd cared for him since the beating, he said, "My pleasure, I owe you more."

"No, Mike, you don't owe me anything. I'm so sorry I got you into this mess. I wish there was something I could do to make it right."

"You didn't do anything wrong, I did. I wasn't careful."

"Maybe you should quit. There's nothing wrong with

that. It's not your problem anymore. They tried to kill you. It's just luck that you're still alive."

Tate moved his jaw around. "You're right, it probably was a 'they'. It would have been difficult for one man to load me in a car and dump me in Skandia. Not impossible, but difficult. Dead weight is hard to move. Could have been Earl and his crudsack roommate. Or Earl and Harlan. Or, well, there are a number of possibilities."

"Other possibilities?"

"Sure. Though Harlan and Earl are the most likely suspects, it's too early to rule out others."

Gayla straightened. "Like who?"

"At this stage, I'd say everyone. We're talking about a truckload of money here, and from what I've seen, money can cause people, even otherwise good people, to rationalize the most heinous behavior. To cross anyone off the list just because they seem nice or innocent or aren't that kind of person would be naive."

"But Earl has to be a suspect."

"Absolutely. Earl and Harlan. But would Harlan really hole up at Earl's place? I suppose if their actions were spontaneous and they couldn't think of anyplace better. But if anyone saw him, the scheme would unravel in an instant. Seems mighty risky. Too risky for someone who's played it as smart as Barzoon. But you never know, if he thinks he's gotten away with two murders, he may believe he's immune to making bad decisions."

"That guy you call crudsack, got a name on him yet?"

"No, that's one thing I forgot to ask when I was talking to Clyde, but it's on my list. I'll find out tomorrow. He and Earl must be pals or they wouldn't have been sharing the house and he wouldn't have been watching the girl."

"You didn't fill me in on that. Find anything of interest?"

Tate shook his head. "The creep wouldn't open the door. I did check out the garage, though. There was a blue Jeep inside that had to be Lila's. There were a couple dings and scratches, and the roof was damaged, but other than that, it was in good shape. Didn't seem to have been used since the accident."

Gayla pulled away excited. "Mike, there might be evidence in the Jeep!"

"I didn't have much time, so I wasn't what you'd call thorough, but I did take a look. There were a couple of personal items. Nothing out of the ordinary."

She became pensive . . . then alert. "Mike, forget about the inside. For Lila to have been thrown, the door must have come open. You told me she hit the snow bank on the right side of the road and the Jeep rolled up on it."

"Yeah. So where are you going with this?"

"Was the windshield broken?"

"No."

"Any other windows broken?"

"No."

"That means if she was thrown from the Jeep, it had to be through a door."

"Okay. So?"

"Which door?"

Tate shrugged. "The driver's side."

"That would mean the driver's side door would be open."

"Yeah. So?"

"And if it was open when the Jeep rolled, wouldn't it have been damaged?"

Tate stopped to think. "Maybe."

"Was it damaged?"

He tried to remember. "It was closed when I went in the garage. I opened it, took a quick look inside, tested the brake, then closed it. Seemed to work fine, I guess. Then I left. There wasn't much light, and I was in a hurry because I didn't want the crudsack to catch me snooping and call the cops. That's about the last thing I need. So, like I said, I wasn't thorough. But you're making a good point. If Lila was thrown through a door, either door, it would have been open when the Jeep was rolling. Those doors are kind of flimsy. You'd think there'd be some damage. Maybe I should take another look."

Suddenly afraid for him, "Don't you think it would be better if the police did it?"

"Sure, but they won't. Lila's accident is a closed case. They're not going to start poking around and stirring up trouble just because of some theory you or I may have about damage to a door. I'll need to do it myself."

"If you're going, *I'm* going too."

His brow wrinkled. "What? Not a chance. Too dangerous."

"You're right, Mike, it's too dangerous for you to do it alone. I can be a lookout and warn you if someone's coming."

Tate groaned. She had a point. If she were far enough away so she couldn't be caught up in anything, but still in a position to warn him if anyone was coming, it would work. Reluctantly, he said, "Yeah, maybe."

Gayla bounced off the couch. "We're going to need walkie-talkies. They must have some at Target. They have everything."

"You mean two-way radios? Yeah, they probably do."

"It's only eight. They're still open."

"Now?" said Tate. "I was thinking tomorrow. I was thinking tonight maybe we—"

"What better time than the present? We could check and see. If there's no one's home, we could do it." She grabbed his hand and tugged him off the couch.

# Safety First

TARGET DID HAVE walkie-talkies. They were kids' toys, not the pro-quality sets Tate had used, but the packaging claimed a half-mile range and they were only $39.95. They bought a pair, along with ten dollars' worth of batteries, and tested the units in the parking lot. Not bad, thought Tate. Scratchy, but they work.

On the drive to Barzoon's house, Tate explained, "First we make a pass to see if anyone's home. If the house is dark, we find a place for you to park that's near the limit of radio range. I want you as far away as possible. That'll keep *you* out of trouble and give *me* the maximum amount of time if someone's coming. Remember, if a car comes, any car, I want you to assume it's them and warn me."

"Right, Chief. Will do," said Gayla, grinning.

Tate rolled his eyes. "You gotta take this seriously."

"I am, Mike, but you have to admit it's kind of fun."

"Yeah, fun," said Tate deadpan. "The kind of fun that can land you in jail."

Because the crudsack might have seen the Lincoln on Tate's first visit to Hewitt Street, they'd taken Gayla's Chevy Caprice. With her at the wheel, they drove west on 41 to the Midway Drive turnoff and then north up 510 to Nash Lake Drive, slowing as they cruised past Barzoon's house. They saw no lights, rolled another hundred yards, found a driveway, turned around.

"Drop me at Barzoon's then go a quarter mile further. Find a driveway and back into it. Keep the front end near the road so you can see. Keep the engine running and lights on as though you're leaving home. Earl owns a Corvette, but he or the crudsack could be driving a gray pickup. There's not much traffic on this road, so if you see a car, any car, radio and I'll get out of the garage until it passes. If it's Earl or the sack, the most important thing is that I'm outside so it's only trespassing, not breaking and entering. Assuming they don't see me, after they park and go in the house I can find my way to the road. In any event, communication is key. And remember, safety first. We can always come back later."

"Safety first," repeated Gayla, slowing to drop him off.

The night was cool and damp with just a trace of a hazy moon. A fine mist hung in the air like a dewy cobweb and coated Tate's face with a cold sweat as he walked. The driveway was dark and soggy with snowmelt. He sloshed on wondering if his running shoes would leave footprints. As he neared the house, he became more cautious. There were no lights on, but that didn't mean no one was home. Arriving at a low porch, he crept to the front door on soft feet and peeked through the window next to it. Total darkness. Ear to the glass. No sounds. Satisfied, he hurried in the direction of the garage. The door was unlocked. He opened it, entered, closed it behind him, then switched on a small Maglite he'd brought, cuffing it so only a thin beam was shining through a gap between finger and thumb. The first two stalls were empty so he strode directly to the Jeep. But before beginning his inspection, he pulled out his radio and keyed the mic. "Ninety-nine, are you there?" The ninety-nine was Gayla's idea.

"Ten-four, Chief," came the chuckling reply.

This is the dumbest thing I've ever done, thought Tate. "I'm in. Any traffic?"

"None."

"Good. Out."

The place to begin was at the driver's side door. Trying the latch, he found it worked well and the door opened easily. He closed the door, and the latch clicked securely in place. He went around the vehicle and tried the passenger door. Same result. Back on the driver's side again, he opened the door and shined his light around the interior. It was surprisingly clean. An empty Coke can and a colorful winter scarf lay abandoned on the floor in front of the passenger seat. Other than these two items and ornaments hanging from the mirror, the interior was both empty and spotless. Tate checked the ashtray. It, too, was clean. The key was in the ignition. He reached in and switched it on to see if the battery had any life. None of the gauges moved. He looked at the headlight switch. It was on. Probably on since the night of the accident. A living, breathing Lila Barzoon had turned it on. Tate was jerked back to the here-and-now by a sound from outside. He shut off the Mag, yanked his body from the Jeep, and then stood there listening to his heart pound. The nose of the vehicle was facing out. He felt his way around it to the overhead door. Peering through a dusty window, he saw no movement in the yard or up the drive. Cuffing the Mag so there was only the thinnest of beams, he switched it on and made his way to the side door, and through its window centered his vision on the house, but there was nothing to see, no lights, no sound, no movement. His inner voice said, 'Do what's necessary and get out.'

Back at Lila's Jeep, he inspected the interior again, scanning every inch, but there was simply nothing out of the ordinary. Closing the door, he shined the Mag along the edge near the handle. The gap between door and frame seemed factory perfect, but as he raised the beam to the top of the door, he noticed something, a thin vertical line of scratches in the paint, the line extending over the edge of the hardtop and ending where it became concave. He shined his light down the door to the rocker panel below it and found scratches there as well. On his haunches, he followed the line inward until it disappeared under the car. Then he was on his hands and knees, but still too high to see under the Jeep. With a sigh of resignation, he lay down on the cold, gritty concrete, swiveled his body around, and slid his head under the Jeep. Shining the light upward, he located the scratches on the rocker panel then followed the logical line inward to the Jeep's frame. Scratches there too. He shined the beam at the center of the undercarriage but didn't see marks. "Nuts." Using his hands and heels to push him, he shinnied further under the Jeep and again shined his light on the section of frame with the scratches, but he still couldn't see where they terminated. Wiggling and pushing some more, he crammed himself in even further under the Jeep and was finally able to see the other side of the frame. There was a hole, about the size of a silver dollar, that had been punched out during manufacture. On the edge of that hole was a mark, a place where force had scraped away the grime and created a tiny dent in the tough steel. A hook, thought Tate.

Someone put a hook in that hole and a cable went under the rocker panel, up the door, and over the edge of the roof. Then the cable was pulled tight, leaving the scratches. That's how he did it. Satisfaction at his discovery gave way to panic as his radio crackled to life. "They're coming!" said a breathless Gayla. "Mike! Get out!"

# Go! Go! Go!

ADRENALIN POURED INTO his system. He was wedged beneath the Jeep, his jacket acting as a Chinese finger puzzle against his escape. He clawed at the concrete with his fingertips, grunting and sweating, inching his way out. With a last pull, he was free, banging his head on the rocker panel as he swiveled into a crouch. The Mag was still on, he switched it off. He had to get out, *now!* But before he could even rise, a brilliant glow lit the garage like an operating room and an electric motor began to whir—the middle door was rolling up! Tate challenged himself to think: Three car garage, two vacant spaces, Lila's Jeep farthest from the side door. He could hear the vehicle coming up the drive, tires splashing through puddles, they'd be inside in seconds. With the garage interior so brightly lit, there was no way to escape unseen. His only option was to hide behind the Jeep, stay quiet, and hope that after garaging the car, whoever it was would leave by the side door and go the house.

His walkie-talkie crackled to life. "Did you hear me, Mike? They're coming!"

Tate fumbled the radio out of his pocket. Dropped it, picked it up, keyed the mic. "I hear you, Gayla. Don't talk. They're here."

Crouching beside the Jeep, body pressed against it, he listened as the car noise became louder. The glare of headlights blinded him as the vehicle rolled into the garage, filling the space next to the Jeep. There was rock music playing. He sensed the room dim as the car lights went off. The music stopped. The engine stopped. The garage door motor whined as it closed the overhead. A door opened. Only one. Tate heard the crunch of a bag, clink of bottles. The door slammed shut, footsteps on the concrete, one man, the side door opened, it closed, footsteps away. Just one man. But the garage lights were still on. Timer, he thought. Wait it out. He didn't move for the three long minutes until the light dimmed to nothingness. Gotta be careful, he thought, real careful.

Tate listened to the truck engine ticking as it cooled for another one minute, two minutes, three minutes. It was time to get out. He rose on stiff legs and gazed around. The porch light at the house had been turned on and a tired yellow glow filtered through the dozen dusty windows in the roll-ups. Lila's Jeep was a dark blob, Tate recognized Barzoon's pickup as the blob next to it. He cautiously made his way around to the cab and looked inside. Nothing there. Then he went to the side door and peered through the window toward the house. Lights on in the living room shining off nearby trees, none in any window facing the garage. He pulled out the walkie-talkie and thumbed the transmit button. "It's me, click twice if you hear." He released the button and listened. *Click, click.* "Go back up the road and turn around where we did before. When you're ready, click twice then slowly drive to the end of the driveway. I'll be there. Click twice if you understand." He released the transmit button and heard *click, click.*

While waiting for Gayla's signal, Tate tried to decide

which would be the best way out. He could circle around the back of the garage and slip into the trees rimming the yard and get to the road that way. But there were patches of unmelted snow and he'd leave tracks. And, it would be slow. Probably better to just hustle up the drive and hope for the best. He'd risk being seen, but he'd be in the car and gone before anyone could react.

*Click, click.* She was ready. He opened the door, stepped outside, listened. There was a stereo on in the house, rock not rap this time, and not as loud as on his last visit. He closed the door and began to run. Six steps later, his still-tender ribs screamed *Big mistake!* and he slowed to a fast walk. Tate glanced back as he left the yard, but he didn't see anyone. He looked over his shoulder again when halfway up the long drive, still no one. The lights from Gayla's car were moving left to center. Then she was at the driveway, and he was climbing in. As he did, his eyes glanced back at the house. This time he saw the silhouette of a man—a black shadow bathed in shimmering yellow mist. He was running toward them on the drive. There was something in his hand. Tate did not want to find out what it was. "Go! Go! Go!" he commanded.

Gayla had the wheels spinning before his door was closed.

# Clues

"THAT WAS CLOSE."

Tate didn't speak.

They were back at Tate's house warming themselves in front of the fireplace.

"I'm sorry. I shouldn't have suggested it."

"Gayla, for twenty years I was on the right side of the law and barely got a scratch. Now, in less than two months, I've committed three B & E's, been chased, beaten up, and even told someone I was the gas man."

She brightened. "You used the gas man line? That's good. You're learning."

"Learning! Of course, I'm learning. Learning I'll soon be making license plates."

"But you found something, right? I can tell."

"How? How can you tell?"

"I told you before, I read you like a book."

"Then you know I need a beer."

After drinking one in silence and beginning his second, Tate opened up. "Yeah, you're right. I did find something, but I'm not sure what it means, if anything."

"What? Tell me."

"There were marks on the Jeep, as though a cable had been attached to it."

"Attached where?"

"I think someone stuck a hook in a hole on the frame then ran a cable up the driver's side door and over the roof."

Gayla's eyes grew wide. "He used it to tip the Jeep over!"

Tate nodded. "Barzoon could have used a come-along tied to a tree and run the cable over the top of the Jeep and down the driver's side to the frame. Then he cranks the come-along and rolls the Jeep on its roof."

"That's gotta be it, Mike. That's the way he did it."

"I'm inclined to agree. But there are a couple of ifs."

"Like what?"

"I read the accident report. Lila was going around a left-hand curve and rolled over the bank on the right side of the road, with the Jeep ending up on its roof. The tow truck guys would've rolled it back on its wheels before winching it up on their truck. But maybe they had to use a cable and roll it the other way first to get Lila's body out. I'll need to ask them to know for sure."

"Makes sense."

"And we need to know the marks weren't there before the night she died. We're not talking about major damage, it's minor cosmetic stuff most people would miss. Establishing they weren't there before she died could be a problem."

"Is it time to get the police involved?"

Tate took another swig of his brew. "Not yet. We'll need more than scratches to get them lathered up. But if we can establish the marks weren't there before the night she died, we'll have something. So, right now, the tow truck guys are number one on my list."

"Oooh, we're getting close, Mike, really close."

"Yeah, maybe too close. Earl or the sack or whoever was running up Barzoon's drive tonight may have seen your car. So, I think, you know, for your own protection and all, maybe you should spend the night here."

She grinned. "For my own protection."

When morning dawned, the weather report promised the warmest day of the new spring. Gayla had long since slipped out of bed, made coffee, and left for work, leaving Tate to sleep and recover from the previous night's Wrestlemania.

After two cups of coffee, a bowl of warmed chili, and some stretching to work out the kinks, Tate called the Sheriff's Department and asked the ever-present Fugman if he'd check the file to see who did the towing on Lila Barzoon's Jeep. A minute later he had the answer.

Northern Towing was on US 41 west of Marquette. In twenty minutes, he was there.

"Only got two guys," said the middle-aged woman across the counter. "My husband, Danny, and Lew Tonella. They're out back working on the truck."

Tate used the back door and ambled across a gravel parking area to a detached metal building. He found the men busy welding a cracked brace on the business end of the truck. When the sparks stopped flying, the welder flipped up his mask. "What can I do for you?"

"Year ago March, the cops called you to pick up a Jeep involved in a rollover about half way up 510 to Big Bay. Recall that?"

The welder nodded. "Yeah, sure. What about it?"

"I've been trying to get a bead on what happened that

night. I was wondering if you'd tell me what you saw when you got there and what you did to get the Jeep rolled over and onto your flatbed."

"You sayin' we did something wrong?"

Why is everyone so defensive? thought Tate. "No, nothing like that. I'm just looking into the accident, that's all. You guys were there. I'd like to know what you saw."

The welder pulled off his heavy mask and set it on the bed of the truck. He ran his fingers through thick black hair then wiped his mouth with the back of his hand. "We see a lot of bad stuff. Usually, I try to forget."

Tate nodded.

"It was early morning when the cops called. They have our home number for afterhours jobs. So I get dressed and go pick up Lew here," his head nodded toward the other man, "and we head on out. When we get there, we find out a woman driving a Jeep had rolled on a turn. She musta got thrown, 'cause she ended up underneath."

"Was she still underneath when you guys got there?"

"Nope. Cops had pushed the Jeep back over and it was sittin' on the road. Probably thought she might be alive."

"How'd they do it? I mean, how'd they roll it over?"

"Just lifted and pushed on it. Them things ain't that heavy. If it's sitting right, a couple strong guys can do it."

"So it hadn't rolled very far over the snow bank?"

"No, it hadn't. Kinda strange really. The bank wasn't very high right there, but it musta caught the tires just right and it rolled."

"Did it only do a half roll, not a one and a half?"

"Yeah, that's the way it looked."

"If it only did a half roll, how did the woman end up underneath?"

The welder sucked on his teeth. "Couldn't say. Kinda wondered about that myself."

"Last question. You said the Jeep was on its wheels on the road when you got there."

"Yeah."

"So you'd have no reason to put a cable around it?"

"Nope. Just backed up Bluto," he jerked his thumb toward the truck, "put the hooks on and winched her up on the bed."

"You see any cables or winches lying around that the cops might have used?"

He thought about it briefly, shook his head. "Nope. Like I told you, the cops pushed it over by hand."

"They tell you that?"

"Yeah. No reason for them to lie."

Tate's next stop was the Sheriff's Department.

"How's it hangin', Fugman?"

"Like a baby's arm with an apple in its fist. What about you, Tate? Senior Center closed today?"

Tate laughed in spite of himself. "When I read the report on Lila Barzoon, I forgot to make a note of who it was responded to the call."

Fugman scratched his neck. "I think Kevela and Johnson. Let me take a look to be sure." He walked away, disappearing into the file room. When he returned, he said, "Yeah, Kevela and Johnson."

"They around?"

"Kevela's gone. Took a job in Oklahoma City six months ago. Johnson's out on road patrol."

"Do me a favor. Call Johnson and ask him something."

"What?"

"Did he and Kevela use their hands to roll the Jeep off Lila Barzoon, or did they use a cable and winch?"

"You got something I oughta know?"

"Maybe. There are marks on the Jeep that suggest a cable was wrapped around it and pulled tight. Tight enough to leave scratches."

"Like maybe to pull it off the snow bank?"

"Like maybe to pull it on."

Fugman gave a low whistle. "You seen the Jeep?"

"Let's say I'm guessing."

Fugman nodded. "And you want to make sure no one at the accident scene used a cable on it."

"Yeah, that's it."

Fugman turned toward the dispatcher's office. When he came back, he said, "Johnson claims he and Kevela rolled the Jeep over by hand on the chance the woman might still be alive. No ropes, no cables, no winch."

"Anything new on Barzoon?"

"Uh-uh. Another week or two of weather like this and the snow's gonna be all gone around Echo Lake. Probably do another search. He's either out there or he's not. Warms up enough, the dogs should be able to find him."

"Thanks, Fugman." Tate turned to leave.

"You really think he did it?" asked Fugman.

"Starting to look that way."

Thinking Nicole and Clyde would be his best source of information on the condition of Lila's Jeep, Tate drove south out of Marquette to Lakewood Lane. Pulling into their drive, he saw only one car, the Plymouth. He parked next to it and strolled to the door. He knocked. Heard footsteps. The door opened. It was Clyde.

"What do you want?"

Not too friendly, thought Tate. "I'd like to ask you a question about Lila's Jeep."

"What?" He was standing in the half-opened door as though guarding it.

"Did it have any damage before the accident?"

"Damage? Like what?"

"Anything. Anything you can think of."

Clyde shook his head. "No, nothing. Lila loved that Jeep. Babied it. She'd get mad if you dropped a gum wrapper on the floor."

"How about the outside? Any dings or scratches?"

"Uh-uh. It wasn't like she was out four-wheeling in the mud. It was a car for her. She kept it clean and shiny. Even waxed it."

"Why so particular?"

"It was the only thing that was hers. I mean, really hers. She bought it herself. It was the only new car she'd ever owned. It was special to her. Now, if you don't mind . . . ."

"One last thing. That house you were sharing with Earl and another guy. What's the other person's name?"

Clyde's eyes went up, as though thinking, then he said, "I can't recall."

Tate laughed. "You were living in the same house and you can't recall his name?"

"No," said Clyde, curtly. "And I'd rather you not come by anymore." He began to close the door but Tate's hand went up, stopping it.

"Somebody tell you not to talk?"

"Take your hand off my door."

"Did someone threaten you? Was it Earl? Harlan?"

"No one threatened me and there's nothing going on. You're just making things up, you and your wild theories. I'm not talking to you anymore. Leave or I'll call the cops."

Tate didn't move. "Do you think that if I go away it'll end? It won't end." Tate removed his hand, and the door slammed shut.

Back in the Lincoln, Tate made for home to mull things over. Once inside his house, he pulled a pad from a kitchen drawer and sat at the table to write a to-do list.

*What caused the change in Clyde's demeanor?*
*Get further verification the cable marks weren't on the Jeep before Lila's accident.*
*Who was taking care of Jenna when Barzoon went missing.*
*Where is Barzoon?*
*Talk to Barzoon's friends, Halliwell and Kent.*
He paused for a moment, then added,
*Check out Monica Adams' cottage on Shag Lake.*

Then he stopped. Something was bothering him; something that didn't make sense. If Barzoon was scamming the insurance company, running out of gas was set up to provide a reason to abandon the machine. If that's the case, why pull out the tool kit and tinker with the engine? He didn't need it for an excuse, and it would take up valuable time on that dark, cold night when he could be setting up phony tracks and doubling back to 550. But then what? He couldn't very well walk back to town. He'd risk being seen. He couldn't travel through the woods.

Too much snow and too far. Maybe he had another car parked at the road. Or maybe he got a ride from someone. That someone would almost certainly have been Earl or Monica. But that still leaves the question of who was taking care of Jenna? Monica Adams didn't answer him when he'd asked about it. Earl told the police he was supposed to meet his father at his Harlan's place on Sunday at 1:00, and when he arrived, Harlan wasn't home, and a couple hours later he went looking for him. It doesn't seem reasonable that he'd have had Jenna for an extra day without wondering where Harlan was. And if he *was* taking care of Jenna, what did he do with her when he went out looking for his father? That leaves Monica Adams and perhaps Nicole and/or a nanny as the most likely person or persons to have been taking care of her. Theresa Barzoon said Monica would do anything Harlan asked. Damn! As much as he didn't want to do it, he had to call her. Tate dialed, hoping for the best but not expecting it.

"Ms. Adams."

"You! I told you I don't want to talk to you anymore."

"Just one question and I won't bother you again. Just one."

Silence. "All right, but only one, then I never hear from you. Understood?"

"Understood."

"What is it?"

"Were you taking care of Harlan's daughter the night he went missing? And if you weren't, who was?"

"I wasn't, and I don't know."

"Ms. Adams, if you're lying you'll be setting yourself up for an aiding and abetting charge." He knew it wasn't true, but why not try?

"I'm not lying. It was a Friday night. I went out. I had dinner in town with a friend and then we went to a movie."

"Who's the friend?"

"You've more than used up your one question, Mr. Tate."

"Who was that friend, Ms. Adams. Let me confirm it and I'm off your back."

He heard her let out a sigh, pause, and then say, "Nicole Barzoon. Not that it's any of your business." Then she hung up.

What? Nicole Barzoon had dinner with Monica Adams the night her father disappeared? That doesn't make sense. Other than the obvious common denominator of Harlan, what could they possibly have in common? Monica must know I'll check with Nicole, so she's probably telling the truth. And that still leaves the question of who was taking care of Jenna?

His next call was to Orville Dorian. A woman answered, identifying herself as Martha.

"My name's Tate. I'm trying to reach Orville. Is he around?"

"He's at work."

"Oh, yeah. I should have thought of that. Can you tell me where he works?"

"Harris Painting."

"Where's it located?"

"Between Marquette and Negaunee on 41, about three miles west of Marquette."

Tate had a thought. "Say, are you taking care of Jenna?"

"Yes, why?"

"I'm an investigator (he purposely left off the private)

working on her father's disappearance. Would you ask Jenna if she remembers who was taking care of her the night her father disappeared?"

"I don't know, Mr. Tate. Orville told me not to let anyone talk to her."

"I wouldn't be talking to her, you would. I just need to have this one question answered. That's all. Okay?"

There was a hesitation. "Well . . ."

"I wouldn't ask if it weren't important."

"All right, but don't expect much. She's a very bright child, but she's only four."

Tate heard her call Jenna and ask the question. Then a tiny voice answered, "Uncle Clyde."

# New Information

TATE WAS NONPLUSSED. Clyde Dorian? Clyde Dorian was watching Jenna the night Harlan went missing?

He dialed Orville's number again.

"Hello, ma'am. This is Mike Tate again. I'm sorry to bother you, but there's just one more simple question I'd like you to ask Jenna."

"And what would that be?"

"Did Uncle Clyde stay at her house, or did she go to his?"

"Mr. Tate, I'm not sure—"

Tate cut her off. "Please, it's very important."

"Oh, all right."

Tate heard her call the girl again and ask the question, but he couldn't hear the answer.

"What did she say, ma'am?"

"She said they stayed home. Uncle Clyde stayed at her house."

"Thank you. I won't bother you again."

Tate sat at his kitchen table sipping lukewarm coffee and digesting this latest revelation. So Clyde was taking care of Jenna. But didn't Fugman say Barzoon told people he was going to his camp for *the* night? Not two nights, *the* night. And he left on Friday. So, if Clyde was watching Jenna and Barzoon was only supposed to be gone for one night, why wasn't he concerned when Harlan didn't show on Saturday?

Tate tossed the rest of his coffee in the sink and rinsed his cup, placing it on the drain board, a long established bachelor habit—eat over the sink, don't use unnecessary dishes, clean everything immediately.

Tate strode to the door, opened it, and was only half-surprised to see Greg standing there, sunglasses shading his eyes, a toy pistol dangling from a front pocket of his jeans.

"Good afternoon, Agent Greg. Out on a case?"

The boy nodded. "There are bad guys around."

Tate affected concern. "What makes you think so?"

"I can tell," said the boy, not offering more.

"Keeping an eye on 'em?"

"You bet, Mr. Tate."

"What's going on? Bank robbery? Kidnapping? Counterfeiting?"

"What's counterfeiting?"

"That's when people make fake money and pretend it's real and use it to buy things."

Greg wondered if he and his friends were counterfeiters. They always used play money, buying and selling stuff back and forth between them. He reasoned since they were kids it was okay, just not okay for grownups. "No, not those things. Spying."

"Umm," said Tate. "That's pretty serious stuff. Someone in the neighborhood?"

"Yeah," said the kid. "You."

Tate smiled. "You think I'm a spy?"

"Uh-uh," replied Greg, vigorously shaking his head. "It's *them*!"

"Them?"

"Yeah, them!"

"Who's them?"

"I don't know. But I can tell. They're spying."

Tate was confused. "But you just said it was me."

"No," said the boy, frustrated. "They're spying on you."

Tate's friendly smile disappeared. "You're serious?"

The boy nodded.

"Why do you think they're spying on me?"

"I saw them. I was behind your garage watching the neighborhood when I saw a car drive along the road. Then it came back real slow. They were looking around. Then they came in your driveway." He paused to collect himself. "I got scared." Another pause. "Agents aren't supposed to get scared, are they?" He hung his head.

Tate reflected on the times he'd felt the cold grip of fear. "Scared? Sure agents get scared. That's normal. Being scared keeps you from doing things that could get you hurt."

"Really?" said the boy, brightening. Then his brow furrowed. "But how can you fight bad guys if you're scared?"

"Being scared makes you careful. And when you're dealing with bad guys, you always want to be careful. The FBI trains you to be careful and not to rush in and try to arrest them all alone in a situation where you might get hurt. It's better to call headquarters and have your friends come and help. Then the bad guys see they don't have a chance and give up." Tate raised his hand for emphasis.

"I guess," said the boy, thinking fighting bad guys wouldn't be nearly as much fun if he were scared all the time and always had to call for help. He turned to leave.

"Greg, wait! You said someone came in my drive. Did you see them?"

Happy for the recognition, he said, "Sure, Mr. Tate. I saw them . . . kind of."

"Was it more than one person?"

"No, just one."

"Man or a woman," asked Tate, thinking it may have been Gayla.

"A man, I think," he replied. "It was hard to see."

Maybe it was Noon, thought Tate. "Do you remember what kind of car he was driving?"

"It wasn't a car, it was a pickup truck."

Noon drove a black Ford Crown Victoria. Crown Vic's being the car of choice for countless police agencies, they were never purchased for personal transportation by officers. Thus, it'd been a source of great amusement to the veteran agents at the office when, fresh from training, Noon arrived driving one.

"Remember the color?"

"Umm . . . white."

"You didn't happen to catch the tag number, did you?"

"What's a tag?"

"The license plate."

Greg shook his head in failure.

"That's okay."

"If they come back, I'll write it down," he said, patting the pocket where he kept his pad and pencil.

Tate chewed on this for a moment. There was probably nothing to it. Greg had a vivid imagination. Might not have been anyone in his drive at all, or maybe someone turning around . . . or the gas man. "Tell you what,

Agent Greg, if you see that truck come back, here's what I want you to do. First, keep your distance. That's the most important thing. Don't get too close. And don't let on that you're watching. You need to stay undercover on this assignment. That's really important. But if you can get a look at the license plate, write down the number. That way I can check it with the Bureau and see who it is. Writing down license numbers is an important part of FBI work."

"Sure thing, Mister Tate." Greg was beaming. "Don't you worry. I'll take care of it." Then he bolted from the porch, disappearing into the jack pines beyond Tate's garage.

Tate wondered if he might have made a mistake with Greg. He thought he'd better stop by and speak with the boy's parents later on to let them know what they'd talked about. There was nothing to it, but the last thing he wanted was upset neighbors.

Stoking the Brontocarus to life, Tate drove west along winding Lakewood Lane until he reached Clyde and Nicole's cottage. Pulling in the yard, he noted Clyde's Plymouth was gone but Nicole's Mustang was there. When he knocked, she answered.

"Clyde around?"

She shook her head. "Not here."

"Know where he went?"

"I just got home a few minutes ago. The house was empty when I arrived."

"Got an extra minute?"

She shrugged. "Sure, come in."

She led him into the small living room, taking a seat

on the couch and pulling her legs up. Tate opted for one of the chairs.

"The night your father disappeared, it was a Friday, do you remember what you were doing that night?"

"Of course, how could I forget. I had dinner with Monica Adams at L'Attitudes and then we went to a movie."

"Good movie?"

She crinkled her brow. "Do I need an alibi?"

"I'm just trying to cover all bases."

"It was okay. *Another Time*. A chick flick. I don't think you'd like it."

She was probably right. "You and Monica good friends?"

"Not really. We're friends."

"Seems kind of odd, age difference and all."

She didn't respond.

"You call her or she call you?"

"What do you mean?"

"Who's idea was it to have dinner and a movie?"

"It was Monica's. She'd called a couple of days earlier and suggested it."

"And you agreed?"

She shrugged. "Sure, why not?"

"Seems you'd have better things to do with your Friday nights."

"I'm a psychology major, Mr. Tate. I think it's important to get to know and understand people, all kinds of people, not just those my own age."

"You didn't think it was odd that she called?"

"She was in love with my father. I'm sure she was trying to get closer to the family. That's something women do. It's normal."

"Do you like her?"

"I try not to be judgmental."

"I understand Clyde was taking care of Jenna that night."

"Yes."

"Did he do that often?"

"I couldn't say. He was living with Earl on Hewitt Street and I didn't see him much."

"How is it that he's living here now?"

"My roommate moved out. I needed someone to share the rent. Clyde called and said he'd moved out of Hewitt Street and was staying with his father while looking for a new place to live."

"He wasn't happy living with your brother?"

"He said there was too much partying going on. He's not really the party type."

"How's it working out?"

"It's working fine. He's a good housemate. Does his own dishes, cleans, buys food, sometimes even cooks. I've had roommates who weren't nearly so considerate."

"If Clyde was watching Jenna that Friday night and your father was supposed to be back on Saturday, when Saturday came and went, why wasn't Clyde concerned enough to call someone?"

"He did. He called me Saturday afternoon."

"You?"

"Yes. Monica mentioned Harlan had been under some pressure, and I assumed he'd decided to stay at camp another night to unwind. I told Clyde if he had plans, I'd drive over and take care of Jenna, but he said he didn't and he'd stay. I thought it was pretty nice of him, but that's just the way he is."

"Clyde and Harlan get along?"

She shrugged. "So, so."

"I'm surprised your father would ask Clyde to take care of Jenna."

"He didn't, I did."

"You?"

"Yes. Harlan had a nanny for her, but she only worked during the week. He called Earl and asked if he'd do it, but Earl doesn't have the patience for it and called me. I'd already made plans with Monica, so I asked Earl if Clyde was there. Earl put him on and I asked Clyde if he'd do it. He said he would. Simple as that."

Tate thought most any man would do anything Nicole Barzoon asked. Clyde Dorian would be no exception.

"I stopped by earlier. Clyde was here. He was upset and didn't want to talk. Actually slammed the door in my face. Got any idea why?"

Her face registered surprise. "That doesn't sound like Clyde."

"Have any idea where he might be now? I'd like to talk to him again."

Nicole shrugged. "School maybe, the library, his dad's place, shopping? Could be anywhere."

"He's in college?"

"Yes. He's very bright. A physics major."

Tate rose to leave. "Thanks for your time, Ms. Barzoon."

"You can call me Nicole. Calling me Ms. Barzoon makes me feel as though I should be wearing opaque stockings and cooking a casserole."

Tate came under her spell. "Try as I might, that's something I cannot imagine."

He drove away less certain than when he'd arrived. Everything Nicole told him was plausible. Monica Adams could have called suggesting a night out. Nicole could have accepted. The chain of events could have ended with Clyde watching Jenna. He could have called Nicole and been assured all was well and agreed to watch the child for another night. Maybe it was all true, and maybe Harlan Barzoon's body would turn up in the woods during the next search, but that wouldn't explain his own 'accident'. He still had a score to settle. He wasn't with the Bureau anymore. It was something he'd take care of himself.

With time to kill, he thought he'd track down Harlan's pals and find out what they had to say, something he should have done earlier to get a better feel for Barzoon. People tend to hang with their kind, and his friends are likely to have witnessed, or at least sensed, the essence of his character. After driving home to get their business addresses from the phonebook, he was back in the Lincoln and headed to town. First stop, Halliwell Plumbing and Heating.

He's in the warehouse, said the counterman. Straight down the hall and through the door.
Short and stocky, clipboard in hand, Pug Halliwell was inventorying a bin of PVC fittings. Tate introduced himself, said he was looking into Barzoon's disappearance, and asked Halliwell if he'd mind talking about him. Halliwell set the clipboard in the bin. "Harlan? Sure, what do you want to know?"
"You were friends with him?"

"Good friends. Shame what happened. He was one of a kind. I'm going to miss him."

"No offense, Mr. Halliwell, but I've spoken to a number of people who feel just the opposite."

Halliwell dismissed it with a wave of his hand. "Envy, that's all it is. Harlan was larger than life. When he stepped into a room, you knew something was happening. The guy had charisma, big time. He was a force. Some people saw that as ego. And sure, he had an ego, but he could back up his bluster with results. Some people are threatened by men like him. Makes 'em feel small. So they bad-mouth guys like Harlan to try to make themselves seem bigger."

"Ever hear any of it?"

"'Course I have. Ninety-nine percent bullshit. Look, Tate, I knew Harlan since high school. Played cards once or twice a month. Went to camp together, hunting, fishing, stuff like that. We were close. Me and Harlan and Jeff Kent. Kevin, too, before he died. We were tight." He paused. "Harlan, I'll tell you about Harlan. Salt of the earth. He'd do things for others, give his time, give his money, never expected anything in return. And he didn't trumpet it around town like most would. Saw it myself. Many times. Sure, Harlan was human. He had flaws. He was maybe a little too interested in the ladies." He gave a self-deprecating shrug. "You know, guy like me, I'm lucky to have the wife I got. Not takin' any chances. But Harlan, him being handsome and smooth with words, well, women were a lot friendlier to him. And he wasn't always as careful with his money as he should be. But that was part of his personality. He was an optimist, a dreamer, I don't think he ever imagined things wouldn't turn out right, somehow. And they usually did, because he was always in motion, always making it happen. He was a good guy, Tate, and a good friend. I'll miss him."

"How was he after the Adams accident?"

"Shook up. A little scared too, but he tried to hide it. He really wasn't a builder, you know, he was a salesman. Whole different world. Takes a different mindset. I'm a little of both and it works for me, but I'll never be big time. He was all of one. Pure salesman. Heck, I knew he'd have trouble with the business. Tried to tell him so, but he was blind to it. His confidence trumping his common sense."

"Think Harlan Barzoon would ever commit a crime?"

"Harlan? Nooo." Halliwell vigorously shook his head. "He'd push things to the limit, but he knew where the line was and wouldn't cross it."

"Thanks for your time, Mr. Halliwell."

After the interview with Halliwell, Tate drove to Third Street and the dental practice of Dr. Jeffrey Kent. Kent graciously made time for him between patients.

"Loved him," said Kent. "Fun to be around. Always upbeat. Pug and Harlan and I had some damn good times. Canoe trips, fishing, hunting, poker games. Before he split with Theresa, we all did a lot of family stuff together too. Holidays, things like that. Afterword, you know, later when he was married to Lila, not so much." He shrugged an apology. "It was the wives. They didn't really take to Lila. Whenever she was around, she was the center of attention and I think it made them uncomfortable. Well, it's more than think, I know it did. Not that they had anything to worry about, you understand, but, well, you know."

"How was Harlan after Lila died?"

"Broken up. Heck, he knew their marriage wasn't going to last. Talked about it with me and Pug. Said he loved her but it wasn't going to be enough. I felt sorry for him. Especially after talk started getting around about her and some guy in Big Bay."

"Think Harlan would ever do anything to Lila out of anger?"

Kent tilted his head. "Anyone's capable. Get pushed too far. Lose your temper. But Harlan? I'd say no. It wasn't his style. He knew he could win by talking, so that's what he'd do."

"Toward the end, when his business was in trouble, did he ever mention it?"

"Oh, sure. We'd be talking business and he'd bitch and moan like the rest of us. But I never got the impression he couldn't handle it. You'd have to have known him to understand. The guy was really something."

"Yeah, seems he was."

After leaving the dentist's office, with nothing left to do, Tate motored toward home. Pug Halliwell and Jeff Kent seemed solid, honest, and brighter than average. They did not seem like the kind of men who'd condone criminal activity. They both liked Barzoon, respected him, and they were almost identical to Monica Adams in their praise of him. And though most people will shield a friend, that's not the impression he'd gotten from either of them. There was no shielding, just honest opinion. Maybe Barzoon wasn't dirty. Maybe he'd just been talking to the wrong people, people with an axe to grind, like Orville and Johnny and Theresa. Or maybe Harlan Barzoon was a far better salesman than even his closest friends gave him credit for.

Turning into his tree-lined drive, he saw Gayla's light-blue Caprice in front of his house. She'd just arrived. He pulled in, parked, and walked over to her.

A smile danced on her face. "Let's have a picnic."

# Presque Isle

"HUH?"

"A picnic. You know, where you go somewhere and eat outside."

His eyes lit up. "Like with a basket and cold fried chicken?"

"How about a paper sack with pasties and beer?"

"Works for me." Tate was a meat and potatoes man and a pasty is man food. Beef, pork, potatoes, onions and a few chunks of rutabaga thrown in for gas, baked in a pie crust and eaten with your hands, the way a man should eat.

"I called Laura and Bill. They said they'd meet us at Sunset Point on the Island at 5:30." Suddenly shy because she'd never made plans for them without asking, "Hope that's okay? You don't mind, do you?"

"Heck, no. Pasties and beer at the Island sounds great."

Gayla smiled. Another hurdle overcome.

Strictly speaking, Presque Isle isn't an island, it's an oblong knob of peninsula extending into Lake Superior from the northernmost extremity of Marquette. But everyone calls it the Island. There's a rustic band shell, marina, and hiking trail. It's a perennial favorite for a walk, a picnic, or simply to relax watching the waves of the lake as they scrub the shoreline or crash against the breakwater that juts the eastern shore.

Mike and Gayla arrived early. They parked by the picnic tables at Sunset Point then walked the perimeter loop, stopping from time to time to watch breakers explode against the Island's red sandstone cliffs. Finishing their stroll, they found Laura and Bill relaxing at the Point.

Noon called Tate several times while he was recovering, but otherwise left him alone. Theirs was an unusual friendship. When they met, Tate was a veteran agent sent to pasture after disciplinary issues in Detroit. Noon was a rookie straight from the academy whose zeal was both an irritation and a source of great mirth to the other agents at the Marquette office. Noon and Tate were thrown together on a case that ended in a gun battle at the very house Tate now owned. It was Noon's first case and Tate's last, and on it they forged a bond that bridged their twenty-five year age difference. And ever since Tate's retirement, every few weeks they'd get together to hoist a beverage and shoot the breeze.

Still air and warm sunshine. Sun low in the west. The four friends sat at an ancient wooden table near the water's edge and wolfed warm pasties, washing them down with cold Labatts Blue. Afterward, Gayla and Laura went for a stroll along the beach while Tate and Noon stayed behind sipping beer and making small talk. Tate asked Noon about his work, and Noon, always willing to oblige, went on about the latest investigation he was involved in, illegal drugs distributed throughout the Upper Peninsula.

"Making any progress?"

Noon exhaled. "Yeah, a little. We know who the local low-level guys are, but that's about it. Boletto asked if

I'd go undercover. He said since I'm still relatively new around here, I wouldn't be recognized."

First one gone, Tate pulled a fresh pasty out of a bag, broke off a chunk of crust and popped it in his mouth. "That's the kind of decision you have to make for yourself," he said between chews. "But remember, no matter what anyone tells you, no matter what limits you set for yourself, once you get inside, you're going to have to prove you're one of them to gain their trust. The low level dealers aren't that smart, otherwise they wouldn't be low level dealers. But if you get past the first layer, you'll be dealing with men who stay in business by being wary. They can smell a cop by the way you turn a phrase, treat a woman, or any of a hundred other things. They perceive the world in a different way than we do. Their attitudes will be jarring to your senses. And the only way to get close to them is to be like them, to empathize. Once you do that, it's easy to make friends, easy get to into the life, and later on, it can be hard to forget. Living two lives and lying to people all day, every day is not healthy. You didn't ask for advice, but I'm giving it. Don't do it. Don't risk losing part of yourself just to bust some punk whose shoes will be filled before the day is out."

Noon nodded. Tate knew what he was talking about, knew first hand. "I'm not going to jump into anything. Anyway, when it's over I'd probably be transferred, and I'm kind of liking it here."

Tate knew what Noon was liking. She was up the beach talking woman talk with Gayla. They'd met shortly after Noon came to town and had been cozy ever since.

"What about you, Tate? What's going on with the Barzoon thing? Making any headway?"

"Yes and no. Everything ties up neat but it doesn't feel right. Two people dead in vehicle accidents so obviously accidental that no one bothers to investigate. Now Barzoon is missing and presumed dead, but no one can find the body. He could have died in the woods, but I'm not buying it."

"Still think it's an insurance scam?"

Tate gave a nod as he chewed another piece of crust. "Yeah, that's the most logical explanation. But there are a couple people with reason to want him dead, so I can't rule out homicide."

Tate gave Noon an abbreviated version of his investigation to date. When through, he asked, "What do you think? Anything jump out at you?"

Noon stared out over expanse of Lake Superior. "Who knew Barzoon was going to his camp that night?"

Tate thought for a moment. "Earl, Clyde, Nicole." He sucked on his cheeks. "Monica Adams might have known. Maybe even Orville Dorian or Theresa Barzoon. And, by extension, Johnny Nolen."

"You said the machine ran out of gas but Barzoon had a tool kit out and was messing with the engine. That doesn't make sense. It wouldn't further his storyline. Just run the machine out of gas and leave tracks that would make people believe you wandered into the forest. What's the point of fooling with the engine? He didn't need that."

"Yeah, the tool kit bothers me. If I were on a snowmobile and it quit running, my first thought would be gas, but Barzoon began tinkering with the engine. Why wouldn't he check the gas? Particularly if he hadn't gassed up, which he obviously hadn't."

Noon nodded. "Who was there when he left his house?"

"Clyde Dorian."

He stroked his thin mustache. "What if Barzoon asked Clyde to top off the tank and Clyde says he will but doesn't, or even drains some gas out to guarantee Barzoon won't make it to camp? If Clyde suspected Barzoon in his sister's death, he'd have motive."

"Umm . . . Clyde was there, but only by chance."

"How about Earl? With a million dollars of insurance money in play, he'd certainly have a motive. And the way you describe him, he doesn't seem above it."

Tate ripped the pasty in half, loaded it with ketchup from a disposable packet, and took a large bite. After swallowing, he said, "That's a thought. It'd be interesting to know if Earl was at Harlan's before Harlan left for camp. Earl could have followed him, done the deed then driven home to party. I'll need to see if he has an alibi. Did I mention he left town?"

Noon shook his head.

"Supposedly, for some rest and relaxation. Probably hangin' with the old man, trying to decide between Belize or the Caymans for when the insurance money comes through."

"How about Johnny Nolen? You said Lila was planning on leaving her husband for him. His suspicion about Barzoon being responsible for her death would give him cause."

"Could be. Nicole or Theresa might have mentioned Harlan's plans, and Nolen may have seen it as an opportunity."

"How about Nicole?"

"She was with Monica Adams."

"Orville Dorian?"

Tate shook his head. "Don't think so. If he had, he wouldn't have encouraged me to start digging."

"So what you have is Earl, Clyde, Johnny or Harlan himself."

"Yeah, that's what I figure. Which puts me about where I started. It's probably Earl and his old man running a scam, but I gotta check out the rest."

"T and T?" said Noon, meaning tail and tap.

"No chance of a tap, but a tail on Earl might be productive. That is, if he ever comes back." Tate produced a salesman's smile. "Want a part-time job?"

"Sure. I could do six to midnight. You'd have to find someone else for the day shift."

"What day shift?" asked Laura, as she and Gayla strolled toward the table.

"Mike's putting me to work on the Barzoon case. He's management. I'm labor."

Laura's face lit up. "Surveillance? Is that it?"

"Yup," said Noon. He turned to Tate. "When do you want me to start?"

Laura said, "It'll take more than one person."

"I'll do it," offered Gayla, enthusiastic.

Tate's face fell. "No, you won't. These people are dangerous."

"I'll do it," said Laura. "Get my story the hard way."

Tate grimaced. "Didn't you hear what I just said? This isn't playtime. These are bad characters who do ugly things to people who get in their way. If they catch you following them, you can't scare them off by threatening to pen a derogatory review."

"We could do it together," said Gayla, excited. "That would be safe. I could take some time off."

Laura nodded. "It's a plan."

"No, it's not a plan," insisted Tate. But after swimming upstream for the next fifteen minutes and using every argument he could come up with, exhausted, he succumbed to the current and grudgingly said, "All right, you win. We'll start tomorrow morning at six."

"Six?" chimed the women in unison, brows crinkling. "Kind of early, don't you think?"

"Routine," said Noon. "Can't risk letting the suspect drive off before you're in position."

Tate said, "Meet at my place. We'll discuss the ground rules and decide where you should park to pick up Clyde."

"Clyde?" said Gayla. "I thought we'd be tailing Earl?"

"Nicole told me Earl's out of town. Didn't I mention that?" His face was the picture of innocence.

"No," said the women in unison.

Right, thought Tate. They can tail boring Clyde until they're tired of the chore and quit. He and Noon can do the real work when Earl comes back.

"Clyde?" said Gayla again, clearly disappointed.

"Yes, Clyde. He's developed an attitude and doesn't want to talk. He may lead us to the reason." Tate didn't believe it, but it would keep the ladies safe.

"Six it is," said Laura. Then to Noon, "We'd better be going. I need my beauty rest."

Tate and Gayla stayed behind, casually strolling the rocky shoreline all the way to where the park ended and a row of residences crowded a picturesque cove with a wide, sandy beach. They skipped rocks on shallow swells and talked about small things and good things until the sun was a yellow halo over Middle Island Point. Only after the last golden rays faded into a tattered ribbon of lavender and rose did they pack what remained of their picnic and depart. Tate drove, Gayla sat close, his arm around her, her head on his shoulder. He powered the windows down and warm scented air swirled though the car, buffing their skin and adding to a sense of anticipation.

Back at the beach house they made love, not wild like the night before, but tender. When it was over, she lay with her head on his chest. "Mike, you could have done anything, why the FBI? From what you've told me, it doesn't seem as though you enjoyed it."

He thought about it for a moment then laughed. "I wanted to fight the bad guys." Slowly his smile melted away and he became serious. "What I wanted to do was help stop the criminals who prey on the weak and the innocent. They're the ones who need laws and law enforcement the most. The strong and bright and wealthy, hell, they can take care of themselves. Always have and always will. It's the weak and the innocent who are most easily taken advantage of and suffer the most harm. They need society's protection. I wanted to help. I wanted to make a difference."

"You *have*, Mike, and you still are." She kissed his chest and snuggled closer.

# The Tail

THE ALARM WENT off at 5:15, but Gayla was already up. Tate could hear her humming a tune in the kitchen. The aroma of coffee and bacon levitated him to the table. He was becoming accustomed to breakfasts consisting of more than milk on something crunchy. Women are like a drug, he thought, easy to start, and before you know it, you're hooked. Finishing his plate, he asked for seconds.

Fields arrived precisely at 6:00. A cold front had passed through during the night, bringing with it thick dark clouds and a steady cold rain. Shedding her raincoat in the porch, Laura entered the kitchen and proclaimed she was "Ready to rock!"

Her enthusiasm made Tate nervous. "You don't want to get too excited," he cautioned. "Stay cool. Stay detached. Stay healthy. Do the job and go home, not to the hospital."

"Right, Mike," she said bouncing around.

Gayla was equally exuberant. It was like being in a TV movie. Better, because it was real.

The women stood at the front door tapping their toes long before Tate was emotionally ready to cut them loose. "Communication is essential," he grunted.

Gayla said, "Here, Mike, take my cell so we can keep you posted."

Tate eyed the tiny pink phone with suspicion. He couldn't escape the feeling that having a cell phone impinged upon his freedom by chaining him to the whims of others. He'd studiously avoided ever having one. And if he ever did have one, it would not be pink. But with no radio communication available, he grudgingly conceded that the cell might be an acceptable alternative.

Laura giggled as Gayla showed him how to use it. When she was through, Laura said, "Welcome to the twenty-first century."

Tate scowled. "Listen, here's how it works. Almost no one suspects a tail unless you make yourself obvious. How often do you check for cars tailing you?"

The women turned to each other in surprise. "It's different with women," said Laura. "Sometimes there are creeps, you know. So, um, once in a while, but not too often." Gayla nodded agreement.

"With men, it's almost never. But when someone's involved in a criminal activity, they're more cautious. Still, if you keep your distance and act casual, no one will make you. The key is to keep your distance and make your presence plausible. Nobody's going to notice one more woman in a shopping mall, but you can't follow the subject into the men's room. Nobody's going to notice you driving behind them if you're a quarter-mile back with a couple cars in between, but tailgate for a block and they'll make you for sure. Nobody's going to pay attention if your parked in a normal parking place, talking to each other or searching in your purse or starting your car and driving off or anything else that seems normal and routine, but sit stone faced and stare directly at the suspect and he'll make you in a second. Got it?"

They nodded.

"One more thing. You're both too attractive."

Fields smirked. Gayla posed, patting her hair.

"I'm serious. If you're a woman and you're tailing a man, you don't want him to give you a second glance. You need to frump yourselves up."

"You're joking," said Gayla.

"I'm not. Your makeup's perfect. Your hair's perfect. You're too pretty. You'll call attention to yourselves. Get moving or the deal's off."

The women trudged toward the bathroom, flattered and complaining. Reappearing several minutes later, Gayla asked, "How's this?"

Gazing from one woman to the other, Tate couldn't tell anything had changed. He sighed in resignation. "A quarter-mile away, three cars back. Don't get any closer."

Gayla's hand went up in a salute. "Right, Chief."

"Just follow Clyde and see where he goes. Make some notes: times, addresses, contacts. If you know the person, fine. If not, jot down a description. Get the make, model, color, and tag number of any relevant vehicles, as well as anything else that seems important. Don't be seen doing it. It's better to miss something or lose the tail than to be made. You can always pick him up later. Got it?" They nodded. Tate thought for a moment. "Laura, you have your Volkswagen, right?"

"Yes."

"Volkswagens are too distinctive. Especially yours. It's like a mutant lemon on wheels. Might as well tail him in a low-rider and bounce the front end at stoplights. Gayla's Caprice is a better choice."

Gayla said, "Shouldn't we take both and leapfrog like they do on TV?"

Tate frowned. "I want you two together. It's safer that way. Plus, you gave me your phone so you only have one left. Communication is essential. One car, ladies. Plus, tails involve a lot of down time sitting around waiting for the subject to do something. Trust me, you'll want someone to talk to. And be sure to bring magazines and snacks."

"Already packed," said Gayla, pointing to a tote leaning against the wall by the door.

"Okay. Clyde lives at 367 on the west end of the Lane. It's a small cottage on the beach side. He's a about six-two, medium build, 180, curly reddish hair with a scraggly goatee, no mustache. He drives a brown Plymouth with rust around the wheel wells. I've made contact with him twice. The first time he seemed normal, but yesterday when I tried to talk to him, he became upset. I sensed fear. Might have been nothing, but that was my impression." Tate paused for emphasis. "I can't stress this enough. Even someone like Clyde, who seems meek and mild, can turn on you if he feels threatened. Don't put yourself in that situation."

The women were edging closer to the door. Turning the knob. Pulling it open. Backing out. Tate got the hint. "There's only one obvious route from his house into town. Find an inconspicuous place to park on Main Street between Green Bay and US 41. Pick him up there."

With the speed and determination of prisoners escaping a gulag, Gayla and Laura fled before Tate could remind them for the hundredth time to be careful. "Call me if you pick him up," he yelled as they hurried to Gayla's car, arms shielding their hair from the downpour. "And be careful."

After the Caprice turned right at the end of the drive and disappeared down the lane, Tate ambled back into the kitchen. It was only 6:20, too early to get in touch with anyone. He had another cup of coffee, straightened up the house, and then spent an hour exercising, taking care not to re-injure mending tissue. Afterward, he took a long, hot shower. At 9:00 he was back where he began, sitting in the kitchen munching on a sandwich and staring at his notes. He'd answered the first question—Clyde was watching Jenna—so he made a new list, adding two new questions to answer.

*Check out the Adams cottage on Shag Lake.*
*Was there anyone else at Barzoon's house before he left for camp?*
*Gas level in the snowmobile.*
*Get further verification that the scratch marks weren't on Lila's Jeep before the accident.*
*Name and whereabouts of the crudsack.*

Might as well start at the top, he thought. Grabbing a phonebook from the kitchen counter, he thumbed through the pages until he came to Adams. There it was, a second number listed under *Adams, M.* The Shag Lake cottage had a number, and an address. It was a long shot, but Barzoon might be hiding there. Criminals have been known to do dumber things. Cover all bases, thought Tate as he snatched a jacket from its hook and hobbled through the rain to his car.

# Bad Business

SHAG LAKE IS thirty miles south of Marquette, just beyond the village of Gwinn. The terrain is flat and sandy, covered by thick stands of pines and dotted with numerous lakes ringed by cottages for getaways in a land where the fleeting summer is cherished and enjoyed to the fullest. Tate had never been to Shag Lake and had a map open on the seat. After forty minutes of driving, he spied a carved wooden sign swinging in the wind at the entrance to a sandy drive: *Kevin and Monica Adams*. As with Theresa Barzoon, Tate felt a twinge of sympathy for Kevin Adams, a man who'd built his life around an unfaithful wife, and he wondered again if it could have been Monica who'd come up with the idea of having Barzoon buy into her husband's business? If so, his death, accidental or not, could be laid directly at her feet.

Pulling to the side of the road just past the driveway, Tate twisted in his seat to appraise the layout. The cottage, a one-story with yellow vinyl siding, was roughly a hundred feet from the road and forty from the lake. There were two small out-buildings between Tate and the cottage, one obviously a shed, the other most likely a sauna.

After giving the place the once over, he turned his attention to the task. The rain was drumming on the roof of the Lincoln and all he had was a summer-weight jacket. Getting drenched didn't appeal to him, but there was no other way, so he opened the door and climbed out of the car into the downpour, and then slogged up the driveway, skirting puddles as he made his way to the cottage. There was no door and only one window facing the drive, but a fieldstone walk led from a grassy parking area around the left of the cottage to the side facing the lake. Standing in the parking area, he searched for signs of recent habitation. The rain and general gloom made it difficult. There were traces of tire tracks on the drive. He couldn't tell if they were recent. Though the day was gray and cold, there was no light showing in the lone window and no smoke rising from the chimney.

He walked forward, rounding the corner to the lake side of the cottage, and saw an untended lawn sloping down to a wooden dock, choppy water lapping its pilings, the lake beyond uninviting in the rain. Turning his gaze to the cottage, he viewed the true front. Facing the water were two large picture windows with a small porch and door in between. Moving close to the first of the windows, he peered inside. Knotty pine interior. Patterned vinyl flooring. Oval weave rug. Early American coffee table in front of a basic couch and chair set. Brick fireplace at the left end of the room, a second couch facing it. Inexpensive woodland prints on the walls: a sunset, ducks in flight. There were no clothes or other items strewn about and nothing to suggest anyone was inside or had recently been there. Tate stepped onto the small wooden porch, went to the door, tried the handle. As expected, it was locked. Stepping off the porch, he went to the second window for a different view. Now he could see into a kitchen on the left side behind the living room. No pots on the stove or dishes on the drain board. No—

"Looking for something?"

The voice startled him. Adrenaline flowed. He swiveled toward the threat. Twenty feet away, at the corner of the building, was a tall, heavyset sheriff's deputy in rain gear. Tate's mind raced. "Thought I'd stop by and see if Monica Adams was home." It was as good a lie as any.

"You a friend of hers?"

"Acquaintance."

"Didn't see a car so you thought you'd look in the windows and try the door?"

He must have been watching, thought Tate. "Thought she might be here."

"No lights on? No car in the drive? You thought she might be here?"

This is bullshit, thought Tate. He began walking toward the deputy to explain.

"Hold it right there!" His hand moved to his gun.

Tate stopped. "There's nothing going on here, Deputy."

"Let's see some ID."

Tate pulled out his wallet, slid the driver's license out, held it up. "Name's Mike Tate. I live on Lakewood Lane in Marquette."

"Put it on the ground, Mr. Tate, then step back."

Tate did. Then the deputy made a tactical error. He should have had Tate lean against the wall or lie on the ground, but he hadn't. As the deputy moved forward and leaned down to picked up the license, Tate knew he could have taken him. But, of course, he didn't.

Eyeing the license, the deputy asked, "What do you do for a living?"

"Just retired from the FBI," said Tate, thinking that would be enough.

The expression on the deputy's face turned unfriendly. "You some kind of smartass?"

"I'm ex FBI, Deputy. You can call the Marquette office and talk to anyone there, they'll tell you it's true."

"Sure."

"Call Logan Fugman, he'll tell you the same."

The deputy's demeanor softened. "You know Fugman?"

"Yeah, I was just talking to him yesterday."

"When?"

"Yesterday."

"No, I mean what time?"

"Mid-morning."

"What were you asking him?"

"Personal business."

"About the accident?"

Then it clicked. "Are you Johnson?"

"Yeah," said the deputy, relaxing. He reached out, handing the license back to Tate. "Raining like hell. Let's go in the cruiser."

Johnson got behind the wheel, Tate slid in the passenger side. He knew if Johnson had any doubts about him, he wouldn't be sitting up front, he'd be back behind the mesh.

"Kind of a coincidence you'd be by here same time as me," said Tate.

"Been keeping an eye on the place."

"Any reason in particular?"

"Maybe," said Johnson, playing it close to the vest. "What about you?"

"Like I said, thought Ms. Adams might be here."

"Cut the bull, Tate. You thought Harlan Barzoon might be here."

"Yeah, maybe," said Tate, surprised. "That why you're here?"

"Maybe," said Johnson, mirroring Tate.

Neither spoke. Tate broke the silence. "You and your partner were the first responders at the Lila Barzoon accident."

"Yeah."

"Anything seem unusual about it?"

"Like what?"

"If I knew, I'd say."

Johnson moved his jaw around then stared at Tate. "You ever work traffic accidents?"

"No."

"It's bad business. People cut up, busted up, moaning, crying, screaming, or not moving at all. Or maybe they're drunk and belligerent, or they run, or they just start wandering off in shock and you have to corral 'em before they get hurt. Most of the time they're young, but sometimes not. Sometimes whole families. Little kids lying there dead, parents wailing, sick with grief. It's bad business, Tate. Real bad. After you get an accident call, you have to steel yourself to what you might find so you won't get too emotional and not be able to do your job. First priority is to care for the injured; last is to protect the scene. Understand?"

"Yeah."

"So, Kevela and I get up there and we see the overturned Jeep and a pair of legs sticking out from underneath. Didn't know how long the vic had been under it, probably too long because after we got the call, it took us a half-hour to get there. It was snowing hard, couple inches on the legs already. It didn't look good, but you never know. So without talking about it, we started pushing on the Jeep, trying to roll it off her. Kevela's big, like me, and the bank had a some incline toward the road, so I guess we figured we could do it. On the first try, it started to roll, so we on kept lifting and pushing and it ended up going all the way over on its wheels. Didn't make any difference, though, she was long dead."

"I was up there when the snow was still deep. If the Jeep went over the bank—"

Johnson cut him off. "Wasn't much of a bank at that spot. You'd think so because of the curve and snowplows and all, but it was at a place where a logging road joins 510. The road wasn't plowed, but wind whipping down the channel between the trees caused most of the snow to blow across 510. What I'm saying is it wasn't that deep. Maybe two feet and packed hard."

"After you knew she was dead, did you check the scene to try to determine what happened?"

Johnson let out a breath. "At the time, it seemed obvious. Going too fast, skidded, hit the bank, rolled, the lady got thrown and ended up underneath."

"At the time."

"Yeah. At the time." Johnson stared ahead at the rain spattering against his windshield. "Like I said, it'd been snowing pretty hard, two, three inches since she went off the road. Wasn't any way to tell exactly what happened, other than the obvious, and we didn't really think anything of it, just wrote down what we saw." Johnson paused. "But later, you know, after the adrenalin wore off and we were back in the cruiser headed toward Marquette, I got to thinking about it and came up with some questions."

"Like what?"

"Like when a car's going too fast and can't make a curve, the inertia generally takes the vehicle straight into whatever's in its path. But Mrs. Barzoon's Jeep was already around the curve before it left the road."

"Anything else?"

"Yeah. When we rolled the Jeep off her, Mrs. Barzoon wasn't all messed up."

Tate didn't understand and said so.

"You see, Tate, people get thrown out of a moving vehicle and get rolled on—and I've seen it before, so I can tell you—they aren't just lying there with their clothes all neat and tidy like they're sleeping."

# Blowin' Smoke

THE TRIP TO Adams' cottage and the conversation with Deputy Johnson consumed Tate's thoughts on his drive back to Marquette. He was soaking wet, and even with the heater on full blast, he was cold. Dry clothes were high on his priority list. It wasn't until he was on US 41 nearing the turnoff toward Lakewood Lane that he remembered Gayla and Laura and the tail on Clyde.

Since he lived on the east end of Lakewood Lane, rather than suffering slow, curvy drive, Tate usually saved a few minutes by taking M-28, the straighter, faster east-west highway paralleling it, and turning off on Hiawatha, the feeder nearest his home. Clyde and Nicole's cottage was near the west end of the Lakewood Lane, much closer to US 41. From there, the shortest way to town was via Green Bay Street to Main Street to 41. Tate was about to turn right on M-28, but changed his mind and went straight three blocks to Main, turned right and cruised eastbound searching for Gayla's car. It was nowhere to be seen.

"They were supposed to call me when they picked him up," he grumbled.

Pulling the Lincoln to the shoulder, he fished the pink phone out of his pocket, flipped it open, and then realized he didn't know Laura's number. Tate scowled, cursed, rammed the gearshift into drive and headed for home.

Arriving, he parked the Lincoln as close as possible to the house and jogged through the rain to the porch. Opening the storm door, he saw a piece of paper taped to the wooden inner door. A note from the ladies, he suspected. Pulling it free, he hurried inside, turned on the lights, shed his dripping jacket, and opened the note. In a child's scrawl was written BZM974.

Greg, thought Tate. The license number of the car. What did he say? Not a car, a pickup truck, a white pickup truck. Probably nothing to it. Kid's imagination. Hmm . . . the pickup next to Lila's Jeep in Barzoon's garage had been what? Gray, he thought? But maybe it was white. It'd been dark and he'd been concentrating on the Jeep and hadn't paid any attention to it. Could be a custom plate. BZM, Barzoon. BZ makes sense, but not the M. He picked up the phone and dialed Fugman.

"No can do, Tate. I've already bent over backward for you. Why not call one of your chums at the Bureau. Or are you afraid you'll interrupt their favorite soap?"

"Yeah, I think *Days of Our Lives* is on. They'd be real upset. C'mon, just one last time?"

"Uh-uh. Nope. Better try someone else."

Tate knew Noon could run the tag, but he didn't want to risk getting him in trouble. Shivering as he stripped off his wet clothing, he took a hot shower, then toweled dry and donned fresh jeans and a shirt.

Back in the kitchen, he poured himself a cup of cold coffee, dragged out the directory, found the number for the Peninsula Journal, dialed, and asked for the editor. When a man identifying himself as Kip Lewis answered, Tate told him he needed to reach Laura about a story on coho fishing in Superior. He said Fields gave him her cell number but he lost it. The editor recited it from memory. Tate jotted it down, said thanks.

The cell was still in his pocket. He despised them but thought he'd better test it to know it worked. Using a fingernail to punch miniscule buttons, he lifted the phone to his ear. Nothing. Then he remembered he had to push SEND. "I hate these damned things!" he muttered, jabbing the SEND button. Laura answered on the second ring. "Hi, Mike. Where have you been?"

"Wha . . ? How'd you know it was me?"

"You're using Gayla's phone. It says Gayla on my display when her number calls."

Miffed at his ignorance, Tate growled, "I thought I told you to call when you picked up the tail!"

"We did, Mister Technology, but you must have been in a dead zone."

"Dead zone?"

"No cell reception."

"Oh."

"Clyde drove past about 9:30 and we followed him to the University parking lot. I guess he had a class, because he was carrying books. He stayed a little over an hour then drove home. We're back on Harvey Street."

"I was by fifteen minutes ago. Must have just missed you."

"Yeah, we just got here."

"Since Clyde's home, I think I'll pay him a visit. If you see him drive by in the next few minutes, call me so I don't waste my time."

Laura said, "Right, Chief. Over and out." He heard the women giggling, then the phone went dead.

The rain was hard and steady as Tate cruised westward on Lakewood Lane. He pulled into Clyde's drive. Both the Plymouth and the Mustang were there. He parked. Hurried to the door. Knocked. Nicole answered.

"Mr. Tate, back so soon? I'm beginning to think you like me."

Chip off the old block, thought Tate. "May I come in? It's pouring."

"Sure." She opened the door wide.

Clyde was standing by the couch in the living room. When he saw Tate, his hackles went up. "What are you doing here? I told you to stay away. Get out, *now*, or I'll call the cops."

"Clyde, it's okay," said Nicole, trying to sooth him.

"He's just here to cause trouble," said Clyde, puffing up and striding toward Tate. "I said get out!"

Tate stayed relaxed. "Settle down, Clyde. Trouble for who?"

Clyde stepped up to him, not close enough to be threatening, but close. "I said out!"

"What are you afraid of, Clyde?"

"Yes, Clyde," it was Nicole. "What *are* you afraid of?"

Clyde stopped short. Nicole had power over him.

Tate asked, "Who was at Harlan's house before he left for camp?"

"None of your damned business." He turned to Nicole, "See? He's just trying to make trouble."

"Clyde, settle down. What does it matter?" Her eyes went to Tate. "I was there that afternoon. I stopped by to see Harlan before meeting Monica for dinner." She made a 'so what' gesture with her hands.

"You and Clyde and Harlan and Jenna were there? Anyone else?"

She feigned thinking. "Um, no, just us."

Tate paused to build the drama. "You see, Nicole, what I'm trying to figure out is this: Who was it that drained the gas out of your father's snowmobile? And the only two names I have right now are you and Clyde."

Nicole's mouth fell open.

Clyde's body straightened. Then he relaxed as a cynical smile appeared. "You're blowing smoke. Last time you were here you said Harlan faked his death for insurance money, and now you're saying somebody drained the gas out of his machine? So that what? he'd be stranded and get lost? You're way off base, Tate. Occam's Razor: the simplest answer is usually the correct one. It was his machine. He forgot to fill it."

Tate shook his head. "Doesn't pass the smell test. Anyone taking a snowmobile in the woods at night is going to check the gas. That is, unless someone else told him they'd filled it but hadn't, or maybe even drained some out."

"What?" His face opened in disbelief. "No!"

"Yes," responded Tate. "Otherwise, when the engine quit, the first thing he'd check would be the gas. But he didn't. He thought it was a mechanical problem and pulled out his tools. Then he ran the battery down trying to get it started. And that was the plan."

Clyde glared at him. "Are you accusing me? You're out of your mind! I was at Harlan's as a favor. And I did *not* touch that machine. Period. End of story."

Tate turned to Nicole. "Who got there first, you or Clyde?"

She glanced at Clyde but didn't speak.

"I did," he said. "But that doesn't prove anything. I told you, I didn't do it."

"Who else was there? Was it Earl? Was he there? Has he threatened you in some way? Is that why you're afraid?"

He folded his arms defiantly. "I'm not saying another word."

"How about Monica Adams?"

Against his will, he shook his head no.

"Nicole's mother, Theresa?"

"You're way off base with this crap. None of them were there."

"How about that crud you were sharing the house with on Hewitt Street? What's his name?"

"Lex," said Clyde. "No, Lex wasn't there."

"What's his last name?"

"Radmiller."

"He from around here?"

"Never asked; never cared."

"Why did you move out of that house?"

"None of your business."

Nicole spoke. "For godsake, what's the big deal? Tell him, Clyde." But he remained mute. Frustrated, Nicole said, "A few days after Harlan disappeared, he and Earl got into some sort of an argument."

Tate turned to Clyde. "What was the argument about?"

"I'm through talking," he said and then stomped off to his room.

Nicole's eyes followed him in bewilderment.

"Why did you go to your father's house that afternoon?"

Her gaze returned to Tate. "He's my father, do I need a reason?"

"The cops will be asking the same question. They'll want a better answer than that."

"I . . . I wanted to see how close he and Monica had become. I was having dinner with her that evening, and I didn't want to say the wrong thing."

"What was his response?"

"He told me they were just friends."

"When you were there, how did he seem?"

"Fine. Normal. You'd have to know him to understand."

"Was he the forgetful type?"

"You mean about the gas?"

"Yes."

She shrugged. "I can't remember him ever running out of gas in the car."

He thanked her and turned for the door.

"Wait," said Nicole. "Why would someone want him to run out of gas? That doesn't make sense."

"Sorry to say this, Nicole, but it does if that someone wanted to kill him."

"Who'd want to kill Harlan? I mean, he could be unreasonable, but . . . ." She let the sentence trail off.

"I'm making a list. If you want to add any names, call me."

Outside, the rain continued falling. Tate pulled the door closed behind him but didn't make a move toward his car. From inside he heard the sound of Clyde yelling, "I told you, he's just here to make trouble. Damn it! You shouldn't have told him anything." Then Nicole's voice, soft and controlled, he couldn't make out the words. Time to go. He dashed to the Lincoln. Opening his car door, he glanced back. The door to the cottage was open a crack, then it closed.

He drove eastward on the Lane for two blocks before stopping to call Laura on the pink phone. He briefed her about his conversation with Clyde and Nicole, described Nicole's car, and said they should watch for it. "Forget about Clyde for now, keep an eye out for the Mustang." Then he drove home, the interaction churning in his mind. He'd barely stepped inside when he got the call. "Mike, it's me. We're behind her on 41. She's traveling toward Marquette. Going damn fast too. Laura can hardly keep up."

"Stay back. Don't let her see you."

"She won't."

"Be careful."

"She's a woman, Mike, it's not like she's dangerous."

Tate eyed the phone in exasperation. "If she turns up 550 toward Big Bay, call me."

"What makes you think she's going there?"

"Just a hunch."

Gayla called fifteen minutes later. "You were right, she just made the turn onto 550. What do you want us to do?"

"You can break it off and come home. We know where she's going."

"Where's that?"

"To see Johnny Nolen."

# Out of Gas

IT WAS ONLY two in the afternoon, but Tate popped the cap off a bottle of beer, wandered into the living room, and stood at his picture window, sheets of water sliding down the glass. Gazing through the sodden gloom toward Lake Superior, he saw line after line of sizzling white caps on powerful rollers laying siege to the shores of Gitche Gumee. The storm was increasing.

He didn't have a plan and never had. He'd been fishing, making things up as he went along, using stories for bait, trying to get a reaction, and now he'd gotten one. Nicole had lied to him, of that he was sure. Now she was speeding north to see her lover, Johnny Nolen. Was Nolen with her that Friday afternoon at Barzoon's? Did he drain the gas from Harlan's snowmobile then follow his track on the camp road until he found him? What then? Pull out a gat and march him into the woods far enough so no one would find him?

He'd appraised Nolen's physical abilities when they first met. A longstanding habit. Not muscled up but fit, the kind of fitness that comes from regular exercise. And there were cross country skis on his porch. Maybe Nolen didn't walk in the camp road, maybe he skied in. It would be easier and faster. And as Barzoon tired himself running away through the snowy forest, Nolen could ski leisurely behind, gun at the ready, until they were far enough in the woods so the body wouldn't be found. And after the dirty work was over, he could have obscured the trail on his way out or simply taken another route. It was possible.

What about Nicole? Did she know? Was she part of the plan? She and Harlan hadn't been close, but is that enough reason for a daughter to kill her own father? Odds were against it, but add money into the mix and things change. Maybe she knew Harlan had a megabuck life insurance policy but didn't know Earl was the only beneficiary. And speaking of Earl, where is he? Supposedly on some spur of the moment getaway. Him being a dickhead, it's easy, almost gratifying, to think of him as a suspect, but maybe he's simply the former and nothing more. Nolen, on the other hand, is bright, smooth, and a talented artist. It reminded Tate of an old joke. What's the difference between an artist and a large pizza? Answer: The pizza can feed a family of four. Handsome and talented but probably poor, Nolen was used as a boy toy for women who wanted more out of life. But what did he get in exchange? Sex, to be sure, and at first that'd be more than enough. But how about later? How could he support the woman of his choice on an artist's income? Could it be that Nicole mentioned Harlan's insurance policy to Johnny, and Johnny thought he could pad his bank account by loving her up then bumping off dad? And now Nicole is running to him. But for what? To confront him with accusations? Tell him to be careful because I'd stumbled onto their scheme? Or to cry and plead for help because she did it and now she needs him? Regardless of which scenario was playing out, the result would be the same; the guilty party would lie, run, hide, and lawyer up. If Nicole, Johnny, or both lawyered up, time would be on their side. Much better to confront them now.

Tate left his beer on the mantle and went into his bedroom. His .38 was on a shelf in the closet. He still didn't have his license, but that didn't matter. Safety first. Back in the kitchen, he grabbed a dry jacket from the coat rack and made for the door. Taking the Lane to Hiawatha to M-28, he turned eastbound toward the junction with US 41. Halfway there he passed Gayla and Laura. They waved as he sped by.

With gusting wind, heavy rain, and slick roads, nearly an hour elapsed before he was guiding the Lincoln along the curving pavement around Lake Independence. As he neared Nolen's drive, he saw Nicole's Mustang parked next to Johnny's pickup. Rather than alert them by pulling in, Tate rolled to a stop just beyond the house then reluctantly left the climate control of the car. Windblown rain pelted his face, he hurried to Nolen's door. Arriving, he didn't knock, just listened. There was conversation inside, but it was muted. Time to do it. He knocked.

When the door opened, Nolen's face told him he hadn't wasted his time. The friendly demeanor was missing, in its place was surprise and discomfort. "Tate! What are you doing here?"

"In the neighborhood, Johnny. Thought I'd drop by."

"I'm kind of busy right now. Maybe some other time." He began to close the door.

Tate blocked it with his foot. "Now's better for me."

Nolen glanced down at Tate's foot. "What the hell are you doing? Do you want me to call the cops? I will."

"Yeah, do that. And while you're at it, why not tell them how it was you who killed Harlan Barzoon."

Nolen's face went wide. "You're crazy. I did no such thing. I told you before, I've never even met the man."

"That right? Then how'd you know where his camp was?"

"Huh? I never said—"

"Sorry, wrong answer. First time I was here I began to explain where it was and you said you knew."

"Yeah? Well maybe I do. That doesn't mean anything."

"Oh, but it does, Johnny. How are you going to explain that in court?"

"Maybe I was there with Nicole."

"But you weren't." It was her voice from behind him. He turned around to face her.

With Nolan distracted, Tate pushed his way inside and closed the door.

"What are you talking about, Nicole? Of course we were there."

He was lying. Tate knew it. Trying to coax Nicole into lying too.

"But we weren't. Ever. You know it and I know it." Anger building as she stepped up to him. Eyes glaring like hot Klieg lights. "Did you do it, Johnny? Did you kill my father?"

Nolen's mouth fell open. "You don't believe him, do you? That's insane! Why would I do it? Why?"

"Why are you lying about us going to camp when you know it's not true?"

"I didn't do it!" said Nolen, almost pleading.

"You knew daddy was going to camp for the night. You knew because you were with me when I went to his house."

"What are you talking about? You're mistaken. I was

never at your father's house."

"Yes you were, Johnny. You were there with me. I drove you there."

"Nicole, what are you trying to do to me?"

"Clyde was there too. He'll tell the truth. He'll say he saw you."

"You know he didn't," said Nolen, a shard of composure returning.

"You just think he didn't because when he and I came out of the house, you were hiding in the car. The snowmobile was on daddy's pickup when we got there. It was right next to where I parked. You must have gotten out and drained the gas while I was inside. How could you? How could you kill my father?" Nicole's hand flashed toward Nolen's face. The slap was hard and sharp.

"You don't know anything," said Nolen, backing out of range. "Nothing at all. Now get out! Both of you." He turned and strode across the room to the windows overlooking the lake and then stood, back to his accusers, staring at the rain.

Nicole grabbed her coat then pushed past Tate, flung the door open, and dashed toward her car.

After he heard her car door slam and the engine rev up, Tate said, "Don't run, Nolen. It doesn't work." He turned to leave, but before he was out the door, Nolen said, "Wait!"

Tate stepped back inside as Nolen strode over to him. "There's something I couldn't say. Not in front of Nicole."

"Yeah? What's that?"

"I *have* been to Harlan's camp . . . but not with Nicole."

"With who then?" But he already knew.

Nolen sucked in a breath. "With her mother, Theresa.

She still has a key and suggested we go there one day." He exhaled, shaking his head. "Don't you see? There's no way Nicole would understand. You had me trapped. I *had* to lie. But I swear to you, I've never met Harlan Barzoon. I didn't drain any gas. I didn't follow him. And I absolutely did not kill him. Tate, you have to believe me!"

"Were you at his house that Friday with Nicole?"

He gave a frustrated sighed. "Yes, but it was completely by accident. I ran into Nicole in town and she asked if I wanted to go for a ride. I thought we were going for a cruise around the Island. It was only after we were on our way that she told me she had to stop at Harlan's first. Jesus! That's the last place in the world I wanted to go. I'd slept with his wife. He probably knew it. His ex-wife too. And now I show up at his door with his daughter! It's not like he's gonna say, 'Hey, Johnny! Good to see you, bro. Come on in. Let's have a beer and compare notes.' Simply being there would have been tantamount to spitting in his face. The only thing he'd be thinking about is whether to use a baseball bat or a tire iron on me. I couldn't believe it when Nicole said that's where we were going. I told her to let me out on the side of the road and pick me up on her way back, but she swore she was just running in and out and I could duck down in the car and no one would see me. Drain the gas out of his snowmobile? Screw that. I just wanted to get the hell out of there before he came out blasting."

"Did Clyde see you?"

"He came out of the house with Nicole. Not all the way to the car, maybe half way. He was staring at the Mustang. I was hunched down, but yeah, maybe he saw me."

The side of Nolen's face was crimson where Nicole slapped it. His normally perfect posture had collapsed into a slump. "I didn't do it, Tate. I told you before, I've never met Harlan Barzoon in my life. If he walked in the door right now, I wouldn't know who he was. I didn't do it."

"Then who did?"

He raised his hands in helplessness. "I don't know."

# BZM974

IT WAS 5:30 by the time Tate arrived home. Gayla, Laura, and Bill Noon were at the kitchen table munching cheese and crackers and chatting about the case. Tate made straight for the refrigerator and a cold brew.

"Stakeout off?" asked Noon, knowing, or at least hoping, Tate wouldn't drink before going on one.

"Yeah," he said, pulling out a chair. "I thought I had this thing figured out, but now I'm not so sure."

"What happened?" asked Gayla. "We saw you pass us on our way back. You went to Johnny Nolen's, didn't you?"

He took a pull on his beverage then nodded.

Laura said, "Don't keep us in suspense."

Tate pulled out a chair and then sat in it backwards, arms resting on the back. "Earlier, I went over to Nicole and Clyde's place and stirred the pot with a story about how someone purposely drained the gas out of Harlan's snowmobile to strand him in the woods so they could follow him, whack him, and make it look like an accident. They both said no one other than the two of them were there at Harlan's before he left for camp. I was certain they were lying and, sure enough, only minutes after I leave, Nicole is burning rubber in the direction of Big Bay. My guess was Johnny Nolen's. When I get there, she's inside. Nolen's on edge, doesn't want to let me in, but I persist."

Noon chuckled at his choice of words.

Laura said, "I'll bet."

"Go on," said Gayla.

"On a previous visit, Nolen told me he knew how to get to Barzoon's camp. When I asked him how he knew, he crossed himself up by saying he'd been there with Nicole. She immediately contradicts him and says they were never there. Then I asked Nolen if he was at Barzoon's house before he disappeared. He said he wasn't. Then Nicole calls him a liar and says he was there with her, and that Clyde saw him. That squared with the impression I'd gotten earlier. Then Nicole and Johnny get into an argument with her accusing him of doing the deed. Then she runs out and drives off. Made sense to me. Johnny was in love with Lila and blamed Barzoon for her death. And Johnny was at Barzoon's house before he left for camp. He could have drained the gas, skied up the camp road behind him, frog marched him into the woods, and left him where he wouldn't be found. Means, motive and opportunity."

"Could have," said Noon. "But your tone says didn't."

"Yeah, there are a couple problems. Johnny told me he just happened to run into Nicole in Marquette and she asked him if he wanted to go for a ride. He said he was shocked when he realized she was driving to her father's house. Makes sense too. Nolen had been messing with his wife, now he's chummy with his daughter. Situation like that, you don't stop by to chat."

"Guess not," said Laura. The others nodded.

"And if he *did* decide on the spur of the moment to drain Harlan's machine, follow him, and kill him, it's not like Barzoon's gonna march to his death just because Johnny's threatening him with a loaded paint brush. Even a knife wouldn't do it, he'd need a gun. And I don't figure Nolen for the type to be carrying a heater just in case. Maybe he is, but instinct tells me no."

Noon pointed at the Labatt. "Got any more of those?"

Tate straightened. "Yeah, sure. Shoulda offered."

Gayla was up before he could move. "All around?" Everyone nodded.

"Go on," coaxed Laura. "I know there's more."

"Yeah. So anyway, I start to leave and Johnny stops me. Wants to explain why he lied about being at Barzoon's camp with Nicole and why he couldn't say it in front of her."

"This has gotta be good," said Laura, hunching forward to hear.

Tate worked to suppress a grin. "It is. The time he was there, it wasn't with Nicole . . . it was with her mother."

The women's eyebrows went up. Noon smirked. "That guy gets around."

"Seems so," replied Tate. "And based on a conversation I had yesterday with Theresa Barzoon, I think he's telling the truth. So, it's only too easy to understand why Johnny wouldn't want the lovely Nicole knowing he'd been spending quality time with her mom."

"Geez, I'll say," agreed Gayla, setting the beverages on the table.

Noon said, "Doesn't sound like Johnny's your man."

"Nope. That only leaves Nicole and Clyde, if indeed gas was drained. Nicole was with someone the whole time, so that rules her out for rigging the gas, and Clyde was watching Jenna. She was too young to leave alone for the amount of time it would take to follow and dispatch Barzoon, so that probably rules him out too. Plus, he was only there as a favor to Nicole. So, after considering it, I think the gas angle is a blind alley. Maybe Barzoon was just careless."

Gayla said, "Or that brings us back to your original theory about him staging his disappearance for insurance money."

"That's right," said Laura. "Since his body hasn't been found, that theory still stands. Anyway, if Nolen did it, who scared Orville into telling you to quit the case? And who was it that beat you up? You're a big guy, Mike. I can't imagine some artsy type like Johnny Nolen giving you trouble."

"Any word on Earl?" asked Noon.

Tate shook his head. "Far as I know, he hasn't come back. Sent an email to Nicole after he left saying he was all broken up over his father's death and needed some time to himself. Seems like a lie. People don't scatter after a death, they cling together. Odds are he's hiding out with Harlan, biding their time until payday."

"Makes sense," said Gayla. "And from what you've uncovered about Lila's accident, it's looking more and more like it wasn't an accident at all."

"There's more on that too," offered Tate. "I ran into the deputy who worked the scene. Won't bore you with the details, but he told me something about it didn't look right. At the time, he was caught up in the emotion of it, dead woman and all, but later on it bothered him."

"Well," said Noon, rising to leave. "The kid will show up sooner or later. Nobody takes a pass on a million bucks. He'll be back. Then he'll lead you to Barzoon."

With no stakeout planned, Bill and Laura said their goodbyes. What little light the day had offered was gone.

Gayla began preparing dinner. Tate opened his third Labatts and then wandered into the living room and toyed at making a fire. Hunched in front of the grate, he constructed an intricate teepee of cedar kindling over balled strips of newspaper, tore it down and then built it again, exactly the same. Striking a match on the stonework, he put flame to paper and watched as the kindling ignited into a crackling yellow fire.

Gayla tuned in a jazz station on the clock-radio on the kitchen counter. The volume was low, but Tate recognized the tune: Billie Holiday singing "Ain't Nobody's Business." He knew the song, reciting one line in particular: *"I swear that I won't call no copper, if I'm beat up by my papa. Ain't nobody's business if I do."* Tate shook his head in disgust. What kind of mindset would it take to believe it was okay to get beaten up? And why would someone write a song to legitimize it? He was drifting into a blue funk and Billie Holiday wasn't helping. It was the Barzoon case, it had him. He couldn't get away.

He'd been involved in countless cases with the Bureau that, even after enormous amounts of effort, remained unsolved. It was frustrating, but in the end he'd rationalized that it was just a job, not a game to be won or lost, and he'd go out every day and do his best and try not to bring the frustration home with him. Back then, the philosophy worked. But this was different. Maybe it was because it was just him, him alone against the bad guys, as Greg would say. A good kid, thought Tate. Then he remembered the note. A plate number. BZM974. Was that it? Rising, he went to the kitchen table and found it lying on his 'to do' list. BZM 974. Fugman wouldn't run it. Noon would, but why risk getting him in trouble. Tate sniffed the air. Gayla was making spaghetti and meatballs, fragrant notes of garlic, oregano, and onion an aromatic opera. His stomach growled. He lost concentration. Later, he thought, tossing the note back on the table.

He ate without speaking. The specter of Lila Barzoon had come to haunt him, spoiling his meal. *"She was wild and full of life,"* said Gordy. *"Adventurous,"* is what Nicole called her and had become friends with Lila even though she'd broken up her mother's marriage. *"My little girl,"* said Orville. *"He killed my little girl."* They all loved her, maybe Barzoon too, but she was leaving him and he knew it, so he murdered her just like he murdered Kevin Adams. Then his brow furrowed. Was that really it? Or . . . was it something entirely different?

Tate set his fork on the edge of his plate and reached for the scrap with the license number on it and then stared as if it were a secret code. BZM 974. His mouth slowly opened with realization. Then his jaw tightened with resolve. *"DAMN IT!"* he roared, pounding the table with his fist.

Startled, the fork slipped from Gayla's hand, bouncing on the floor as she reeled back.

It brought Tate back. "Sorry, hon. Didn't mean to scare you." He pushed out his chair, rising. "Listen, I gotta go out." Grabbing his jacket and a flashlight from the counter, he was gone before Gayla could respond.

Rain pelted him as he jogged to the Lincoln. Then he was on M-28, rolling toward Barzoon's house, the storm battering the car, wipers almost helpless as they labored to scrape away the torrent. He was driving too fast, tires hydroplaning, zero traction, anything could put him into a spin. Headlights appeared, glared, passed into oblivion. Slow down, don't kill anybody. Don't be like him.

Reaching the 41 junction, he turned toward Marquette. Five miles later he took the bypass westbound toward Nash Lake, toward Barzoon's house. Then he was on the two-lane, still going too fast. Then Nash Lake Drive, Barzoon's road, almost missing the driveway in the darkness. He skidded to a stop, backed up, turned in.

There were no lights on in the house. He hadn't expected any. It wouldn't have mattered. Mud splashed as the tires of the heavy car pounded through puddles in the gravel drive. Pulling into the yard, he pointed the headlights directly at the garage, left the motor running, got out. Rain poured down, giant drops soaking him to the skin. Staring through the plastic window of a door, he saw it—Barzoon's pickup. He'd thought it was gray. It wasn't. It was white and needed a wash. Face pressed against the pane, he tried to see the license. The angle was too steep, the plate shrouded in darkness. Returning to the Lincoln, he grabbed his flashlight from the seat and hurried back for another look. No good. Water ran down his forehead and into his eyes. He pawed at it then swabbed his face with a sleeve. The side door was to the left. Slogging through a deep puddle, he rounded the corner. His hand grabbed the knob and twisted. It was locked. Without a second thought, he took a step back and let loose a vicious kick. Metal shrieked, wood splintered, glass cracked, the door flew open.

Once inside, he went directly to the pickup. His flashlight beamed down on the plate, BZN 974. The last letter was an *N* not an *M*. A custom plate for Barzoon. This was the truck Greg had seen. And there was only one person who could have been driving it. It was him all along, thought Tate. But now it's over.

# Party Time

TATE THRUST HIS bulk into the Brontocarus, sodden clothing drenching the seat. He stared through the rain-blurred windshield at the stark white garage doors glaring in the beams of his headlights, the wipers beating water away with a hypnotic *swik, swock, swik, swock.* Slowly, deliberately, he pulled the gearshift into reverse, executed a turn, and drove, machine-like, first toward Marquette then southbound along 41 to the Harvey Road turn off on his path to destiny.

Pulling into the driveway of 367, he saw both the Mustang and Plymouth glittering in the glow of the porch light. He parked behind the Plymouth, shut off the engine, got out. "It's party time."

The wind had increased since he'd left Barzoon's. Jack pines whistled and bent low, a forest of bows pulled taut. On the other side of the cottage he could hear the hammer-mill pounding of giant waves breaking against the shoreline. His jacket whipped and snapped in the wind. A river of rain ran diagonally across his face. Tate leaned into it and went forward.

He was on the concrete stoop that served as a porch. He reached for the knob. Slowly turned it. A gentle push. The door opened a crack. Out of long habit, his right hand went back beneath his jacket for his gun. It wasn't there. He'd put it away after his visit to Nolen's.

It didn't matter. He could handle it.

He eased the door open enough to see inside. Pressure changes swayed the curtains framing the living room picture window that faced the blackness where Superior churned and boiled. There was a light on. Only one. A floor lamp with a curved arm and Tiffany shade. It stood to the right of the couch next to the easy chair. Backed by the darkness of the storm, the picture window was a mirror. In it, Tate saw Clyde Dorian sitting in the chair, watching him. The coffee table was pulled near his knees. On it sat a glass of red wine along with a half-empty bottle. Dorian continued to stare as Tate's frame filled the door.

"Come in."

He stepped inside, water pooling at his feet.

"Close the door."

He swung the door shut, never taking his eyes off his prey.

"Bad night to be out visiting."

"Is that what I'm doing?"

Dorian shifted. "Oh? Not a social call?"

"No," said Tate, moving forward, cutting down the distance.

"Looking for Nicole?"

"No."

"That's good. She's unavailable."

"It's better that way."

"Is it?"

Tate was within ten feet of Dorian. "Yes."

"That's close enough," said Clyde. His hand slipped between the arm and cushion of the chair. "I have a gun."

"Everyone has a gun," said Tate, moving left toward a

chair at the other end of the couch, but he didn't sit. "You did it, Clyde."

"Oh? That what you think?" A smile rippled across his face.

"Yes."

"Have a seat and we'll discuss it."

"I think I'll stand."

Dorian's hand came up, dragging behind it an enormous handgun that Tate immediately recognized as a .44 magnum Smith and Wesson Model 29, the gun made famous by Clint Eastwood as Dirty Harry Callahan. Tate remembered reading about a woman who'd fired one at a shooting range. The blast tore the gun from her grip and the frame struck her in the forehead, killing her. Clyde Dorian was holding the gun in his right hand, relaxed, nonchalantly waving the barrel from Tate to the chair, telling him it was time to sit. Tate knew he could take Dorian. He'd get off one shot before the kick tore the three pounds of steel from his hand, maybe taking a finger or two with it. But if Clyde were lucky, one shot would be all he'd need. A round from a .44 goes in like a dime but comes out like a grapefruit. Tate eased himself down on the edge of the overstuffed chair, purposely keeping his weight forward.

"Now, nice and slow, pull out your gun and set it on the coffee table."

"I'm not carrying," said Tate, opening his jacket to show he was unarmed.

"Let's see the back."

Tate rose, pulled his jacket up, did a three-sixty, and then sat back down. "Plan on killing me too, Clyde?"

Dorian smiled and nodded. "Uh-huh."

"Gonna blast a hole in me? Or am I going to be accident prone?"

His lips tightened, brow furrowing. "I'll need to give it some thought. Spur of the moment and all. I wasn't expecting you."

"Expecting someone else?"

Without taking his eyes off Tate, Dorian reached for his glass of wine and drained it. After setting the glass back on the table, he wiped his mouth with his hand. "You're lucky, Tate."

"Funny, that's what I've always thought."

"Don't be a smartass or your luck will run out." Dorian used his thumb to pull back the large hammer on the .44. *Ka-click!*

"How am I lucky, Clyde?"

A smile slithered onto his face. "You're lucky every moment I let you stay alive."

"That what you told Harlan in the garage before you killed him?"

Clyde's smile crawled away. "How'd you know?"

"I ruled everyone else out, so it had to be you. As far as doing him in the garage, well, that's just a guess. You could have followed him to the camp road, maybe skied up after him, he could have conveniently run out of gas at the halfway point, close enough to camp so it would make sense for him to walk in the rest of the way, then you could've pulled out the artillery and told him he was going for a hike." He glanced at the gun. "And who wouldn't, with a cannon like that pointed at 'em? But to do it that way, you'd have had to calculate exactly how much gas the machine uses and how much is in the tank and lines. It'd be a challenge, but you could have done it.

You're plenty smart enough. But why bother? Barzoon might have been the careful type and checked, then where would you be?" Tate shook his head. "Much easier to take him right there in the garage. Just zap him a couple of times with your stun gun and do to him what you did to me, except maybe a little more. Then what'd you do? Toss a blanket over him while you drove out and set up the snowmobile scene?"

Dorian didn't answer.

"There are a couple things I can't figure."

"What's that?"

"Why'd you take out the tool kit?"

Clyde huffed a laugh. "You were right when you said I could compute the volume of gas to leave in the tank so the machine would stall halfway to camp, but it wouldn't be as easy as driving it there, disconnecting the line, and draining the tank. Then all I had to do was reconnect it and start the engine and let it idle till it died. Occam's Razor, Tate. The simple answer is usually the correct one."

"But you left the tools out when you were done. Why?"

Dorian smiled. "Figured it would make him look like a fool."

Tate nodded. "After you set up the snowmobile scene, how'd you get back to his place?"

"Easy. I walked the snowmobile track back to the road and then hitch-hiked."

"Weren't you worried about footprints?"

"It was snowing, it was night, no one would be along till the next day at the earliest. I figured they'd be covered by snow by then, and they were."

"Weren't you worried about Jenna?"

"She was fine. I locked her in her room so she'd be

safe, safer than she ever was with him. He didn't give a damn about her. Didn't give a damn about anyone but himself."

"Wasn't hard to kill him, was it?"

Dorian's head moved side to side. "No, not hard at all."

"And I don't guess Earl will be coming back from that, ah, vacation any time soon."

"Umm . . . no. That would be unlikely."

"Why him? I thought you two were pals. Oh wait, there was an argument."

Clyde cocked his head. "That fucking cretin put his hands on me. He should *not* have done that. I warned him, but he had to prove how tough he was." A sound came from Dorian's throat, low and ugly. "Wasn't feeling nearly so macho that night in the ice fishing shanty, all trussed up with duct tape, wiggling and squirming. Cried like a baby when I wired the cement blocks to his feet."

"Then you sent an email to Nicole about Earl's vacation plans."

"I didn't think Earl would be needing his computer anymore, so I borrowed it and put it to good use."

"The attorney and pressure on the insurance company."

"You're catching on."

Tate smiled and nodded amiably. He wanted to hear more. "I suppose you did Kevin Adams to help Lila and Harlan out financially. How'd you think up the end-loader stunt? And him being your first, was it hard?"

"Wasn't as hard as you might think. Adams was a fool and his wife a slut, always coming on to Harlan. That was my sister's husband she was messing with!"

"But the end loader?"

"What are you talking about? Any simpleton can drive

one of those things. Watch someone for two minutes and you're an expert."

"So you found Adams working alone, zapped him with the gun, dragged him into position, fired up the loader, fastened your seatbelt and, *presto*, a tragic accident."

"Yeah, that's close."

"What'd I miss?"

"The part where I put the plastic bag over his head."

Tate raised his palms in realization. "Of course! You asphyxiated him. Couldn't have him recover from the stinger and crawl out of the way while you were running the loader up the pile."

"Nooo," said Dorian, shaking his head. "Couldn't have that. Once the loader was on its side, the scene would be set. No way to jack it up and slide him under."

"Yeah, and with him all messed up by the loader, no one would ever suspect the real cause of death. Just an unfortunate accident."

Dorian reached for the wine and poured himself another glass.

"That only leaves Lila. Why her?"

"She was a tramp, Tate. Don't you understand? I was going to fix it so she'd end up with everything: the house, the business, the insurance money. She'd be set. *We'd* be set. The whole family. And the best part was, she didn't care about money. *I'd* be the one controlling it. Life was going to be easy, Tate, real easy. But Lila couldn't keep her pants on. Had to go up to Big Bay and start giving it away to pretty boy Johnny. Then she has the nerve to tell me she's leaving Harlan. Can you believe it? Leave him to shack up with some third-rate artist and live like trailer trash the rest of her life? *No god damned way!* I'd worked too hard. I'd taken too many risks. It was *my* future she was messing with. It was *my* money. I'd *earned* it. So, I had to make an adjustment in my plan."

"You followed her to Big Bay and waited."

"Half the goddamned night."

"How'd it feel when you put the plastic over her face?"

He laughed. "Didn't have to. After I juiced her with the stinger, she went into a coma or something. Her eyes were open and she was breathing, but she couldn't move. You should have seen the look on her face just before the Jeep came down on her."

"You killed your own sister, and you did it for money. That's pathetic."

Dorian was taking a sip of wine. It shot out of his mouth, spraying on the coffee table and rug. The hand with the gun came up, ugly black muzzle pointed at the center of Tate's face, hollow eye promising death. "Don't push your luck."

Tate smiled and forced himself to relax in response. "Must have been a surprise when you discovered Barzoon's insurance policy was made out to Earl."

Dorian eased off. He wanted to talk. He wanted to tell Tate of his greatness, of his beautiful plan, of his triumphs and struggles while executing it. He could share it with Tate and then see wonder and admiration reflected back at him. Tate was one of the few who would fully understand. Then he'd kill him, and his secret would be safe. He leaned back in his chair, the heavy gun resting on the arm.

"Yes, it was a surprise. What an ass, leaves all the insurance money to his suckhead son. But I'll still do okay. All the other assets—the house, the business, the Echo

Lake property, stocks, bonds, cash, everything—will go to Jenna, and I'll be the one calling the shots."

"But with Earl gone, won't the estate be divided between Jenna and Nicole?"

He gave a self-satisfied smirk. "There's a will." He let the sentence hang in the air, gauging Tate's reaction. Seeing Tate's questioning eyes as an acknowledgement of his brilliance, he went on. "I had Lila talk him into doing it. Told her it'd be better for Jenna. I have a copy, of course, which I'll make public in due time. So, with Lila and Harlan gone, everything goes to Jenna, nothing to Nicole."

"Speaking of Nicole, aren't you concerned she'll come home and see this?"

Dorian laughed and then shook his head. "Not really." His demeanor implying more.

"So, Clyde, have you given it some thought? What kind of an accident am I going to have? Tell me now so I can savor the image before it's time to go."

Dorian nodded. "Fine, Tate. You'll like this. Lake Superior is cold. Even at the end of August, it's what, low sixties?"

"Yeah, 'bout there."

"And now, just after the ice break-up, mid-thirties?"

"I suppose."

"Night like tonight, big breakers and all, bad night to go walking on the beach. Might wander too close to the water, a wave catches you, pulls you in, you struggle, you try to swim, but your arms and legs won't work, hypothermia is shutting your body down, wet clothing like an anchor, dragging you under. You gasp for air, but there's only water. Some frantic thrashing. A few convulsions. It's over."

Tate smiled. "The way you tell it, it doesn't sound so bad."

Dorian laughed. "That's funny, Tate." He flicked the barrel of the .44 toward the picture window, indicating Lake Superior raging in the darkness beyond. "I'm gonna put you in right there. With the wind out of the northwest, the tide will drag your carcass a couple miles east before morning. It'll seem like you went for a walk, got too close and, *damn*, bad luck." He smiled. "I know where you live. I know you live alone. Who's gonna think otherwise?"

"Yeah, you've been to my place a couple times to check it out. Maybe thinking you'd drop by and encourage me to end the investigation."

Dorian's face registered surprise. He tried to hide it. "You weren't home. How'd you know?"

"A fellow agent told me. He wrote down the description of the truck you were driving—white Ford F-250 four-by-four—and the license number—BZN974. My pals at the Bureau checked it out." It was a lie, of course, but it might make Dorian pause to consider the consequences. "Barzoon's truck, that was the key. That was your mistake. That's what got me thinking about you. Even if Harlan *were* still alive and pulling an insurance scam, he sure as hell wouldn't be driving around in his own truck. So, the question was, who else had access? Earl? He's gone, and pickups aren't his style. The driver was a man, so it couldn't have been Nicole. It could have been that crudball, Lex, but who'd trust a freak like him with anything important? Orville? Not a chance. Johnny? Wouldn't have access. So, you see, Clyde, with all of them ruled out, that only left you. And, like I said, I had the tag checked and mentioned your name when I did it. That means when I come up missing, the boys at the Bureau are gonna be on you like a rash."

An animal sound came out of Dorian's throat, course and guttural. His face twisted in anger, then he rose from his chair, leg bumping the coffee table, wine bottle falling on the floor, blood-red liquid pooling on the rug.

A gray jacket was draped across the end of the couch. Shifting the gun hand to hand, Dorian pulled it on. "Too bad for you, Tate. I was gonna let you watch as I did Johnny, but I'm sick of your bullshit." With the .44 trained on Tate's chest, Dorian sidled to the kitchen, slid open a drawer, and pulled out a hefty yellow stun gun. Tate saw the size and knew it packed a punch, but he didn't need to see it to know. A shiver ran through him as he vividly recalled the misery of his last encounter. "Ah! So that's who you were waiting for, Johnny Nolen. But why?"

"None of your fucking business. I was going to let you watch the show, let you witness the master at work while Johnny begs for mercy, but you've been rude, so it's time for your swim."

"Fine with me." It was a dumb thing to say, but he had to keep the conversation going.

Dorian slid the stun gun in his jacket pocket then used his free hand to grab a large flashlight from the counter. "Up."

Tate rose.

"Hands behind your head."

He complied.

"Let's go." He waived the muzzle toward the door.

Tate took his time walking across the room. He stopped in front of the door.

"I'm gonna be right behind you. Try to make a move

and I'll blow a hole in you the size of Kansas, but if you walk down to the beach like a good boy and get in the water, I won't shoot. You'll have maybe one chance in a hundred to get out alive, but those are better odds than if you try anything. Understand?"

"Yeah, no problem. I love to swim." But he was thinking there was no way Dorian would put him in the water without 40,000 volts or a bullet to guarantee his fate. Whatever he was going to do, it had to be before that.

"Open it."

Tate opened the door. Immediately, the force of the storm was against him.

"Move."

He stepped into the downpour. Rain streaked past the porch light like rods of glass. There were pools on what passed for a lawn.

"There's a path to the right, take it."

Spotlight on his back, Tate began to walk. Reaching the end of the cottage, the path turned right and he turned with it. As he did, the full fury of the storm hit him. He dug his running shoes in the wet sand and leaned into the wind to keep from being blown backward.

The tempest battered them as they followed a well-worn trail past the last of the jack pines, across a grassy area, and onto the long slope of the beach. The powerful flashlight beam bounced with each of Dorian's steps, illuminating first the beach, then the waves, then the beach again, but always Tate's body. He estimated Dorian was ten feet behind him, too far away to make a move and too close to run from. The beach was wide and open. The sand would make running slow. Ahead of him, in the beam of the flashlight, Tate saw towering white caps on ten-foot breakers crashing against the shoreline, each with the power of a locomotive. Tons of water rushed up the beach to forty feet from where the waves broke. Then, energy expended, it would rush back out, dragging anything hapless enough to be caught in the current to be pummeled by the next wave and dragged even farther out. Once he was in, it would be over. He wouldn't last a minute.

After allowing himself to be herded to the very edge of the in-rushing surf, Tate stopped and turned around.

"Move!" shouted Dorian.

Tate took several cautious steps backward before another monster breaker crashed, sending a surge of water rushing up the shore. It hit him fast, up to his calves, up to his knees, so cold it was a shock, icy water paralyzing his legs as it flowed around them.

The force of the water toppled him toward Dorian. He thrust his arms out, staggering to stay upright. Then the water turned and began rushing out, and Tate had to lean forward to keep from being pulled out with it. Current swirled around his legs and feet, carving sand from beneath his footing, causing him to stumble, nearly fall. I'll never make it, he thought. I have to do something, even if it doesn't work. I have to do something, and I have to do it *now!*

Dorian was twenty feet up the bank, out of the surf, flashlight beam on Tate. The rain fell in milky sheets, blurring the light, Dorian a shimmering wraith behind it. Tate raised his hands to shield his eyes from the glare, and then over the fury of the storm he shouted, "Dorian! I can't do it! Shoot me with the voltage. That'll make it easier."

There was no response.

He tried again. "Dorian! Hit me with the stun gun! It's the only way!" Seconds passed . . . then the beam of light began to bounce.

# Going Down

ANOTHER BREAKER CRASHED, sending a torrent of water rushing at him. He was concentrating on Dorian, and the force knocked him to his knees, freezing water soaking him to the chest, so cold it made him gasp. Then the flow stopped, turned, and began rushing out . . . *pulling him with it!* He dug in his feet and clawed at the sand to keep from being sucked backward to certain death, struggling till the flow abated. The water was low now, almost calm. Tate pushed with frozen hands to right himself. As he stood, he sensed Dorian was closer, maybe ten feet away. He couldn't see him, only the light, but he knew.

"Dorian, do it!" he pleaded. "Make it easy on me. Hit me with the voltage." He held his arms away from his sides in an act of submission, baring his chest for the prongs of death, offering proof he was ready for the end. The light came closer, closer, eight feet, six feet, four feet. He saw the glittering tips of the prongs and the yellow plastic of the handle as it moved into the beam of light. Tate's whole being was fixed on it. Closer. *Closer.* Soon, he thought, one way or the other. Closer. *Closer.* Suddenly, Dorian's hand thrust forward to ram the prongs into his chest. When Tate saw it, his hands came down and he took a step back. Grabbing the bottom of his sodden jacket, he pulled it up and around the stun gun and held on for his life.

"Dorian!" he yelled over the tumult. "If you pull the trigger, we both get zapped." Then the voltage hit him, surging though his wet clothing, rippling through his hands, up his arms, through his chest to his face. His muscles began to spasm and his only thought was *hang on!*

Another breaker crashed and the flood hit them. Tate reeled like a drunk, fighting to stay erect and hold onto the gun at the same time. Don't fall! he pleaded to himself. Don't fall or you'll die! Just as his body began to recover from the icy shock of the last wave, the next rushed forward, pushing him helplessly toward Dorian and the stun gun. Then he saw the flashlight beam swing wildly and fall into the water—the light dimmed, tumbling up the beach, water pushing it. He dropped it! thought Tate. When he pulled the trigger on the stun gun, the voltage went through him too and he dropped it. He must have dropped the gun too, or he would have shot me. No time to think! Push!

Tate pushed as hard as he could on the arm holding the stun gun. Dorian was pushing too. Then Tate felt a kick to the stomach. Blinding pain tightened his chest and abdomen. He couldn't breathe. He couldn't think. *Hold on or die!*

Dorian was pushing forward, using all his strength to ram the prongs into Tate's chest, but Tate was stronger. One step, two steps, he was forcing Dorian backwards. A wave crashed and water surged up the shore. Then, suddenly, instead of pushing, Dorian's arm was pulling away. No! thought Tate. Don't let him go! He couldn't feel his hands, but he willed them to grip like a vice. But Dorian's pull was strong, he pulled then pushed then jerked back again. Tate, with all his weight forward, staggered and teetered on the brink but didn't fall. Now the flow was going out, faster and faster into the murderous surf. His legs were nearly useless, they began to buckle. His hands were blocks of ice. He could barely hold on as Dorian began pulling sideways, struggling to get free. Then out of the blackness came an explosion, and the muzzle flash from Dorian's .44 lit up the beach like a strobe. Tate heard a scream of pain and for an instant saw Dorian next to him, splayed sideways, struggling in the water. Then came darkness.

Leaning against the out-rushing tide, Tate felt Dorian's arm pulling outward, toward the surf. He released his grip and let the hand with the stun gun slip out of his, but an instant later, he felt it grab his pant leg, pulling his left leg backward toward the surf and certain death. His left foot lost traction, and he began to panic as rushing water pulled his leg toward the lake. Instinct made him lean toward the beach. He spun on his right heel, trying to break Dorian's grip, and with his left foot kicked in the direction of the hand. His foot hit something solid. The hand loosened its grip, and Tate felt it slip away as Clyde Dorian's body slid into the surf.

"I'm free!" thought Tate, ecstatic, as he was falling backward into the water. Then he was under, body screaming in misery from the cold. His feet kicked at the churning tide, arms flailing, fingers clawing at the grainy sand, losing the battle as his body was dragged outward. His arms and legs were leaden, each movement more difficult than the last. He was freezing to death. His energy almost gone. A little more, he begged of himself, a little more. Then the flow slowed and stopped.

This is my chance! He tried to stand, but his legs

wouldn't obey, so he willed himself to crawl. Kicking and scraping, he dragged himself up the slope of the beach. He was making headway, but too slowly. Soon he heard the crash of the next big breaker and moments later a fresh surge of ice water washed over his body . . . *pushing him up the beach!* Go with it, he thought. He gulped a breath and went prone, spreading his arms and legs to create the maximum surface area. *Let it push you up the shore. When it stops, hold on for your life.*

It took two more surges before Tate was able to drag his carcass above the tide line. The wind-driven rain lashed him for his effort as he lay panting on the freezing sand. He was shivering uncontrollably. He tried to stand, but couldn't. *Crawl! It's the only way. Must get inside. Must get warm or I'll die.* So he crawled. Slowly at first. Then faster. Then he was on his hands and knees. Halfway across the grass, he was able to stand. He staggered toward the cottage, hunched, dizzy from exhaustion, unable to breathe because of his reinjured ribs. A gust felled him, once, again, then he was around the corner of the cottage and out of the worst of it.

Hands on the building to steady himself, he shuffled to the door. In the glow of the porch light, he clutched the doorknob and twisted, but nothing happened. *His hand was too numb to squeeze the knob!* In desperation, he tried again. Same result. He tried two hands. Nothing. "No!" he moaned, sinking to his knees. *Inches away from heat but I can't get in. What should I do? Rest first. Rest here. So cold. So tired.* As he curled up to rest on the concrete slab, his eyes drifted to the driveway and he saw the Lincoln. *The car!* He'd left it unlocked. The key was in the ignition. It had a heater. Salvation was only thirty feet away. *Move, he thought. Move or you'll never move again.*

For the second time that night, Tate began to crawl. As icy rain cascaded upon him, he dragged himself through puddles in the sparse lawn and across the gravel parking area to the door of the Lincoln. Pushing himself to his knees, he jammed a nearly useless hand under the handle and pulled. To his overwhelming relief, the door popped open and the interior light went on. Overcome by an aching joy, Tate pulled himself into a sitting position in the driver's seat. As soon as he was inside, as if to congratulate him, a strong gust blew the door closed.

It was warmer in the Lincoln, but only marginally. He was out of the rain and wind, but it wasn't enough. He needed heat. The key was in the ignition. His fingers couldn't grasp it, so Tate let his torso fall to the right until he was lying on the seat then thrust his left arm out till his balled fist touched the key. He forced the key between his first and second fingers, clenched his fist as tight as he could, then twisted his arm. The starter made a grinding sound and 250 horses roared to life. Tate groaned in relief. The heater was on, he used his fist to ram the temperature control to high, and as the storm rocked the Lincoln, he lay in the darkness to wait.

# Find Her!

CURLED AND SHIVERING despite the blazing heat in the car, Tate moaned in agony as his frozen hands and feet began to thaw. It was as if they were on fire! Huge throbbing balloons of fire. *Soon,* he thought. *Soon it'll end, and I'll be okay.* The kick in the stomach had re-injured his ribs and shallow breaths were all he could take. He was lying on the seat, panting, time passing in the smallest of increments, when flickering headlights lit up the inside of the Lincoln. Someone was coming in the drive! He heard a vehicle pull in next to his. A car door slammed. Then all he heard was the storm, howling in its fury, each new gust shaking the Lincoln like a toy. Time went by and he began to lose hope. All of a sudden there was a pounding on his window. "Tate! You in there?" It was Johnny Nolen.

Tate tried to shout a yes but his rib cage denied him, so he used a foot and kicked at the inside of the door. A second time. A third time. Then it opened and the light went on.

"Tate?" A pause. "You okay?"

Tate weakly lifted his head. He fixed his eyes on Nolen and whispered, "No."

When Nolen opened the door, a blast of hot air rushed past his face. The heater was on high, it must have been ninety inside, but there was Tate, soaking wet, curled, fetal, shivering on the seat, muddy hands clenched under his chin. Hypothermia, thought Nolen. He'd seen it happen to ice fisherman on Lake Independence. Tate must have been outside too long, got wet, became hypothermic then crawled into the car.

"We need to get you inside. The lights are on, but no one answers. Stay here, I'll try again."

Stay here, thought Tate. Sure.

Nolen was back in seconds. "The door's unlocked. I'll help you in."

Nolen helped Tate out of the Lincoln and supported him as they shuffled to the cottage. Once they were inside, he said, "Gotta get you out of these wet clothes and into a hot shower to bring your body temp up." Tate didn't resist as Nolen maneuvered him into the bathroom and got the shower running, hot spray from the nozzle filling the room with steam. Nolen tried to work Tate's jacket off, but the wet cloth and Tate's rigid posture made it impossible.

"Forget the clothes, let's get you in as you are."

Tate shuffled into the shower, slumping to the floor, leaning against a wall as hot water poured down on him, penetrating the layers of cold and increasing the agony in his hands and feet. But after only a few minutes, he began to feel relief. The heat loosened the tightness in his chest and he was able to take deeper, albeit painful, breaths. And he was able to flex his fingers, and his thinking was returning to normal. Peering through the plastic shower curtain, he saw Nolen sitting on the closed commode, watching him.

"Feeling a little better?" asked Nolan.

He croaked a weak, "Yes."

"Give it another ten minutes and then we'll get you dry and into some blankets."

Dry sounded good. Tate nodded. Then he remembered Nicole and spoke her name. "Nicole." The effort caused him to cough and grimace in pain.

Nolen shook his head. "She's not here. There's no one home."

Tate pushed the shower curtain aside and mouthed the words, "Find her."

Nolen cocked his head in confusion.

Tate screwed his face up in anger and frustration, then he reached out and grabbed Nolen's pant leg. *"Find her!"*

"Okay, Tate! Take it easy, I'll look for her." He rose and left the bathroom, closing the door on his way out. Tate relaxed and let the gloriously warm shower wash over him. Time passed, a minute, two minutes, then he heard voices, one a woman's. The bathroom door opened and there was Nicole, strips of duct tape dangling from her wrists and ankles.

She rushed to him. "Tate! Are you all right?"

He whispered. "Call Gayla."

"Who?"

"Call my house."

Nicole made the call. Gayla answered and was there in fifteen minutes carrying a tote full of dry clothes. The hot shower worked, and Tate was feeling better. Nolen helped him into a bedroom where, with an assist from Gayla, he was able to strip off his wet clothes. After toweling off, he changed into the dry set. As he was buckling his belt, Nolen popped his head in the door. "You should lie down and rest. I put water on for tea."

Tate shook his head. "I want to go home."

"Mike, he's right," said Gayla.

Tate was adamant. "Home."

Nolen drove behind him and steadied him as he walked to the house. Before leaving, he said to Gayla, "Hot soup, that's what he needs. That and rest." She was already pulling out a pan.

# The P.J.

Tate awoke with a feeling that he'd been asleep for years. Lying in bed, he carefully stretched and flexed. Nothing broken or torn, except the ribs again, so his breathing was painful, but at least he could move and speak. And, most importantly, he was alive. He took his time dressing then shuffled into the kitchen where Gayla was sipping coffee and reading the paper. "Yesterday's news," he said, carefully taking a seat at the table.

"Today's news," she replied. "It's six o'clock."

It wasn't morning, it was evening. He'd slept the entire day.

"I'm hungry."

"That's the Mike Tate I know and love." She came around the table and gave him a gentle hug then went to the counter where a crock-pot was steaming. Pot roast, she knew it was his favorite.

By Saturday afternoon Tate was grumpy, which meant he was almost back to normal. The ribs would take time, but other than that and a few cuts and scrapes, he was all right. Bill and Laura stopped by, the four of them sipping cold Labatts by the fireplace in the living room. Through the large picture window they could see leaves and a few fallen branches on the lakeside yard, but the violence of the storm was long gone. A scattering of cottony fair-weather clouds floated effortlessly in the cool blue sky and brilliant sunlight sparkled on Superior's undulating water, creating endlessly varying bands of indigo and silver.

Noon said, "They found his body washed up east of here on the public beach."

Just as Dorian predicted, thought Tate.

"You're lucky. Nolen said when he first saw you in the car, he thought you'd tipped a few and were sleeping it off. His first thought was to let you be. If he had, even with the heat, you might have gone into shock and died."

"I've always been lucky," said Tate, chuckling at the absurdity of the statement.

"Yeah, you're the lucky one," said Laura. "And I am too. Don't forget, you owe me a story."

Tate gave a friendly salute. "I always honor my commitments, ma'am."

Noon said, "Not that Dorian wasn't already unhinged, but it seems an incident with Nicole that afternoon pushed him over the edge. She said Dorian came on to her, saying all sorts of wild things and telling her she belonged with him. She laughed him off, thinking it was a joke. When she did, he became enraged, zapped her with the stun gun, and tied her up. Then Clyde began ranting about Johnny Nolen, saying Nolen was the cause of his problems. He worked himself into a frenzy and then called Johnny and told him Nicole was upset and suicidal and she needed him and he had to come right away or it'd be too late. Dorian was lying in wait for him when you chanced by. Lucky for Johnny you got there first. Lucky for Nicole too, I imagine."

Fields said, "She's already been interviewed by the

police. She heard the entire conversation between you and Clyde and backs you up completely."

Tate said, "Strange as it may seem, part of this has worked out as Dorian planned. With Earl gone and assuming there's a new will, Jenna will inherit what there is of the estate and Nicole and Jenna will split the insurance money." He didn't bother to mention the discouraging part. The policies on Kevin, Lila, and Harlan would no longer be in question, the result being no recovery fee for him.

Noon said, "Only thing undetermined is the whereabouts of Harlan Barzoon's body."

"Modus operandi," said Tate. "He told me he put Earl in the water. My guess is he did the same with Harlan. Probably right there in Nash Lake near Barzoon's place. When the divers go down to look for Earl, they might get a twofer."

"Grim," said Laura.

Noon grinned. "You did good work, Tate. All the guys at the Bureau are talking about it. Boletto's even making noises about trying to get you to come back."

"But he can't go back," said Gayla. She jumped up and dashed into the kitchen, hurrying back a moment later to exclaim, "Look, Mike! It came in the mail while you were asleep. I was so excited, I had to open it." She held up a stiff piece of paper with an official seal and a flourish of writing. Seeing his puzzled expression, she said, "It's your license, silly. Now you're a real P.I."

# Acknowledgements

My sincere thanks to the following friends for their assistance in preparing Lila for publication: Jim Simmons, Dennis Bell, Chris Kitzman, Joanne Spurr, Linda Radmacher, and K.C. Meadows.

by Alan Robertson

The Money Belt

Diamond

Sierra Joe 9

Lila

Man's Work

The Rogue

Summer Moon

CPSIA information can be obtained at www.ICGtesting.com
Printed in the USA
BVOW08s0948100214

344470BV00001B/6/P